Ancient Haunts

Ancient Haunts

The Stoneground Ghost Tales
E. G. Swain

Tedious Brief Tales of Granta and Gramarye
"Ingulphus"
(Arthur Gray, Master of Jesus College)

Coachwhip Publications
Landisville, Pennsylvania

Ancient Haunts: The Stoneground Ghost Tales / Tedious Brief Tales of Granta and Gramarye
Copyright © 2010 Coachwhip Publications

ISBN 1-61646-005-9
ISBN-13 978-1-61646-005-1

Cover: Church © Dale Mitchell
Back Cover: Church Window © Stephen Bonk

CoachwhipBooks.com

All Rights Reserved. No part of this publication may be reproduced, stored in a retrieval system or transmitted in any form or by any means—electronic, mechanical, photocopy, recording or any other—except for brief quotations in printed reviews, without the prior permission of the author or publisher.

Ancient Haunts

THE STONEGROUND GHOST TALES

The Man with the Roller	9
Bone to His Bone	19
The Richpins	28
The Eastern Window	44
Lubrietta	55
The Rockery	67
The Indian Lamp-Shade	79
The Place of Safety	93
The Kirk Spook	109

Ancient Haunts

Tedious Brief Tales of Granta and Gramarye

To Two Cambridge Magicians	119
The Everlasting Club	120
The Treasure of John Badcoke	129
The True History of Anthony Ffryar	139
The Necromancer	148
Brother John's Bequest	157
The Burden of Dead Books	168
Thankfull Thomas	188
The Palladium	198
The Sacrist of Saint Radegund	206

The Stoneground Ghost Tales

Compiled from the Recollections of
the Reverend Roland Batchel,
Vicar of the Parish

E. G. Swain

(1912)

The Man with the Roller

On the edge of that vast tract of East Anglia, which retains its ancient name of the Fens, there may be found, by those who know where to seek it, a certain village called Stoneground. It was once a picturesque village. To-day it is not to be called either a village, or picturesque. Man dwells not in one "house of clay," but in two, and the material of the second is drawn from the earth upon which this and the neighbouring villages stood. The unlovely signs of the industry have changed the place alike in aspect and in population. Many who have seen the fossil skeletons of great saurians brought out of the clay in which they have lain from pre-historic times, have thought that the inhabitants of the place have not since changed for the better. The chief habitations, however, have their foundations not upon clay, but upon a bed of gravel which anciently gave to the place its name, and upon the highest part of this gravel stands, and has stood for many centuries, the Parish Church, dominating the landscape for miles around.

Stoneground, however, is no longer the inaccessible village, which in the middle ages stood out above a waste of waters. Occasional floods serve to indicate what was once its ordinary outlook, but in more recent times the construction of roads and railways, and the drainage of the Fens, have given it freedom of communication with the world from which it was formerly isolated.

The Vicarage of Stoneground stands hard by the Church, and is renowned for its spacious garden, part of which, and that (as might be expected) the part nearest the house, is of ancient date.

To the original plot successive Vicars have added adjacent lands, so that the garden has gradually acquired the state in which it now appears.

The Vicars have been many in member. Since Henry de Greville was instituted in the year 1140 there have been 30, all of whom have lived, and most of whom have died, in successive vicarage houses upon the present site.

The present incumbent, Mr. Batchel, is a solitary man of somewhat studious habits, but is not too much enamoured of his solitude to receive visits, from time to time, from schoolboys and such. In the summer of the year 1906 he entertained two, who are the occasion of this narrative, though still unconscious of their part in it, for one of the two, celebrating his 15th birthday during his visit to Stoneground, was presented by Mr. Batchel with a new camera, with which he proceeded to photograph, with considerable skill, the surroundings of the house.

One of these photographs Mr. Batchel thought particularly pleasing. It was a view of the house with the lawn in the foreground. A few small copies, such as the boy's camera was capable of producing, were sent to him by his young friend, some weeks after the visit, and again Mr. Batchel was so much pleased with the picture, that he begged for the negative, with the intention of having the view enlarged.

The boy met the request with what seemed a needlessly modest plea. There were two negatives, he replied, but each of them had, in the same part of the picture, a small blur for which there was no accounting otherwise than by carelessness. His desire, therefore, was to discard these films, and to produce something more worthy of enlargement, upon a subsequent visit.

Mr. Batchel, however, persisted in his request, and upon receipt of the negative, examined it with a lens. He was just able to detect the blur alluded to; an examination under a powerful glass, in fact revealed something more than he had at first detected. The blur was like the nucleus of a comet as one sees it represented in pictures, and seemed to be connected with a faint streak which extended across the negative. It was, however, so inconsiderable a defect that Mr. Batchel resolved to disregard it. He had a neighbour whose favourite pastime was photography, one who was notably skilled in everything that pertained to the art, and to him he sent the negative, with the request for an enlargement, reminding him of a longstanding promise to do any such service, when as had now happened, his friend might see fit to ask it.

This neighbour who had acquired such skill in photography, was one Mr. Groves, a young clergyman, residing in the Precincts of the Minster near at hand, which was visible from Mr. Batchel's garden. He lodged with a Mrs. Rumney, a superannuated servant of the Palace, and a strong-minded vigorous woman still, exactly such a one as Mr. Groves needed to have about him. For he was a constant trial to Mrs. Rumney, and but for the wholesome fear she begot in him, would have converted his rooms into a mere den. Her carpets and tablecloths were continually bespattered with chemicals; her chimney-piece ornaments had been unceremoniously stowed away and replaced by labelled bottles; even the bed of Mr. Groves was, by day, strewn with drying film and mounts, and her old and favourite cat had a bald patch on his flank, the result of a mishap with the pyrogallic acid.

Mrs. Rumney's lodger, however, was a great favourite with her, as such helpless men are apt to be with motherly women, and she took no small pride in his work. A life-size portrait of herself, originally a, peace-offering, hung in her parlour, and had long excited the envy of every friend who took tea with her.

"Mr. Groves," she was wont to say, "is a nice gentleman, *and* a gentleman; and chemical though he may be, I'd rather wait on him for nothing than what I would on anyone else for twice the money."

Every new piece of photographic work was of interest to Mrs. Rumney, and she expected to be allowed both to admire and to criticism. The view of Stoneground Vicarage, therefore, was shown to her upon its arrival. "Well may it want enlarging," she remarked, "and it no bigger than a postage stamp; it looks more like a doll's house than a vicarage," and with this she went about her work, whilst Mr. Groves retired to his dark room with the film, to see what he could make of the task assigned to him.

Two days later, after repeated visits to his dark room, he had made something considerable; and when Mrs. Rumney brought him his chop for luncheon, she was lost in admiration. A large but unfinished print stood upon his easel, and such a picture of Stoneground Vicarage was in the making as was calculated to delight both the young photographer and the Vicar.

Mr. Groves spent only his mornings, as a rule, in photography. His afternoons he gave to pastoral work, and the work upon this enlargement was over for the day. It required little more than "touching up," but it was this "touching up" which made the difference between the enlargements of Mr. Groves and those of other men. The print, therefore, was to be left upon the easel until the morrow, when it was to be finished. Mrs. Rumney and he, together, gave it an admiring inspection as she was carrying away the tray, and what they agreed in admiring most particularly was the smooth and open stretch of lawn, which made so excellent a foreground for the picture. "It looks," said Mrs. Rumney, who had once been young, "as if it was waiting for someone to come and dance on it."

Mr. Groves left his lodgings—we must now be particular about the hours—at half-past two, with the intention of returning, as usual, at five. "As reg'lar as a clock," Mrs. Rumney was wont to say, "and a sight more reg'lar than some clocks I knows of."

Upon this day he was, nevertheless, somewhat late, some visit had detained him unexpectedly, and it was a quarter-past five when he inserted his latch-key in Mrs. Rumney's door.

Hardly had he entered, when his landlady, obviously awaiting him, appeared in the passage: her face, usually florid, was of the colour of parchment, and, breathing hurriedly and shortly, she pointed at the door of Mr. Groves' room.

In some alarm at her condition, Mr. Groves hastily questioned her; all she could say was: "The photograph! the photograph!" Mr. Groves could only suppose that his enlargement had met with some mishap for which Mrs. Rumney was responsible. Perhaps she had allowed it to flutter into the fire. He turned towards his room in order to discover the worst, but at this Mrs. Rumney laid a trembling hand upon his arm, and held him back. "Don't go in," she said, "have your tea in the parlour."

"Nonsense," said Mr. Groves, "if that is gone we can easily do another."

"Gone," said his landlady, "I wish to Heaven it was."

The ensuing conversation shall not detain us. It will suffice to say that after a considerable time Mr. Groves succeeded in quieting his landlady, so much so that she consented, still trembling violently, to enter the room with him. To speak truth, she was as much concerned for him as for herself, and she was not by nature a timid woman.

The room, so far from disclosing to Mr. Groves any cause for excitement, appeared wholly unchanged. In its usual place stood every article of his stained and ill-used furniture, on the easel stood the photograph, precisely where he had left it; and except that his tea was not upon the table, everything was in its usual state and place.

But Mrs. Rumney again became excited and tremulous, "It's there," she cried. "Look at the lawn."

Mr. Groves stopped quickly forward and looked at the photograph. Then he turned as pale as Mrs. Rumney herself.

There was a man, a man with an indescribably horrible suffering face, rolling the lawn with a large roller.

Mr. Groves retreated in amazement to where Mrs. Rumney had remained standing. "Has anyone been in here?" he asked.

"Not a soul," was the reply, "I came in to make up the fire, and turned to have another look at the picture, when I saw that dead-alive face at the edge. It gave me the creeps," she said, "particularly from not having noticed it before. If that's anyone in Stoneground, I said to myself, I wonder the Vicar has him in the garden with that awful face. It took that hold of me I thought I must come and look at it again, and at five o'clock I brought your tea in. And then I saw him moved along right in front, with a roller dragging behind him, like you see."

Mr. Groves was greatly puzzled. Mrs. Rumney's story, of course, was incredible, but this strange evil-faced man had appeared in the photograph somehow. That he had not been there when the print was made was quite certain.

The problem soon ceased to alarm Mr. Groves; in his mind it was investing itself with a scientific interest. He began to think of suspended chemical action, and other possible avenues of investigation. At Mrs. Rumney's urgent entreaty, however, he turned the photograph upon the easel, and with only its white back presented to the room, he sat down and ordered tea to be brought in.

He did not look again at the picture. The face of the man had about it something unnaturally painful: he could remember, and still see, as it were, the drawn features, and the look of the man had unaccountably distressed him.

He finished his slight meal, and having lit a pipe, began to brood over the scientific possibilities of the problem. Had any other photograph upon the original film become involved in the one he had enlarged? Had the image of any other face, distorted by the enlarging lens, become a part of this picture? For the space of two hours he debated this possibility, and that, only to reject them all. His optical knowledge told him that no conceivable accident could have brought into his picture a man with a roller. No negative of his had ever contained such a man; if it had, no natural causes would suffice to leave him, as it were, hovering about the apparatus.

His repugnance to the actual thing had by this time lost its freshness, and he determined to end his scientific musings with another inspection of the object. So he approached the easel and turned the photograph round again. His horror returned, and with good cause. The man with the roller had now advanced to the middle of the lawn. The face was stricken still with the same indescribable look of suffering. The man seemed to be appealing to the spectator for some kind of help. Almost, he spoke.

Mr. Groves was naturally reduced to a condition of extreme nervous excitement. Although not by nature what is called a nervous man, he trembled from head to foot. With a sudden effort, he turned away his head, took hold of the picture with his outstretched hand, and opening a drawer in his sideboard thrust the thing underneath a folded tablecloth which was lying there. Then he closed the drawer and took up an entertaining book to distract his thoughts from the whole matter.

In this he succeeded very ill. Yet somehow the rest of the evening passed, and as it wore away, be lost something of his alarm. At ten o'clock, Mrs. Rumney, knocking and receiving answer twice, lest by any chance she should find herself alone in the room, brought in the cocoa usually taken by her lodger at that hour. A hasty glance at the easel showed her that it stood empty, and her face betrayed her relief. She made no comment, and Mr. Groves invited none.

The latter, however, could not make up his mind to go to bed. The face he had seen was taking firm hold upon his imagination, and seemed to fascinate him and repel him at the same time. Before long, he found himself wholly unable to resist the impulse to look at it once more. He took it again, with some indecision, from the drawer and laid it under the lamp.

The man with the roller had now passed completely over the lawn, and was near the left of the picture.

The shock to Mr. Groves was again considerable. He stood facing the fire, trembling with excitement which refused to be suppressed. In this state his eye lighted upon the calendar hanging before him, and it furnished him with some distraction. The next day was his mother's birthday. Never did he omit to write a letter which should lie upon her breakfast-table, and the pre-occupation of this evening had made him wholly forgetful of the matter. There was a collection of letters, however, from the pillar-box near at hand, at a quarter before midnight, so he turned to his desk, wrote a letter which would at least serve to convey his affectionate greetings, and having written it, went out into the night and posted it.

The clocks were striking midnight as he returned to his room. We may be sure that he did not resist the desire to glance at the photograph he had left on his table. But the results of that glance, he, at any rate, had not anticipated. The man with the roller had disappeared. The lawn lay as smooth and clear as at first, "looking," as Mrs. Rumney had said, "as if it was waiting for someone to come and dance on it."

The photograph, after this, remained a photograph and nothing more. Mr. Groves would have liked to persuade himself that it had never undergone these changes which he had witnessed, and which we have endeavoured to describe, but his sense of their reality was too insistent. He kept the print lying for a week upon his easel. Mrs. Rumney, although she had ceased to dread it, was obviously relieved at its disappearance, when it was carried to Stoneground to be delivered to Mr. Batchel. Mr. Groves said nothing of the man with the roller, but gave the enlargement, without comment, into his friend's hands. The work of enlargement had been skilfully done, and was deservedly praised.

Mr. Groves, making some modest disclaimer, observed that the view, with its spacious foreground of lawn, was such as could not have failed to enlarge well. And this lawn, he added, as they sat looking out of the Vicar's study, looks as well from within your house as from without. It must give you a sense of responsibility, he added, reflectively, to be sitting where your predecessors have sat for so many centuries and to be continuing their peaceful work. The mere presence before your window, of the turf upon which good men have walked, is an inspiration.

The Vicar made no reply to these somewhat sententious remarks. For a moment he seemed as if he would speak some words of conventional assent. Then he abruptly left the room, to return in a few minutes with a parchment book.

"Your remark, Groves," he said as he seated himself again, "recalled to me a curious bit of history: I went up to the old library to get the book. This is the journal of William Longue who was Vicar here up to the year 1602. What you said about the lawn will give you an interest in a certain portion of the journal. I will read it."

Aug. 1, 1600.—I am now returned in haste from a journey to Brightelmstone whither I had gone with full intention to remain about the space of two months. Master Josiah Wilburton, of my dear College of Emmanuel, having consented to assume the charge of my parish of Stoneground in the meantime. But I had intelligence, after 12 days' absence, by a messenger from the Churchwardens, that Master

Wilburton had disappeared last Monday sennight, and had been no more seen. So here I am again in my study to the entire frustration of my plans, and can do nothing in my perplexity but sit and look out from my window, before which Andrew Birch rolleth the grass with much persistence. Andrew passeth so many times over the same place with his roller that I have just now stepped without to demand why he so wasteth his labour, and upon this he hath pointed out a place which is not levelled, and hath continued his rolling.

Aug. 2.—There is a change in Andrew Birch since my absence, who hath indeed the aspect of one in great depression, which is noteworthy of so chearful a man. He haply shares our common trouble in respect of Master Wilburton, of whom we remain without tidings. Having made part of a sermon upon the seventh Chapter of the former Epistle of St. Paul to the Corinthians and the 27th verse, I found Andrew again at his task, and bade him desist and saddle my horse, being minded to ride forth and take counsel with my good friend John Palmer at the Deanery, who bore Master Wilburton great affection.

Aug. 2 continued.—Dire news awaiteth me upon my return. The Sheriff's men have disinterred the body of poor Master W. from beneath the grass Andrew was rolling, and have arrested him on the charge of being his cause of death.

Aug. 10.—Alas! Andrew Birch hath been hanged, the Justice having mercifully ordered that he should hang by the neck until he should be dead, and not sooner molested. May the Lord have mercy on his soul. He made full confession before me, that he had slain Master Wilburton in heat upon his threatening to make me privy to certain peculation of which I should not have suspected so old a servant. The poor man bemoaned his evil temper in great contrition, and beat his breast, saying that he knew himself doomed for ever to roll the grass in the place where he had tried to conceal his wicked fact.

"Thank you," said Mr. Groves. "Has that little negative got the date upon it?" Yes, replied Mr. Batchel, as he examined it with his glass. The boy has marked it August 10. The Vicar seemed not to remark the coincidence with the date of Birch's execution. Needless to say that it did not escape Mr. Groves. But he kept silence about the man with the roller, who has been no more seen to this day.

Doubtless there is more in our photography than we yet know of. The camera sees more than the eye, and chemicals in a freshly prepared and active state, have a power which they afterwards lose. Our units of time, adopted for the convenience of persons dealing with the ordinary movements of material objects, are of course conventional. Those who turn the instruments of science upon nature will always be in danger of seeing more than they looked for. There is such a disaster as that of knowing too much, and at some time or another it may overtake each of us. May we then be as wise as Mr. Groves in our reticence, if our turn should come.

Bone to His Bone

William Whitehead, Fellow of Emmanuel College, in the University of Cambridge, became Vicar of Stoneground in the year 1731. The annals of his incumbency were doubtless short and simple: they have not survived. In his day were no newspapers to collect gossip, no Parish Magazines to record the simple events of parochial life. One event, however, of greater moment then than now, is recorded in two places. Vicar Whitehead failed in health after 23 years of work, and journeyed to Bath in what his monument calls "the vain hope of being restored." The duration of his visit is unknown; it is reasonable to suppose that he made his journey in the summer, it is certain that by the month of November his physician told him to lay aside all hope of recovery.

Then it was that the thoughts of the patient turned to the comfortable straggling vicarage he had left at Stoneground, in which he had hoped to end his days. He prayed that his successor might be as happy there as he had been himself. Setting his affairs in order, as became one who had but a short time to live, he executed a will, bequeathing to the Vicars of Stoneground, for ever, the close of ground he had recently purchased because it lay next the vicarage garden. And by a codicil, he added to the bequest his library of books. Within a few days, William Whitehead was gathered to his fathers.

A mural tablet in the north aisle of the church, records, in Latin, his services and his bequests, his two marriages, and his fruitless journey to Bath. The house he loved, but never again saw, was taken down 40 years later, and re-built by Vicar James Devie. The garden, with Vicar Whitehead's "close of ground" and other adjacent lands, was opened out and planted, somewhat before 1850, by Vicar Robert Towerson. The aspect of everything has changed But in a convenient chamber on the first floor of the present vicarage the library of Vicar Whitehead stands very much as he used it and loved it, and as he bequeathed it to his successors "for ever."

The books there are arranged as he arranged and ticketed them. Little slips of paper, sometimes bearing interesting fragments of writing, still mark his places. His marginal comments still give life to pages from which all other interest has faded, and he would have but a dull imagination who could sit in the chamber amidst these books without ever being carried back 180 years into the past, to the time when the newest of them left the printer's hands.

Of those into whose possession the books have come, some have doubtless loved them more, and some less; some, perhaps, have left them severely alone. But neither those who loved them, nor those who loved them not, have lost them, and they passed, some century and a half after William Whitehead's death, into the hands of Mr. Batchel, who loved them as a father loves his children. He lived alone, and had few domestic cares to distract his mind. He was able, therefore, to enjoy to the full what Vicar Whitehead had enjoyed so long before him. During many a long summer evening would he sit poring over long-forgotten books; and since the chamber, otherwise called the library, faced the south, he could also spend sunny winter mornings there without discomfort. Writing at a small table, or reading as he stood at a tall desk, he would browse amongst the books like an ox in a pleasant pasture.

There were other times also, at which Mr. Batchel would use the books. Not being a sound sleeper (for book-loving men seldom are), he elected to use as a bedroom one of the two chambers which opened at either side into the library. The arrangement enabled him to beguile many a sleepless hour amongst the books, and in view of these nocturnal visits he kept a candle standing in a sconce above the desk, and matches always ready to his hand.

There was one disadvantage in this close proximity of his bed to the library. Owing, apparently, to some defect in the fittings of the room, which, having no mechanical tastes, Mr. Batchel had never investigated, there could be heard, in the stillness of the night, exactly such sounds as might arise from a person moving about amongst the books. Visitors using the other adjacent room would often remark at breakfast, that they had heard their host in the library at one or two o'clock in the morning, when, in fact, he had not left his bed. Invariably Mr. Batchel allowed them to suppose that he had been where they thought him. He disliked idle controversy, and was unwilling to afford an opening for supernatural talk. Knowing well enough the sounds by which his guests had been deceived, he wanted no other explanation of them than his own, though it was of too vague a character to count as an explanation. He conjectured that the window-sashes, or the doors, or "something", were defective, and was too phlegmatic and too unpractical to make any investigation. The matter gave him no concern.

Persons whose sleep is uncertain are apt to have their worst nights when they would like their best. The consciousness of a special need for rest seems to bring enough mental disturbance to forbid it. So on Christmas Eve, in the year 1907, Mr. Batchel, who would have liked to sleep well, in view of the labours of Christmas Day, lay hopelessly wide awake. He exhausted all the known devices for courting sleep, and, at the end, found himself wider awake than ever. A brilliant moon shone into his room, for he hated window-blinds. There was a light wind blowing, and the sounds in the library were more than usually suggestive of a person moving about. He almost determined to have the sashes "seen to", although he could seldom be induced to have anything "seen to". He disliked changes, even for the better, and would submit to great inconvenience rather than have things altered with which he had become familiar.

As he revolved these matters in his mind, he heard the clocks strike the hour of midnight, and having now lost all hope of falling asleep, he rose from his bed, got into a large dressing gown which hung in readiness for such occasions, and passed into the library, with the intention of reading himself sleepy, if he could.

The moon, by this time, had passed out of the south, and the library seemed all the darker by contrast with the moonlit chamber he had left. He could see nothing but two blue-grey rectangles formed by the windows against the sky, the furniture of the room being altogether invisible. Groping along to where the table stood, Mr. Batchel felt over its surface for the matches which usually lay there; he found, however, that the table was cleared of everything. He raised his right hand, therefore, in order to feel his way to a shelf where the matches were sometimes mislaid, and at that moment, whilst his hand was in mid-air, the matchbox was gently put into it!

Such an incident could hardly fail to disturb even a phlegmatic person, and Mr. Batchel cried "Who's this?" somewhat nervously. There was no answer. He struck a match, looked hastily round the room, and found it empty, as usual. There was everything, that is to say, that he was accustomed to see, but no other person than himself.

It is not quite accurate, however, to say that everything was in its usual state. Upon the tall desk lay a quarto volume that he had certainly not placed there. It was his quite invariable practice to replace his books upon the shelves after using them, and what we may call his library habits were precise and methodical. A book out of place like this, was not only an offence against good order, but a sign that his privacy had been intruded upon. With some surprise, therefore, he lit the candle standing ready in the sconce, and proceeded to examine the book, not sorry, in the disturbed condition in which he was, to have an occupation found for him.

The book proved to be one with which he was unfamiliar, and this made it certain that some other hand than his had removed it from its place. Its title was "The Compleat Gard'ner" of M. de la Quintinye made English by John Evelyn Esquire. It was not a work in which Mr. Batchel felt any great interest. It consisted of divers reflections on various parts of husbandry, doubtless entertaining enough, but too deliberate and discursive for practical purposes. He had certainly never used the book, and growing restless now in mind, said to himself that some boy having the freedom of the house, had taken it down from its place in the hope of finding pictures.

But even whilst he made this explanation he felt its weakness. To begin with, the desk was too high for a boy. The improbability that any boy would place a book there was equalled by the improbability that he would leave it there. To discover its uninviting character would be the work only of a moment, and no boy would have brought it so far from its shelf.

Mr. Batchel had, however, come to read, and habit was too strong with him to be wholly set aside. Leaving "The Compleat Gard'ner" on the desk, he turned round to the shelves to find some more congenial reading.

Hardly had he done this when he was startled by a sharp rap upon the desk behind him, followed by a rustling of paper. He turned quickly about and saw the quarto lying open. In obedience to the instinct of the moment, he at once sought a natural cause for what he saw. Only a wind, and that of the strongest, could have opened the book, and laid back its heavy cover; and though he accepted, for a brief moment, that explanation, he was too candid to retain it longer. The wind out of doors was very light. The window sash was closed and latched, and, to decide the matter finally, the book had its back, and not its edges, turned towards the only quarter from which a wind could strike.

Mr. Batchel approached the desk again and stood over the book. With increasing perturbation of mind (for he still thought of the matchbox) he looked upon the open page. Without much reason beyond that he felt constrained to do something, he read the words of the half completed sentence at the turn of the page—

> "at dead of night he left the house and
> passed into the solitude of the garden."

But he read no more, nor did he give himself the trouble of discovering whose midnight wandering was being described, although the habit was singularly like one of his own. He was in no condition for reading, and turning his back upon the volume he slowly paced the length of the chamber, "wondering at that which had come to pass."

He reached the opposite end of the chamber and was in the act of turning, when again he heard the rustling of paper, and by the time he had faced round, saw the leaves of the book again turning over. In a moment the volume lay at rest, open in another place, and there was no further movement as he approached it. To make sure that he had not been deceived, he read again the words as they entered the page. The author was following a not uncommon practice of the time, and throwing common speech into forms suggested by Holy Writ: "So dig," it said, "that ye may obtain."

This passage, which to Mr. Batchel seemed reprehensible in its levity, excited at once his interest and his disapproval. He was prepared to read more, but this time was not allowed. Before his eye could pass beyond the passage already cited, the leaves of the book slowly turned again, and presented but a termination of five words and a colophon.

The words were, "to the North, an Ilex." These three passages, in which he saw no meaning and no connection, began to entangle themselves together in Mr. Batchel's mind. He found himself repeating them in different orders, now beginning with one, and now with another. Any further attempt at reading he felt to be impossible, and he was in no mind for any more experiences of the unaccountable. Sleep was, of course, further from him than ever, if that were conceivable. What he did, therefore, was to blow out the candle, to return to his moonlit bedroom, and put on more clothing, and then to pass downstairs with the object of going out of doors.

It was not unusual with Mr. Batchel to walk about his garden at nighttime. This form of exercise had often, after a wakeful hour, sent him back to his bed refreshed and ready for sleep. The convenient access to the garden at such times lay through his study, whose French windows opened on to a short flight of steps, and upon these he now paused for a moment to admire the snow-like appearance of the lawns, bathed as they were in the moonlight. As he paused, he heard the city clocks strike the half-hour after midnight, and he could not forbear repeating aloud

> "At dead of night he left the house,
> and passed into the solitude of the garden."

It was solitary enough. At intervals the screech of an owl, and now and then the noise of a train, seemed to emphasise the solitude by drawing attention to it and then leaving it in possession of the night. Mr. Batchel found himself wondering and conjecturing what Vicar Whitehead, who had acquired the close of land to secure quiet and privacy for a garden, would have thought of the railways to the west and north. He turned his face northwards, whence a whistle had just sounded, and saw a tree beautifully outlined against the sky. His breath caught at the sight. Not because the tree was unfamiliar. Mr. Batchel knew all his trees. But what he had seen was "to the north, an Ilex."

Mr. Batchel knew not what to make of it all. He had walked into the garden hundreds of times and as often seen the Ilex, but the words out of "The Compleat Gard'ner" seemed to be pursuing him in a way that made him almost afraid. His temperament, however, as has been said already, was phlegmatic. It was commonly said, and Mr. Batchel approved the verdict, whilst he condemned its inexactness, that "his nerves were made of fiddle-string", so he braced himself afresh and set upon his walk round the silent garden, which he was accustomed to begin in a northerly direction, and was now too proud to change. He usually passed the Ilex at the beginning of his perambulation, and so would pass it now.

He did not pass it. A small discovery, as he reached it, annoyed and disturbed him. His gardener, as careful and punctilious as himself, never failed to house all his tools at the end of a day's work. Yet there, under the Ilex, standing upright in moonlight brilliant enough to cast a shadow of it, was a spade.

Mr. Batchel's second thought was one of relief. After his extraordinary experiences in the library (he hardly knew now whether they had been real or not) something quite commonplace would act sedatively, and he determined to carry the spade to the tool-house.

The soil was quite dry, and the surface even a little frozen, so Mr. Batchel left the path, walked up to the spade, and would have drawn it towards him. But it was as if he had made the attempt upon the trunk of the Ilex itself. The spade would not be moved. Then, first with one hand, and then with both, he tried to raise it, and still it stood firm. Mr. Batchel, of course, attributed this to the frost, slight as it was. Wondering at the spade's being there, and annoyed at its being frozen, he was about to leave it and continue his walk, when the remaining works of "The Compleat Gard'ner" seemed rather to utter themselves, than to await his will—

"So dig, that ye may obtain."

Mr. Batchel's power of independent action now deserted him. He took the spade, which no longer resisted, and began to dig. "Five spadefuls and no more," he said aloud. "This is all foolishness."

Four spadefuls of earth he then raised and spread out before him in the moonlight. There was nothing unusual to be seen. Nor did Mr. Batchel decide what he would look for, whether coins, jewels, documents in canisters, or weapons. In point of fact, he dug against what he deemed his better judgement, and expected nothing. He spread before him the fifth and last spadeful of earth, not quite without result, but with no result that was at all sensational. The earth contained a bone. Mr. Batchel's knowledge of anatomy was sufficient to show him that it was a human bone. He identified it, even by moonlight, as the *radius*, a bone of the forearm, as he removed the earth from it, with his thumb.

Such a discovery might be thought worthy of more than the very ordinary interest Mr. Batchel showed. As a matter of fact, the presence of a human bone was easily to be accounted for. Recent excavations within the church had caused the upturning of numberless bones, which had been collected and reverently buried. But an earth-stained bone is also easily overlooked, and this *radius* had obviously found its way into the garden with some of the earth brought out of the church.

Mr. Batchel was glad, rather than regretful at this termination to his adventure. He was once more provided with something to do. The reinterment of such bones as this had been his constant care, and he decided at once to restore the bone to consecrated earth. The time seemed opportune. The eyes of the curious were closed in sleep, he himself was still alert and wakeful. The spade remained by his side and the bone in his hand. So he betook himself, there and then, to the churchyard. By the still generous light of the moon, he found a place where the earth yielded to his spade, and within a few minutes the bone was laid decently to earth, some 18 inches deep.

The city clocks struck one as he finished. The whole world seemed asleep, and Mr. Batchel slowly returned to the garden with his spade. As he hung it in its accustomed place he felt stealing over him the welcome desire to sleep. He walked quietly on to the house and ascended to his room. It was now dark: the moon had passed on and left the room in shadow. He lit a candle, and before undressing passed into the library. He had an irresistible curiosity to see the passages in John Evelyn's book which had so strangely adapted themselves to the events of the past hour.

In the library a last surprise awaited him. The desk upon which the book had lain was empty. "The Compleat Gard'ner" stood in its place on the shelf. And then Mr. Batchel knew that he had handled a bone of William Whitehead, and that in response to his own entreaty.

The Richpins

Something of the general character of Stoneground and its people has been indicated by stray allusions in the preceding narratives. We must here add that of its present population only a small part is native, the remainder having been attracted during the recent prosperous days of brickmaking, from the nearer parts of East Anglia and the Midlands. The visitor to Stoneground now finds little more than the signs of an unlovely industry, and of the hasty and inadequate housing of the people it has drawn together. Nothing in the place pleases him more than the excellent train-service which makes it easy to get away. He seldom desires a long acquaintance either with Stoneground or its people.

The impression so made upon the average visitor is, however, unjust, as first impressions often are. The few who have made further acquaintance with Stoneground have soon learned to distinguish between the permanent and the accidental features of the place, and have been astonished by nothing so much as by the unexpected evidence of French influence. Amongst the household treasures of the old Inhabitants are invariably found French knick-knacks: there are pieces of French furniture in what is called "the room" of many houses. A certain ten-acre field is called the "Frenchman's meadow." Upon the voters' lists hanging at the church door are to be found French names, often corrupted; and boys who run about the streets can be heard shrieking to each other such names as Bunnum, Dangibow, Planchey, and so on.

Mr. Batchel himself is possessed of many curious little articles of French handiwork—boxes deftly covered with split straws, arranged ingeniously in patterns; models of the guillotine, built of carved meat-bones, and various other pieces of handiwork, amongst them an accurate road-map of the country between Stoneground and Yarmouth, drawn upon a flyleaf torn from some book, and bearing upon the other side the name of Jules Richepin. The latter had been picked up, according to a pencilled-note written across one corner, by a shepherd, in the year 1811.

The explanation of this French influence is simple enough. Within five miles of Stoneground a large barracks had been erected for the custody of French prisoners during the war with Bonaparte. Many thousands were confined there during the years 1808-14. The prisoners were allowed to sell what articles they could make in the barracks; and many of them, upon their release, settled in the neighbourhood, where their descendants remain. There is little curiosity amongst these descendants about their origin. The events of a century ago seem to them as remote as the Deluge, and as immaterial. To Thomas Richpin, a weakly man who blew the organ in church, Mr. Batchel shewed the map. Richpin, with a broad, black-haired skull and a narrow chin which grew a little pointed beard, had always a foreign look about him: Mr. Batchel thought it more than possible that he might be descended from the owner of the book, and told him as much upon showing him the fly-leaf. Thomas, however, was content to observe that "his name hadn't got no E," and shewed no further interest in the matter. His interest in it, before we have done with him, will have become very large.

For the growing boys of Stoneground, with whom he was on generally friendly terms, Mr. Batchel formed certain clubs to provide them with occupation on winter evenings; and in these clubs, in the interests of peace and good-order, he spent a great deal of time. Sitting one December evening, in a large circle of boys who preferred the warmth of the fire to the more temperate atmosphere of the tables, he found Thomas Richpin the sole topic of conversation.

"We seen Mr. Richpin in Frenchman's Meadow last night," said one.

"What time?" said Mr. Batchel, whose function it was to act as a sort of fly-wheel, and to carry the conversation over dead points. He had received the information with some little surprise, because Frenchman's Meadow was an unusual place for Richpin to have been in, but his question had no further object than to encourage talk.

"Half-past nine," was the reply.

This made the question much more interesting. Mr. Batchel, on the preceding evening, had taken advantage of a warmed church to practise upon the organ. He had played it from nine o'clock until ten, and Richpin had been all that time at the bellows.

"Are you sure it was half-past nine?" he asked.

"Yes," (we reproduce the answer exactly), "we come out o' nightschool at quarter-past, and we was all goin' to the Wash to look if it was friz."

"And you saw Mr. Richpin in Frenchman's Meadow?" said Mr. Batchel.

"Yes. He was looking for something on the ground," added another boy.

"And his trousers was tore," said a third.

The story was clearly destined to stand in no need of corroboration.

"Did Mr. Richpin speak to you?" enquired Mr. Batchel.

"No, we run away afore he come to us," was the answer.

"Why?"

"Because we was frit."

"What frightened you?"

"Jim Lallement hauled a flint at him and hit him in the face, and he didn't take no notice, so we run away."

"Why?" repeated Mr. Batchel.

"Because he never hollered nor looked at us, and it made us feel so funny."

"Did you go straight down to the Wash?"

They had all done so.

"What time was it when you reached home?"

They had all been at home by ten, before Richpin had left the church.

"Why do they call it Frenchman's Meadow?" asked another boy, evidently anxious to change the subject.

Mr. Batchel replied that the meadow had probably belonged to a Frenchman whose name was not easy to say, and the conversation after this was soon in another channel. But, furnished as he was with an unmistakeable alibi, the story about Richpin and the torn trousers, and the flint, greatly puzzled him.

"Go straight home," he said, as the boys at last bade him goodnight, "and let us have no more stone-throwing." They were reckless boys, and Richpin, who used little discretion in reporting their misdemeanours about the church, seemed to Mr. Batchel to stand in real danger.

Frenchman's Meadow provided ten acres of excellent pasture, and the owners of two or three hard-worked horses were glad to pay three shillings a week for the privilege of turning them into it. One of these men came to Mr. Batchel on the morning which followed the conversation at the club.

"I'm in a bit of a quandary about Tom Richpin," he began.

This was an opening that did not fail to command Mr. Batchel's attention. "What is it?" he said.

"I had my mare in Frenchman's Meadow," replied the man, "and Sam Bower come and told me last night as he heard her gallopin' about when he was walking this side the hedge."

"But what about Richpin?" said Mr. Batchel.

"Let me come to it," said the other. "My mare hasn't got no wind to gallop, so I up and went to see to her, and there she was sure enough, like a wild thing, and Tom Richpin walking across the meadow."

"Was he chasing her?" asked Mr. Batchel, who felt the absurdity of the question as he put it.

"He was not," said the man, "but what he could have been doin' to put the mare into that state, I can't think."

"What was he doing when you saw him?" asked Mr. Batchel.

"He was walking along looking for something he'd dropped, with his trousers all tore to ribbons, and while I was catchin' the mare, he made off."

"He was easy enough to find, I suppose?" said Mr. Batchel.

"That's the quandary I was put in," said the man. "I took the mare home and gave her to my lad, and straight I went to Richpin's, and found Tom havin' his supper, with his trousers as good as new."

"You'd made a mistake," said Mr. Batchel.

"But how come the mare to make it too?" said the other.

"What did you say to Richpin?" asked Mr. Batchel.

"Tom," I says, "when did you come in? 'Six o'clock,' he says, 'I bin mendin' my boots'; and there, sure enough, was the bobbin' iron by his chair, and him in his stockin'-feet. I don't know what to do."

"Give the mare a rest," said Mr. Batchel, "and say no more about it."

"I don't want to harm a pore creature like Richpin," said the man, "but a mare's a mare, especially where there's a family to bring up." The man consented, however, to abide by Mr. Batchel's advice, and the interview ended. The evenings just then were light, and both the man and his mare had seen something for which Mr. Batchel could not, at present, account. The worst way, however, of arriving at an explanation is to guess it. He was far too wise to let himself wander into the pleasant fields of conjecture, and had determined, even before the story of the mare had finished, upon the more prosaic path of investigation.

Mr. Batchel, either from strength or indolence of mind, as the reader may be pleased to determine, did not allow matters even of this exciting kind, to disturb his daily round of duty. He was beginning to fear, after what he had heard of the Frenchman's Meadow, that he might find it necessary to preach a plain sermon upon the Witch of Endor, for he foresaw that there would soon be some ghostly talk in circulation. In small communities, like that of Stoneground, such talk arises upon very slight provocation, and here was nothing at all to check it. Richpin was a weak and timid man, whom no one would suspect, whilst an alternative remained open, of wandering about in the dark; and Mr. Batchel knew that the alternative of an apparition, if once suggested, would meet with general acceptance, and this he wished, at all costs, to avoid. His own view of the matter he held in reserve, for the reasons already stated, but he could not help suspecting that there might be a better explanation of the name "Frenchman's Meadow" than he had given to the boys at their club.

Afternoons, with Mr. Batchel, were always spent in making pastoral visits, and upon the day our story has reached he determined to include amongst them a call upon Richpin, and to submit him to a cautious cross-examination. It was evident that at least four persons, all perfectly familiar with his appearance, were under the impression that they had seen him in the meadow, and his own statement upon the matter would be at least worth hearing.

Richpin's home, however, was not the first one visited by Mr. Batchel on that afternoon. His friendly relations with the boys has already been mentioned, and it may now be added that this friendship was but part of a generally keen sympathy with young people of all ages, and of both sexes. Parents knew much less than he did of the love affairs of their young people; and if he was not actually guilty of matchmaking, he was at least a very sympathetic observer of the process. When lovers had their little differences, or even their greater ones, it was Mr. Batchel, in most cases, who adjusted them, and who suffered, if he failed, hardly less than the lovers themselves.

It was a negotiation of this kind which, on this particular day, had given precedence to another visit, and left Richpin until the later part of the afternoon. But the matter of the Frenchman's Meadow had, after all, not to wait for Richpin. Mr. Batchel was calculating how long he should be in reaching it, when he found himself unexpectedly there. Selina Broughton had been a favourite of his from her childhood; she had been sufficiently good to please him, and naughty enough to attract and challenge him; and when at length she began to walk out with Bob Rockfort, who was another favourite, Mr. Batchel rubbed his hands in satisfaction. Their present difference, which now brought him to the Broughtons' cottage, gave him but little anxiety. He had brought Bob half-way towards reconciliation, and had no doubt of his ability to lead Selina to the same place. They would finish the journey, happily enough, together.

But what has this to do with the Frenchman's Meadow? Much every way. The meadow was apt to be the rendezvous of such young people as desired a higher degree of privacy than that afforded by the public paths; and these two had gone there separately the night before, each to nurse a grievance against the other. They had been at opposite ends, as it chanced, of the field; and Bob, who believed himself to be alone there, had been awakened from his reverie by a sudden scream. He had at once run across the field, and found Selina sorely in need of him. Mr. Batchel's work of reconciliation had been there and then anticipated, and Bob had taken the girl home in a condition of great excitement to her mother. All this was explained, in breathless sentences, by Mrs. Broughton, by way of accounting for the fact that Selina was then lying down in "the room."

There was no reason why Mr. Batchel should not see her, of course, and he went in. His original errand had lapsed, but it was now replaced by one of greater interest. Evidently there was Selina's testimony to add to that of the other four; she was not a girl who would scream without good cause, and Mr. Batchel felt that he knew how his question about the cause would be answered, when he came to the point of asking it.

He was not quite prepared for the form of her answer, which she gave without any hesitation. She had seen Mr. Richpin "looking for his eyes." Mr. Batchel saved for another occasion the amusement to be derived from the curiously illogical answer. He saw at once what had suggested it. Richpin had until recently had an atrocious squint, which an operation in London had completely cured. This operation, of which, of course, he knew nothing, he had described, in his own way, to anyone who would listen, and it was commonly believed that his eyes had ceased to be fixtures. It was plain, however, that Selina had seen very much what had been seen by the other four. Her information was precise, and her story perfectly coherent. She preserved a maidenly reticence about his trousers, if she had noticed them; but added a new fact, and a terrible one, in her description of the eyeless sockets. No wonder she had screamed. It will be observed that Mr. Richpin was still searching, if not looking, for something upon the ground.

Mr. Batchel now proceeded to make his remaining visit. Richpin lived in a little cottage by the church, of which cottage the Vicar was the indulgent landlord. Richpin's creditors were obliged to shew some indulgence, because his income was never regular and seldom sufficient. He got on in life by what is called "rubbing along," and appeared to do it with surprisingly little friction. The small duties about the church, assigned to him out of charity, were overpaid. He succeeded in attracting to himself all the available gifts of masculine clothing, of which he probably received enough and to sell, and he had somehow wooed and won a capable, if not very comely, wife, who supplemented his income by her own labour, and managed her house and husband to admiration.

Richpin, however, was not by any means a more dependent upon charity. He was, in his way, a man of parts. All plants, for instance, were his friends, and he had inherited, or acquired, great skill with fruit-trees, which never failed to reward his treatment with abundant crops. The two or three vines, too, of the neighbourhood, he kept in fine order by methods of his own, whose merit was proved by their success. He had other skill, though of a less remunerative kind, in fashioning toys out of wood, cardboard, or paper; and every correctly-behaving child in the parish had some such product of his handiwork. And besides all this, Richpin had a remarkable aptitude for making music. He could do something upon every musical instrument that came in his way, and, but for his voice, which was like that of the pea-hen, would have been a singer. It was his voice that had secured him the situation of organ-blower, as one remote from all incitement to join in the singing in church.

Like all men who have not wit enough to defend themselves by argument, Richpin had a plaintive manner. His way of resenting injury was to complain of it to the next person he met, and such complaints as he found no other means of discharging, he carried home to his wife, who treated his conversation just as she treated the singing of the canary, and other domestic sounds, being hardly conscious of it until it ceased.

The entrance of Mr. Batchel, soon after his interview with Selina, found Richpin engaged in a loud and fluent oration. The fluency was achieved mainly by repetition, for the man had but small command of words, but it served none the less to shew the depth of his indignation.

"I aren't bin in Frenchman's Meadow, am I?" he was saying in appeal to his wife—this is the Stoneground way with auxiliary verbs— "What am I got to go there for?" He acknowledged Mr. Batchel's entrance in no other way than by changing to the third person in his discourse, and he continued without pause— "if she'd let me out o' nights, I'm got better places to go to than Frenchman's Meadow. Let policeman stick to where I am bin, or else keep his mouth shut. What call is he got to say I'm bin where I aren't bin?"

From this, and much more to the same effect, it was clear that the matter of the meadow was being noised abroad, and even receiving official attention. Mr. Batchel was well aware that no question he could put to Richpin, in his present state, would change the flow of his eloquence, and that he had already learned as much as he was likely to learn. He was content, therefore, to ascertain from Mrs. Richpin that her husband had indeed spent all his evenings at home, with the single exception of the one hour during which Mr. Batchel had employed him at the organ. Having ascertained this, he retired, and left Richpin to talk himself out.

No further doubt about the story was now possible. It was not twenty-four hours since Mr. Batchel had heard it from the boys at the club, and it had already been confirmed by at least two unimpeachable witnesses. He thought the matter over, as he took his tea, and was chiefly concerned in Richpin's curious connexion with it. On his account, more than on any other, it had become necessary to make whatever investigation might be feasible, and Mr. Batchel determined, of course, to make the next stage of it in the meadow itself.

The situation of "Frenchman's Meadow" made it more conspicuous than any other enclosure in the neighbourhood. It was upon the edge of what is locally known as "high land"; and though its elevation was not great, one could stand in the meadow and look sea-wards over many miles of flat country, once a waste of brackish water, now a great chess-board of fertile fields bounded by straight dykes of glistening water. The point of view derived another interest from looking down upon a long straight bank which disappeared into the horizon many miles away, and might have been taken for a great railway embankment of which no use had been made. It was, in fact, one of the great works of the Dutch Engineers in the time of Charles I., and it separated the river basin from a large drained area called the "Middle Level," some six feet below it. In this embankment, not two hundred yards below "Frenchman's Meadow," was one of the huge water gates which admitted traffic through a sluice, into the lower level, and the picturesque thatched cottage of the sluice-keeper formed a pleasing addition to the landscape. It was a view with which Mr. Batchel was naturally very familiar. Few of his surroundings were pleasant to the eye, and this was about the only place to which he could take a visitor whom he desired to impress favourably. The way to the meadow lay through a short lane, and he could reach it in five minutes: he was frequently there.

It was, of course, his intention to be there again that evening: to spend the night there, if need be, rather than let anything escape him. He only hoped he should not find half the parish there also. His best hope of privacy lay in the inclemency of the weather; the day was growing colder, and there was a north-east wind, of which Frenchman's Meadow would receive the fine edge.

Mr. Batchel spent the next three hours in dealing with some arrears of correspondence, and at nine o'clock put on his thickest coat and boots, and made his way to the meadow. It became evident, as he walked up the lane, that he was to have company. He heard many voices, and soon recognised the loudest amongst them. Jim Lallement was boasting of the accuracy of his aim: the others were not disputing it, but were asserting their own merits in discordant chorus. This was a nuisance, and to make matters worse, Mr. Batchel heard steps behind him.

A voice soon bade him "Good evening." To Mr. Batchel's great relief it proved to be the policeman, who soon overtook him. The conversation began on his side.

"Curious tricks, sir, these of Richpin's."

"What tricks?" asked Mr. Batchel, with an air of innocence.

"Why, he's been walking about Frenchman's Meadow these three nights, frightening folk and what all."

"Richpin has been at home every night, and all night long," said Mr. Batchel.

"I'm talking about where he was, not where he says he was," said the policeman. "You can't go behind the evidence."

"But Richpin has evidence too. I asked his wife."

"You know, sir, and none better, that wives have got to obey. Richpin wants to be took for a ghost, and we know that sort of ghost. Whenever we hear there's a ghost, we always know there's going to be turkeys missing."

"But there are real ghosts sometimes, surely?" said Mr. Batchel.

"No," said the policeman, "me and my wife have both looked, and there's no such thing."

"Looked where?" enquired Mr. Batchel.

"In the 'Police Duty' Catechism. There's lunatics, and deserters, and dead bodies, but no ghosts."

Mr. Batchel accepted this as final. He had devised a way of ridding himself of all his company, and proceeded at once to carry it into effect. The two had by this time reached the group of boys.

"These are all stone-throwers," said he, loudly.

There was a clatter of stones as they dropped from the hands of the boys.

"These boys ought all to be in the club instead of roaming about here damaging property. Will you take them there, and see them safely in? If Richpin comes here, I will bring him to the station."

The policeman seemed well pleased with the suggestion. No doubt he had overstated his confidence in the definition of the "Police Duty." Mr. Batchel, on his part, knew the boys well enough to be assured that they would keep the policeman occupied for the next half-hour, and as the party moved slowly away, felt proud of his diplomacy.

There was no sign of any other person about the field gate, which he climbed readily enough, and he was soon standing in the highest part of the meadow and peering into the darkness on every side.

It was possible to see a distance of about thirty yards; beyond that it was too dark to distinguish anything. Mr. Batchel designed a zigzag course about the meadow, which would allow of his examining it systematically and as rapidly as possible, and along this course he began to walk briskly, looking straight before him as he went, and pausing to look well about him when he came to a turn. There were no beasts in the meadow—their owners had taken the precaution of removing them; their absence was, of course, of great advantage to Mr. Batchel.

In about ten minutes he had finished his zig-zag path and arrived at the other corner of the meadow; he had seen nothing resembling a man. He then retraced his steps, and examined the field again, but arrived at his starting point, knowing no more than when he had left it. He began to fear the return of the policeman as he faced the wind and set upon a third journey.

The third journey, however, rewarded him. He had reached the end of his second traverse, and was looking about him at the angle between that and the next, when he distinctly saw what looked like Richpin crossing his circle of vision, and making straight for the sluice. There was no gate on that side of the field; the hedge, which seemed to present no obstacle to the other, delayed Mr. Batchel considerably, and still retains some of his clothing, but he was not long through before he had again marked his man. It had every appearance of being Richpin. It went down the slope, crossed the plank that bridged the lock, and disappeared round the corner of the cottage, where the entrance lay.

Mr. Batchel had had no opportunity of confirming the gruesome observation of Selina Broughton, but had seen enough to prove that the others had not been romancing. He was not a half-minute behind the figure as it crossed the plank over the lock—it was slow going in the darkness—and he followed it immediately round the corner of the house. As he expected, it had then disappeared.

Mr. Batchel knocked at the door, and admitted himself, as his custom was. The sluicekeeper was in his kitchen, charring a gate post. He was surprised to see Mr. Batchel at that hour, and his greeting took the form of a remark to that effect.

"I have been talking an evening walk," said Mr. Batchel. "Have you seen Richpin lately?"

"I see him last Saturday week," replied the sluice-keeper, "not since."

"Do you feel lonely here at night?"

"No," replied the sluice-keeper, "people drop in at times. There was a man in on Monday, and another yesterday."

"Have you had no one to-day?" said Mr. Batchel, coming to the point.

The answer showed that Mr. Batchel had been the first to enter the door that day, and after a little general conversation he brought his visit to an end.

It was now ten o'clock. He looked in at Richpin's cottage, where he saw a light burning, as he passed. Richpin had tired himself early, and had been in bed since half-past eight. His wife was visibly annoyed at the rumours which had upset him, and Mr. Batchel said such soothing words as he could command, before he left for home.

He congratulated himself, prematurely, as he sat before the fire in his study, that the day was at an end. It had been cold out of doors, and it was pleasant to think things over in the warmth of the cheerful fire his housekeeper never failed to leave for him. The reader will have no more difficulty than Mr. Batchel had in accounting for the resemblance between Richpin and the man in the meadow. It was a mere question of family likeness. That the ancestor had been seen in the meadow at some former time might perhaps be inferred from its traditional name. The reason for his return, then and now, was a matter of more conjecture, and Mr. Batchel let it alone.

The next incident has, to some, appeared incredible, which only means, after all, that it has made demands upon their powers of imagination and found them bankrupt.

Critics of story-telling have used severe language about authors who avail themselves of the short-cut of coincidence. "That must be reserved, I suppose," said Mr. Batchel, when he came to tell of Richpin, "for what really happens; and that fiction is a game which must be played according to the rules."

"I know," he went on to say, "that the chances were some millions to one against what happened that night, but if that makes it incredible, what is there left to believe?"

It was thereupon remarked by someone in the company, that the credible material would not be exhausted.

"I doubt whether anything happens," replied Mr. Batchel in his dogmatic way, "without the chances being a million to one against it. Why did they choose such a word? What does 'happen' mean?"

There was no reply: it was clearly a rhetorical question.

"Is it incredible," he went on, "that I put into the plate last Sunday the very half-crown my uncle tipped me with in 1881, and that I spent next day?"

"Was that the one you put in?" was asked by several.

"How do I know?" replied Mr. Batchel, "but if I knew the history of the half-crown I did put in, I know it would furnish still more remarkable coincidences."

All this talk arose out of the fact that at midnight on the eventful day, whilst Mr. Batchel was still sitting by his study fire, he had news that the cottage at the sluice had been burnt down. The thatch had been dry; there was, as we know, a stiff east-wind, and an hour had sufficed to destroy all that was inflammable. The fire is still spoken of in Stoneground with great regret. There remains only one building in the place of sufficient merit to find its way on to a postcard.

It was just at midnight that the sluice-keeper rung at Mr. Batchel's door. His errand required no apology. The man had found a night-fisherman to help him as soon as the fire began, and with two long sprits from a lighter they had made haste to tear down the thatch, and upon this had brought down, from under the ridge at the South end, the bones and some of the clothing of a man. Would Mr. Batchel come down and see?

Mr. Batchel put on his coat and returned to the place. The people whom the fire had collected had been kept on the further side of the water, and the space about the cottage was vacant. Near to the smouldering heap of ruin were the remains found under the thatch. The fingers of the right hand still firmly clutched a sheep bone which had been gnawed as a dog would gnaw it.

"Starved to death," said the sluice-keeper, "I see a tramp like that ten years ago."

They laid the bones decently in an out-house, and turned the key, Mr. Batchel carried home in his hand a metal cross, threaded upon a cord. He found an engraved figure of Our Lord on the face of it, and the name of Pierre Richepin upon the back. He went next day to make the matter known to the nearest Priest of the Roman Faith, with whom he left the cross. The remains, after a brief inquest, were interred in the cemetery, with the rites of the Church to which the man had evidently belonged.

Mr. Batchel's deductions from the whole circumstances were curious, and left a great deal to be explained. It seemed as if Pierre Richepin had been disturbed by some premonition of the fire, but had not foreseen that his mortal remains would escape; that he could not return to his own people without the aid of his map, but had no perception of the interval that had elapsed since he had lost it. This map Mr. Batchel put into his pocket-book next day when he went to Thomas Richpin for certain other information about his surviving relatives.

Richpin had a father, it appeared, living a few miles away in Jakesley Fen, and Mr. Batchel concluded that he was worth a visit. He mounted his bicycle, therefore, and made his way to Jakesley that same afternoon.

Mr. Richpin was working not far from home, and was soon brought in. He and his wife shewed great courtesy to their visitor, whom they knew well by repute. They had a well-ordered house, and with a natural and dignified hospitality, asked him to take tea with them. It was evident to Mr. Batchel that there was a great gulf between the elder Richpin and his son; the former was the last of an old race, and the latter the first of a new. In spite of the Board of Education, the latter was vastly the worse.

The cottage contained some French kickshaws which greatly facilitated the enquiries Mr. Batchel had come to make. They proved to be family relies.

"My grandfather," said Mr. Richpin, as they sat at tea, "was a prisoner—he and his brother."

"Your grandfather was Pierre Richepin?" asked Mr. Batchel.

"No! Jules," was the reply. "Pierre got away."

"Shew Mr. Batchel the book," said his wife.

The book was produced. It was a Book of Meditations, with the name of Jules Richepin upon the title-page. The fly-leaf was missing. Mr. Batchel produced the map from his pocketbook. It fitted exactly. The slight indentures along the torn edge fell into their place, and Mr. Batchel left the leaf in the book, to the great delight of the old couple, to whom he told no more of the story than he thought fit.

The Eastern Window

It may well be that Vermuyden and the Dutchmen who drained the fens did good, and that it was interred with their bones. It is quite certain that they did evil and that it lives after them. The rivers, which these men robbed of their water, have at length silted up, and the drainage of one tract of country is proving to have been achieved by the undraining of another.

Places like Stoneground, which lie on the banks of these defrauded rivers, are now become helpless victims of Dutch engineering. The water which has lost its natural outlet, invades their lands. The thrifty cottager who once had the river at the bottom of his garden, has his garden more often in these days, at the bottom of the river, and a summer flood not infrequently destroys the whole produce of his ground.

Such a flood, during an early year in the 20th century, had been unusually disastrous to Stoneground, and Mr. Batchel, who, as a gardener, was well able to estimate the losses of his poorer neighbours, was taking some steps towards repairing them.

Money, however, is never at rest in Stoneground, and it turned out upon this occasion that the funds placed at his command were wholly inadequate to the charitable purpose assigned to them. It seemed as if those who had lost a rood of potatoes could be compensated for no more than a yard.

It was at this time, when he was oppressed in mind by the failure of his charitable enterprise, that Mr. Batchel met with the happy adventure in which the Eastern window of the Church played so singular a part.

The narrative should be prefaced by a brief description of the window in question. It is a large painted window, of a somewhat unfortunate period of execution. The drawing and colouring leave everything to be desired. The scheme of the window, however, is based upon a wholesome tradition. The five large lights in the lower part are assigned to five scenes in the life of Our Lord, and the second of these, counting from the North, contains a bold erect figure of St. John Baptist, to whom the Church is dedicated. It is this figure alone, of all those contained in the window, that is concerned in what we have to relate.

It has already been mentioned that Mr. Batchel had some knowledge of music. He took an interest in the choir, from whose practices he was seldom absent; and was quite competent, in the occasional absence of the choirmaster, to act as his deputy. It is customary at Stoneground for the choirmaster, in order to save the sexton a journey, to extinguish the lights after a choir-practice and to lock up the Church. These duties, accordingly, were performed by Mr. Batchel when the need arose.

It will be of use to the reader to have the procedure in detail. The large gas-meter stood in an aisle of the Church, and it was Mr. Batchel's practice to go round and extinguish all the lights save one, before turning off the gas at the meter. The one remaining light, which was reached by standing upon a choir seat, was always that nearest the door of the chancel, and experience proved that there was ample time to walk from the meter to that light before it died out. It was therefore an easy matter to turn off the last light, to find the door without its aid, and thence to pass out, and close the Church for the night.

Upon the evening of which we have to speak, the choir had hurried out as usual, as soon as the word had been given. Mr. Batchel had remained to gather together some of the books they had left in disorder, and then turned out the lights in the manner already described. But as soon as he had extinguished the last light, his eye fell, as he descended carefully from the seat, upon the figure of the Baptist. There was just enough light outside to make the figures visible in the Eastern Window, and Mr. Batchel saw the figure of St. John raise the right arm to its full extent, and point northward, turning its head, at the same time, so as to look him full in the face. These movements were three times repeated, and, after that, the figure came to rest, in its normal and familiar position.

The reader will not suppose, any more than Mr. Batchel supposed, that a figure painted upon glass had suddenly been endowed with the power of movement. But that there had been the appearance of movement admitted of no doubt, and Mr. Batchel was not so incurious as to let the matter pass without some attempt at investigation. It must be remembered, too, that an experience in the old library, which has been previously recorded, had pre-disposed him to give attention to signs which another man might have wished to explain away. He was not willing, therefore, to leave this matter where it stood. He was quite prepared to think that his eye had been deceived, but was none the less determined to find out what had deceived it. One thing he had no difficulty in deciding. If the movement had not been actually within the Baptist's figure, it had been immediately behind it. Without delay, therefore, he passed out of the church and locked the door after him, with the intention of examining the other side of the window.

Every inhabitant of Stoneground knows, and laments, the ruin of the old Manor House. Its loss by fire some fifteen years ago was a calamity from which the parish has never recovered. The estate was acquired, soon after the destruction of the house, by speculators who have been unable to turn it to any account, and it has for a decade or longer been "let alone," except by the forces of Nature and the wantonness of trespassers. The charred remains of the house still project above the surrounding heaps of fallen masonry, which have long been overgrown by such vegetation as thrives on neglected ground; and what was once a stately house, with its garden and park in fine order, has given place to a scene of desolation and ruin.

Stoneground Church was built, some 600 years ago, within the enclosure of the Manor House, or, as it was anciently termed, the Burystead, and an excellent stratum of gravel such as no builder would wisely disregard, brought the house and Church unusually near together. In more primitive days, the nearness probably caused no inconvenience; but when change and progress affected the popular idea of respectful distance, the Churchyard came to be separated by a substantial stone wall, of sufficient height to secure the privacy of the house.

The change was made with necessary regard to economy of space. The Eastern wall of the Church already projected far into the garden of the Manor, and lay but fifty yards from the south front of the house. On that side of the Churchyard, therefore, the new wall was set back. Running from the north to the nearest corner of the Church, it was there built up to the Church itself, and then continued from the southern corner, leaving the Eastern wall and window within the garden of the Squire. It was his ivy that clung to the wall of the Church, and his trees that shaded the window from the morning sun.

Whilst we have been recalling these facts, Mr. Batchel has made his way out of the Church and through the Churchyard, and has arrived at a small door in the boundary wall, close to the S.E. corner of the chancel. It was a door which some Squire of the previous century had made, to give convenient access to the Church for himself and his household. It has no present use, and Mr. Batchel had some difficulty in getting it open. It was not long, however, before he stood on the inner side, and was examining the second light of the window. There was a tolerably bright moon, and the dark surface of the glass could be distinctly seen, as well as the wirework placed there for its protection.

A tall birch, one of the trees of the old Churchyard, had thrust its lower boughs across the window, and their silvery bark shone in the moonlight. The boughs were bare of leaves, and only very slightly interrupted Mr. Batchel's view of the Baptist's figure, the leaden outline of which was clearly traceable. There was nothing, however, to account for the movement which Mr. Batchel was curious to investigate.

He was about to turn homewards in some disappointment, when a cloud obscured the moon again, and reduced the light to what it had been before he left the Church. Mr. Batchel watched the darkening of the window and the objects near it, and as the figure of the Baptist disappeared from view there came into sight a creamy vaporous figure of another person lightly poised upon the bough of the tree, and almost coincident in position with the picture of the Saint.

It could hardly be described as the figure of a person. It had more the appearance of half a person, and fancifully suggested to Mr. Batchel, who was fond of whist, one of the diagonally bisected knaves in a pack of cards, as he appears when another card conceals a triangular half of the bust.

There was no question, now, of going home. Mr. Batchel's eyes were riveted upon the apparition. It disappeared again for a moment, when an interval between two clouds restored the light of the moon; but no sooner had the second cloud replaced the first than the figure again became distinct. And upon this, its single arm was raised three times, pointing northwards towards the ruined house, just as the figure of the Baptist had seemed to point when Mr. Batchel had seen it from within the Church.

It was natural that upon receipt of this sign Mr. Batchel should step nearer to the tree, from which he was still at some little distance, and as he moved, the figure floated obliquely downwards and came to rest in a direct line between him and the ruins of the house. It rested, not upon the ground, but in just such a position as it would have occupied if the lower parts had been there, and in this position it seemed to await Mr. Batchel's advance. He made such haste to approach it as was possible upon ground encumbered with ivy and brambles, and the figure responded to every advance of his by moving further in the direction of the ruin.

As the ground improved, the progress became more rapid. Soon they were both upon an open stretch of grass, which in better days had been a lawn, and still the figure retreated towards the building, with Mr. Batchel in respectful pursuit. He saw it, at last, poised upon the summit of a heap of masonry, and it disappeared, at his near approach, into a crevice between two large stones.

The timely re-appearance of the moon just enabled Mr. Batchel to perceive this crevice, and he took advantage of the interval of light to mark the place. Taking up a large twig that lay at his feet, he inserted it between the stones. He made a slit in the free end and drew into it one of some papers that he had carried out of the Church. After such a precaution it could hardly be possible to lose the place—for, of course, Mr. Batchel intended to return in daylight and continue his investigation. For the present, it seemed to be at an end. The light was soon obscured again, but there was no re-appearance of the singular figure he had followed, so after remaining about the spot for a few minutes, Mr. Batchel went home to his customary occupation.

He was not a man to let these occupations be disturbed even by a somewhat exciting adventure, nor was he one of those who regard an unusual experience only as a sign of nervous disorder. Mr. Batchel had far too broad a mind to discredit his sensations because they were not like those of other people. Even had his adventure of the evening been shared by some companion who saw less than he did, Mr. Batchel would only have inferred that his own part in the matter was being regarded as more important.

Next morning, therefore, he lost no time in returning to the scene of his adventure. He found his mark undisturbed, and was able to examine the crevice into which the apparition had seemed to enter. It was a crevice formed by the curved surfaces of two large stones which lay together on the top of a small heap of fallen rubbish, and these two stones Mr. Batchel proceeded to remove. His strength was just sufficient for the purpose. He laid the stones upon the ground on either side of the little mound, and then proceeded to remove, with his hands, the rubbish upon which they had rested, and amongst the rubbish he found, tarnished and blackened, two silver coins.

It was not a discovery which seemed to afford any explanation of what had occurred the night before, but Mr. Batchel could not but suppose that there had been an attempt to direct his attention to the coins, and he carried them away with a view of submitting them to a careful examination. Taking them up to his bedroom he poured a little water into a hand basin, and soon succeeded, with the aid of soap and a nail brush, in making them tolerably clean. Ten minutes later, after adding ammonia to the water, he had made them bright, and after carefully drying them, was able to make his examination. They were two crowns of the time of Queen Anne, minted, as a small letter E indicated, at Edinburgh, and stamped with the roses and plumes which testified to the English and Welsh silver in their composition. The coins bore no date, but Mr. Batchel had no hesitation in assigning them to the year 1708 or thereabouts. They were handsome coins, and in themselves a find of considerable interest, but there was nothing to show why he had been directed to their place of concealment. It was an enigma, and he could not solve it. He had other work to do, so he laid the two crowns upon his dressing table, and proceeded to do it.

Mr. Batchel thought little more of the coins until bedtime, when he took them from the table and bestowed upon them another admiring examination by the light of his candle. But the examination told him nothing new: he laid them down again, and, before very long, had lain his own head upon the pillow.

It was Mr. Batchel's custom to read himself to sleep. At this time he happened to be rereading the Waverley novels, and "Woodstock" lay upon the reading-stand which was always placed at his bedside. As he read of the cleverly devised apparition at Woodstock, he naturally asked himself whether he might not have been the victim of some similar trickery, but was not long in coming to the conclusion that his experience admitted of no such explanation. He soon dismissed the matter from his mind and went on with his book.

On this occasion, however, he was tired of reading before he was ready for sleep; it was long in coming, and then did not come to stay. His rest, in fact, was greatly disturbed. Again and again, perhaps every hour or so, he was awakened by an uneasy consciousness of some other presence in the room.

Upon one of his later awakenings, he was distinctly sensible of a sound, or what he described to himself as the "ghost" of a sound. He compared it to the whining of a dog that had lost its voice. It was not a very intelligible comparison, but still it seemed to describe his sensation. The sound, if we may so call it caused him first to sit up in bed and look well about him, and then, when nothing had come of that, to light his candle. It was not to be expected that anything should come of that, but it had seemed a comfortable thing to do, and Mr. Batchel left the candle alight and read his book for half an hour or so, before blowing it out.

After this, there was no further interruption, but Mr. Batchel distinctly felt, when it was time to leave his bed, that he had had a bad night. The coins, almost to his surprise, lay undisturbed. He went to ascertain this as soon as he was on his feet. He would almost have welcomed their removal, or at any rate, some change which might have helped him towards a theory of his adventure. There was, however, nothing. If he had, in fact, been visited during the night, the coins would seem to have had nothing to do with the matter.

Mr. Batchel left the two crowns lying on his table on this next day, and went about his ordinary duties. They were such duties as afforded full occupation for his mind, and he gave no more than a passing thought to the coins, until he was again retiring to rest. He had certainly intended to return to the heap of rubbish from which he had taken them, but had not found leisure to do so. He did not handle the coins again. As he undressed, he made some attempt to estimate their value, but without having arrived at any conclusion, went on to think of other things, and in a little while had lain down to rest again, hoping for a better night.

His hopes were disappointed. Within an hour of falling asleep he found himself awakened again by the voiceless whining he so well remembered. This sound, as for convenience we will call it, was now persistent and continuous. Mr. Batchel gave up oven trying to sleep, and as he grew more restless and uneasy, decided to get up and dress.

It was the entire cessation of the sound at this juncture which led him to a suspicion. His rising was evidently giving satisfaction. From that it was easy to infer that something had been desired of him, both on the present and the preceding night. Mr.

Batchel was not one to hold himself aloof in such a case. If help was wanted, even in such unnatural circumstances, he was ready to offer it. He determined, accordingly, to return to the Manor House, and when he had finished dressing, descended the stairs, put on a warm overcoat and went out, closing his hail door behind him, without having heard any more of the sound, either whilst dressing, or whilst leaving the house.

Once out of doors, the suspicion he had formed was strengthened into a conviction. There was no manner of doubt that he had been fetched from his bed; for about 30 yards in front of him he saw the strange creamy half-figure making straight for the ruins. He followed it as well as he could; as before, he was impeded by the ivy and weeds, and the figure awaited him; as before, it made straight for the heap of masonry and disappeared as soon as Mr. Batchel was at liberty to follow.

There were no dungeons, or subterranean premises beneath the Manor House. It had never been more than a house of residence, and the building had been purely domestic in character. Mr. Batchel was convinced that his adventure would prove unromantic, and felt some impatience at losing again, what he had begun to call his triangular friend. If this friend wanted anything, it was not easy to say why he had so tamely disappeared. There seemed nothing to be done but to wait until he came out again.

Mr. Batchel had a pipe in his pocket, and he seated himself upon the base of a sun-dial within full view of the spot. He filled and smoked his pipe, sitting in momentary expectation of some further sign, but nothing appeared. He heard the hedgehogs moving about him in the undergrowth, and now and then the sound of a restless bird overhead, otherwise all was still. He smoked a second pipe without any further discovery, and that finished, he knocked out the ashes against his boot, walked to the mound, near to which his labelled stick was lying, thrust the stick into the place where the figure had disappeared, and went back to bed, where he was rewarded with five hours of sound sleep.

Mr. Batchel had made up his mind that the next day ought to be a day of disclosure. He was early at the Manor House, this time provided with the gardener's pick, and a spade. He thrust the pick into the place from which he had removed his mark, and loosened the rubbish thoroughly. With his hands, and with his spade, he was not long in reducing the size of the heap by about one-half, and there he found more coins.

There were three more crowns, two half-crowns, and a dozen or so of smaller coins. All these Mr. Batchel wrapped carefully in his handkerchief, and after a few minutes rest went on with his task. As it proved, the task was nearly over. Some strips of oak about nine inches long, were next uncovered, and then, what Mr. Batchel had begun to expect, the lid of a box, with the hinges still attached. It lay, face downwards, upon a flab stone. It proved, when he had taken it up, to be almost unsoiled, and above a long and wide slit in the lid was the gilded legend, "for ye poore" in the graceful lettering and the redundant spelling of two centuries ago.

The meaning of all this Mr. Batchel was not long in interpreting. That the box and its contents had fallen and been broken amongst the masonry, was evident enough. It was as evident that it had been concealed in one of the walls brought down by the fire, and Mr. Batchel had no doubt at all that he had been in the company of a thief, who had once stolen the poor-box from the Church. His task seemed to be at an end, a further rummage revealed nothing new. Mr. Batchel carefully collected the fragments of the box, and left the place.

His next act cannot be defended. He must have been aware that these coins were "treasure trove," and therefore the property of the Crown. In spite of this, he determined to convert them into current coin, as he well knew how, and to apply the proceeds to the Inundation Fund about which he was so anxious. Treating them as his own property, he cleaned them all, as he had cleaned the two crowns, sent them to an antiquarian friend in London to sell for him, and awaited the result. The lid of the poor box he still preserves as a relic of the adventure.

His antiquarian friend did not keep him long waiting. The coins had been eagerly bought, and the price surpassed any expectation that Mr. Batchel had allowed himself to entertain. He had sent the package to London on Saturday morning. Upon the following Tuesday, the last post in the evening brought a cheque for twenty guineas. The brief subscription list of the Inundation Fund lay upon his desk, and he at once entered the amount he had so strangely come by, but could not immediately decide upon its description. Leaving the line blank, therefore, he merely wrote down £21 in the cash column, to be assigned to its source in some suitable form of words when he should have found time to frame them.

In this state he left the subscription list upon his desk, when he retired for the night. It occurred to him as he was undressing, that the twenty guineas might suitably be described as a "restitution," and so he determined to enter it upon the line he had left vacant. As he reconsidered the matter in the morning, he saw no reason to alter his decision, and he went straight from his bedroom to his desk to make the entry and have done with it.

There was an incident in the adventure, however, upon which Mr. Batchel had not reckoned. As he approached the list, he saw, to his amazement, that the line had been filled in. In a crabbed, elongated hand was written, "At last, St. Matt. v. 26."

What may seem more strange is that the handwriting was familiar to Mr. Batchel, he could not at first say why. His memory, however, in such matters, was singularly good, and before breakfast was over he felt sure of having identified the writer.

His confidence was not misplaced. He went to the parish chest, whose contents he had thoroughly examined in past intervals of leisure, and took out the roll of parish constable's accounts. In a few minutes he discovered the handwriting of which he was in search. It was unmistakably that of Salathiel Thrapston, constable from 1705-1710, who met his death in the latter year, whilst in the execution of his duty. The reader will scarcely need to be reminded of the text of the Gospel at the place of reference—

"Thou shalt by no means come out thence till thou hast paid the uttermost farthing."

Lubrietta

For the better understanding of this narrative we shall furnish the reader with a few words of introduction. It amounts to no more than a brief statement of facts which Mr. Batchel obtained from the Lady Principal of the European College in Puna, but the facts nevertheless are important. The narrative itself was obtained from Mr. Batchel with difficulty: he was disposed to regard it as unsuitable for publication because of the delicate nature of the situations with which it deals. When, however, it was made clear to him that it would be recorded in such a manner as would interest only a very select body of readers, his scruples were overcome, and he was induced to communicate the experience now to be related. Those who read it will not fail to see that they are in a manner pledged to deal very discreetly with the knowledge they are privileged to share.

Lubrietta Rodria is described by her Lady Principal as an attractive and high-spirited girl of seventeen, belonging to the Purple of Indian commerce. Her nationality was not precisely known; but drawing near, as she did, to a marriageable age, and being courted by more than one eligible suitor, she was naturally an object of great interest to her schoolfellows, with whom her personal beauty and amiable temper had always made her a favourite. She was not, the Lady Principal thought, a girl who would be regarded in Christian countries as of very high principle; but none the less, she was one whom it was impossible not to like.

Her career at the college had ended sensationally. She had been immoderately anxious about her final examination, and its termination had found her in a state of collapse. They had at once removed her to her father's house in the country, where she received such nursing and assiduous attention as her case required. It was apparently of no avail. For three weeks she lay motionless, deprived of speech, and voluntarily, taking no food. Then for a further period of ten days she lay in a plight still more distressing. She lost all consciousness, and, despite the assurance of the doctors, her parents could hardly be persuaded that she lived.

Her *fiancé* who by this time had been declared, was in despair, not only from natural affection for Lubrietta, but from remorse. It was his intellectual ambition that had incited her to the eagerness in study which was threatening such dire results, and it was well understood that neither of the lovers would survive these anxious days of watching if they were not to be survived by both.

After ten days, however, a change supervened. Lubrietta came back to life amid the frenzied rejoicing of the household and all her circle. She recovered her health and strength with incredible speed, and within three months was married—as the Lady Principal had cause to believe, with the happiest prospects.

* * * * * *

Mr. Batchel had not, whilst residing at Stoneground, lost touch with the University which had given him his degree, and in which he had formerly held one or two minor offices. He had earned no great distinction as a scholar, but had taken a degree in honours, and was possessed of a useful amount of general knowledge, and in this he found not only constant pleasure, but also occasional profit.

The University had made herself, for better or worse, an examiner of a hundred times as many students as she could teach; her system of examinations had extended to the very limits of the British Empire, and her certificates of proficiency were coveted in every quarter of the globe.

In the examination of these students, Mr. Batchel, who had considerable experience in teaching, was annually employed. Papers from all parts of the world were to be found littered about his study, and the examination of these papers called for some weeks of strenuous labour at every year's end. As the weeks passed, he would anxiously watch the growth of a neat stack of papers in the corner of the room, which indicated the number to which marks had been assigned and reported to Cambridge. The day upon which the last of these was laid in its place was a day of satisfaction, second only to that which later on brought him a substantial cheque to remunerate him for his labours.

During this period of special effort, Mr. Batchel's servants had their share of its discomforts. The chairs and tables they wanted to dust and to arrange, were loaded with papers which they were forbidden to touch; and although they were warned against showing visitors into any room where these papers were lying, Mr. Batchel would inconsiderately lay them in every room he had. The privacy of his study, however, where the work was chiefly done, was strictly guarded, and no one was admitted there unless by Mr. Batchel himself.

Imagine his annoyance, therefore, when he returned from an evening engagement at the beginning of the month of January, and found a stranger seated in the study! Yet the annoyance was not long in subsiding. The visitor was a lady, and as she sat by the lamp, a glance was enough to shew that she was young, and very beautiful. The interest which this young lady excited in Mr. Batchel was altogether unusual, as unusual as was the visit of such a person at such a time. His conjecture was that she had called to give him notice of a marriage, but he was really charmed by her presence, and was quite content to find her in no haste to state her errand. The manner, however, of the lady was singular, for neither by word nor movement did she show that she was conscious of Mr. Batchel's entry into the room.

He began at length with his customary formula "What can I have the pleasure of doing for you?" and when, at the sound of his voice, she turned her fine dark eyes upon him, he saw that they were wet with tears.

Mr. Batchel was now really moved. As a tear fell upon the lady's cheek, she raised her hand as if to conceal it—a brilliant sapphire sparkling in the lamp-light as she did so. And then the lady's distress, and the exquisite grace of her presence, altogether overcame him. There stole upon him a strange feeling of tenderness which he supposed to be paternal, but knew nevertheless to be indiscreet. He was a prudent man, with strict notions of propriety, so that, ostensibly with a view to giving the lady a few minutes in which to recover her composure, he quietly left the study and went into another room, to pull himself together.

Mr. Batchel, like most solitary men, had a habit of talking to himself. "It is of no use, B. B.," he said, "to pretend that you have retired on this damsel's account. If you don't take care, you'll make a fool of yourself." He took up from the table a volume of the encyclopedia in which, the day before, he had been looking up Pestalozzi, and turned over the pages in search of something to restore his equanimity. An article on Perspective proved to be the very thing. Wholly unromantic in character, its copious presentment of hard fact relieved his mind, and he was soon threading his way along paths of knowledge to which he was little accustomed. He applied his remedy with such persistence that when four or five minutes had passed, he felt sufficiently composed to return to the study. He framed, as he went, a suitable form of words with which to open the conversation, and took with him his register of Banns of Marriage, of which he thought he foresaw the need. As he opened the study-door, the book fell from his hands to the ground, so completely was he overcome by surprise, for he found the room empty. The lady had disappeared; her chair stood vacant before him.

Mr. Batchel sat down for a moment, and then rang the bell. It was answered by the boy who always attended upon him.

"When did the lady go?" asked Mr. Batchel. The boy looked bewildered.

"The lady you showed into the study before I came."

"Please, sir, I never shown anyone into the study; I never do when you're out."

"There was a lady here," said Mr. Batchel, "when I returned."

The boy now looked incredulous.

"Did you not let someone out just now?"

"No, sir," said the boy. "I put the chain on the front door as soon as you came in."

This was conclusive. The chain upon the hall-door was an ancient and cumbrous thing, and could not be manipulated without considerable effort, and a great deal of noise. Mr. Batchel released the boy, and began to think furiously. He was not, as the reader is well aware, without some experience of the supranormal side of nature, and he knew of course that the visit of this enthralling lady had a purpose. He was beginning to know, however, that it had had an effect. He sat before his fire reproducing her image, and soon gave it up in disgust because his imagination refused to do her justice. He could recover the details of her appearance, but could combine them into nothing that would reproduce the impression she had first made upon him.

He was unable now to concentrate his attention upon the examination papers lying on his table. His mind wandered so often to the other topic that he felt himself to be in danger of marking the answers unfairly. He turned away from his work, therefore, and moved to another chair, where he sat down to road. It was the chair in which she herself had sat, and he made no attempt to pretend that he had chosen it on any other account. He had, in fact, made some discoveries about himself during the last half-hour, and he gave himself another surprise when he came to select his book. In the ordinary course of what he had supposed to be his nature, he would certainly have returned to the article on Perspective; it was lying open in the next room, and he had read no more than a tenth part of it. But instead of that, his thoughts went back to a volume he had but once opened, and that for no more than two minutes. He had received the book, by way of birthday present, early in the preceding year, from a relative who had bestowed either no consideration at all, or else a great deal of cunning, upon its selection. It was a collection of 17th century lyrics, which Mr. Batchel's single glance had sufficed to condemn. Regarding the one lyric he had read as a sort of literary freak, he had banished the book to one of the spare bedrooms, and had never seen it since. And now, after this long interval, the absurd lines which his eye had but once lighted upon, were recurring to his mind:

> "Fair, sweet, and young, receive a prize
> Reserved for your victorious eyes";

and so far from thinking them absurd, as he now recalled them, he went upstairs to fetch the book, in which he was soon absorbed. The lyrics no longer seemed unreasonable. He felt conscious, as he read one after another, of a side of nature that he had strangely neglected, and was obliged to admit that the men whose feelings were set forth in the various sonnets and poems had a fine gift of expression.

> "Thus, whilst I look for her in vain,
> Methinks I am a child again,
> And of my shadow am a-chasing.
> For all her graces are to me
> Like apparitions that I see,
> But never can come near th' embracing."

No! these men were not, as he had formerly supposed, writing with air, and he felt ashamed at having used the term "freak" at their expense.

Mr. Batchel read more of the lyrics, some of them twice, and one of them much oftener. That one he began to commit to memory, and since the household had retired to rest, to recite aloud. He had been unaware that literature contained anything so beautiful, and as he looked again at the book to recover an expression his memory had lost, a tear fell upon the page. It was a thing so extraordinary that Mr. Batchel first looked at the ceiling, but when he found that it was indeed a tear from his own eye he was immoderately pleased with himself. Had not she also shed a tear as she sat upon the same chair? The fact seemed to draw them together.

Contemplation of this sort was, however, a luxury to be enjoyed in something like moderation. Mr. Batchel soon laid down his lyric and savagely began to add up columns of marks, by way of discipline; and when he had totalled several pages of these, respect for his normal self had returned with sufficient force to take him off to bed.

The matter of his dreams, or whether he dreamed at all, has not been disclosed. He awoke, at any rate, in a calmer state of mind, and such romantic thoughts as remained were effectually dispelled by the sight of his own countenance when he began to shave. "Fancy you spouting lyrics," he said, as he dabbed the brush upon his mouth, and by the time he was ready for breakfast he pronounced himself cured.

The prosaic labours awaiting him in the study were soon forced upon his notice, and for once he did not regret it. Amongst the letters lying upon the breakfast table was one from the secretary who controlled the system of examination. The form of the envelope was too familiar to leave him in doubt as to what it contained. It was a letter which, to a careful man like Mr. Batchel, seemed to have the nature of a reproof, inasmuch as it probably asked for information which it had already been his duty to furnish. The contents of the envelope, when he had impatiently torn it open, answered to his expectation—he was formally requested to supply the name and the marks of candidate No. 1004, and he wondered, as he ate his breakfast, how he had omitted to return them. He hunted out the paper of No. 1004 as soon as the meal was over. The candidate proved to be one Lubrietta Rodria, of whom, of course, he had never heard, and her answers had all been marked. He could not understand why they should have been made the subject of enquiry.

He took her papers in his hand, and looked at them again as he stood with his back to the fire, having lit the pipe which invariably followed his breakfast, and then he discovered something much harder to understand. The marks were not his own. In place of the usual sketchy numerals, hardly decipherable to any but himself, he saw figures which were carefully formed; and the marks assigned to the first answer, as he saw it on the uppermost sheet, were higher than the maximum number obtainable for that question.

Mr. Batchel laid down his pipe and seated himself at the table. He was greatly puzzled. As he turned over the sheets of No. 1004 he found all the other questions marked in like manner, and making a total of half as much again as the highest possible number. "Who the dickens," he said, using a meaningless, but not uncommon expression, "has been playing with this; and how came I to pass it over?" The need of the moment, however, was to furnish the proper marks to the secretary at Cambridge, and Mr. Batchel proceeded to read No. 1004 right through.

He soon found that he had read it all before, and the matter began to bristle with queries. It proved, in fact, to be a paper over which he had spent some time, and for a singularly interesting reason. He had learned from a friend in the Indian Civil Service that an exaggerated value was often placed by ambitious Indians and Cingalese upon a European education, and that many aspiring young men declined to take a wife who had not passed this very examination. It was to Mr. Batchel a disquieting reflection that his blue pencil was not only marking mistakes, but might at the same time be cancelling matrimonial engagements, and his friend's communication had made him scrupulously careful in examining the work of young ladies in Oriental Schools. The matter had occurred to him at once as he had examined the answers of Lubrietta Rodria. He perfectly remembered the question upon which her success depended. A problem in logic had been answered by a rambling and worthless argument, to which, somehow, the right conclusion was appended: the conclusion might be a happy guess, or it might have been secured by less honest means, but Mr. Batchel, following his usual practice, gave no marks for it. It was not here that he found any cause for hesitation, but when he came to the end of the paper and found that the candidate had only just failed, he had turned back to the critical question, imagined an eligible bachelor awaiting the result of the examination, and then, after a period of vacillation, had hastily put the symbol of failure upon the paper lest he should be tempted to bring his own charity to the rescue of the candidate's logic, and unfairly add the three marks which would suffice to pass her.

As he now read the answer for the second time, the same pitiful thought troubled him, and this time more than before; for over the edge of the paper of No. 1004 there persistently arose the image of the young lady with the sapphire ring. It directed the current of his thoughts. Suppose that Lubrietta Rodria were anything like that! and what if the arguments of No. 1004 were worthless! Young ladies were notoriously weak in argument, and as strong in conclusions! and after all, the conclusion was correct, and ought not a correct conclusion to have its marks? There followed much more to the same purpose, and in the end Mr. Batchel stultified himself by adding the necessary three marks, and passing the candidate.

"This comes precious near to being a job," he remarked, as he entered the marks upon the form and sealed it in the envelope, "but No. 1004 must pass, this time." He enclosed in the envelope a request to know why the marks had been asked for, since they had certainly been returned in their proper place. A brief official reply informed him next day that the marks he had returned exceeded the maximum, and must, therefore, have been wrongly entered.

"This," said Mr. Batchel, "is a curious coincidence."

Curious as it certainly was, it was less curious than what immediately followed. It was Mr. Batchel's practice to avoid any delay in returning these official papers, and he went out, there and then, to post his envelope. The Post Office was no more than a hundred yards from his door, and in three minutes he was in his study again. The first object that met his eye there was a beautiful sapphire ring lying upon the papers of No. 1004, which had remained upon the table.

Mr. Batchel at once recognised the ring.

"I knew it was precious near a job," he said, "but I didn't know that it was as near as this."

He took up the ring and examined it. It looked like a ring of great value; the stone was large and brilliant, and the setting was of fine workmanship. "Now what on earth," said Mr. Batchel, "am I to do with this?"

The nearest jeweller to Stoneground was a competent and experienced tradesman of the old school. He was a member of the local Natural History Society, and in that capacity Mr. Batchel had made intimate acquaintance with him. To this jeweller, therefore, he carried the ring, and asked him what he thought of it.

"I'll give you forty pounds for it," said the jeweller.

Mr. Batchel replied that the ring was not his. "What about the make of it?" he asked. "Is it English?"

The jeweller replied that it was unmistakably Indian.

"You are sure?" said Mr. Batchel.

"Certain," said the jeweller. "Major Ackroyd brought home one like it, all but the stone, from Puna; I repaired it for him last year."

The information was enough, if not more than enough, for Mr. Batchel. He begged a suitable case from his friend the jeweller, and within an hour had posted the ring to Miss Lubrietta Rodria at the European College in Puna. At the same time he wrote to the Principal the letter whose answer is embodied in the preface to this narrative.

Having done this, Mr. Batchel felt more at ease. He had given Lubrietta Rodria what he amiably called the benefit of the doubt, but it should never be said that he had been bribed.

The rest of his papers he marked with fierce justice. A great deal of the work, in his zeal, he did twice over, but his conscience amply requited him for the superfluous labour. The last paper was marked within a day of the allotted time, Mr. Batchel shortly afterwards received his cheque, and was glad to think that the whole matter was at an end.

* * * * * *

That Lubrietta had been absent from India whilst her relatives and attendants were trying to restore her to consciousness, he had good reason to know. His friends, for the most part, took a very narrow view of human nature and its possibilities, so that he kept his experience, for a long time, to himself; there were personal reasons for not discussing the incident. The reader has been already told upon what understanding it is recorded here.

There remains, however, an episode which Mr. Batchel all but managed to suppress. Upon the one occasion when he allowed himself to speak of this matter, he was being pressed for a description of the sapphire ring, and was not very successful in his attempt to describe it. There was no reason, of course, why this should lay his good faith under suspicion. Few of us could pass an examination upon objects with which we are supposed to be familiar, or say which of our tables have three legs, and which four.

One of Mr. Batchel's auditors, however, took a captious view of the matter, and brusquely remarked, in imitation of a more famous sceptic, "I don't believe there's no sich a thing."

Mr. Batchel, of course, recognised the phrase, and it was his eagerness to establish his credit that committed him at this point to a last disclosure about Lubrietta. He drew a sapphire ring from his pocket, handed it to the incredulous auditor, and addressed him in the manner of Mrs. Gamp.

"What! you bage creetur, have I had this ring three year or more to be told there ain't no sech a thing. Go along with you."

"But I thought the ring was sent back," said more than one.

"How did you come by it?" said all the others.

Mr. Batchel thereupon admitted that he had closed his story prematurely. About six weeks after the return of the ring to Puna he had found it once again upon his table, returned through the post. Enclosed in the package was a note which Mr. Batchel, being now committed to this part of the story, also passed round for inspection. It ran as follows:—

> "Accept the ring, dear one, and wear it for my sake. Fail not to think sometimes of her whom you have made happy.—L. R."

"What on earth am I to do with this?" Mr. Batchel had asked himself again. And this time he had answered the question, after the briefest possible delay, by slipping the ring upon his fourth finger.

The book of Lyrics remained downstairs amongst the books in constant use. Mr. Batchel can repeat at least half of the collection from memory.

He knows well enough that such terms as "dear one" are addressed to bald gentlemen only in a Pickwickian sense, but even with that sense the letter gives him pleasure.

He admits that he thinks very often of "her whom he has made happy," but that he cannot exclude from his thoughts at these times an ungenerous regret. It is that he has also made happy a nameless Oriental gentleman whom he presumptuously calls "the other fellow."

The Rockery

The Vicar's garden at Stoneground has certainly been enclosed for more than seven centuries, and during the whole of that time its almost sacred privacy has been regarded as permanent and unchangeable. It has remained for the innovators of later and more audacious days to hint that it might be given into other hands, and still carry with it no curse that should make a new possessor hasten to undo his irreverence. Whether there can be warrant for such confidence, time will show. The experiences already related will show that the privacy of the garden has been counted upon both by good men and worse. And here is a story, in its way, more strange than any.

By way of beginning, it may be well to describe a part of the garden not hitherto brought into notice. That part lies on the western boundary, where the garden slopes down to a sluggish stream, hardly a stream at all, locally known as the Lode. The Lode bounds the garden on the west along its whole length, and there the moorhen builds her nest, and the kingfisher is sometimes, but in these days too rarely, seen. But the centre of vision, as it were, of this western edge lies in a cluster of tall elms. Towards these all the garden paths converge, and about their base is raised a bank of earth, upon which is heaped a rockery of large stones lately overgrown with ferns.

Mr. Batchel's somewhat prim taste in gardening had long resented this disorderly bank. In more than one place in his garden had wild confusion given place to a park-like trimness, and there were not a few who would say that the change was not for the better. Mr. Batchel, however, went his own way, and in due time determined to remove the rockery. He was puzzled by its presence; he could see no reason why a bank should have been raised about the feet of the elms, and surmounted with stones; not a ray of sunshine ever found its way there, and none but coarse and uninteresting plants had established themselves. Whoever had raised the bank had done it ignorantly, or with some purpose not easy for Mr. Batchel to conjecture.

Upon a certain day, therefore, in the early part of December, when the garden had been made comfortable for its winter rest, he began, with the assistance of his gardener, to remove the stones into another place.

We do but speak according to custom in this matter, and there are few readers who will not suspect the truth, which is that the gardener began to remove the stones, whilst Mr. Batchel stood by and delivered criticisms of very slight value. Such strength, in fact, as Mr. Batchel possessed had concentrated itself upon the mind, and somewhat neglected his body, and what he called help, during his presence in the garden, was called by another name when the gardener and his boy were left to themselves, with full freedom of speech.

There were few of the stones rolled down by the gardener that Mr. Batchel could even have moved, but his astonishment at their size soon gave place to excitement at their appearance. His antiquarian tastes were strong, and were soon busily engaged. For, as the stones rolled down, his eyes were feasted, in a rapid succession, by capitals of columns, fragments of moulded arches and mullions, and other relics of ecclesiastical building.

Repeatedly did he call the gardener down from his work to put these fragments together, and before long there were several complete lengths of arcading laid upon the path. Stones which, perhaps, had been separated for centuries, once more came together, and Mr. Batchel, rubbing his hands in excited satisfaction, declared that he might recover the best parts of a Church by the time the rockery had been demolished.

The interest of the gardener in such matters was of a milder kind. "We must go careful," he merely observed, "when we come to the organ." They went on removing more and more stones, until at length the whole bank was laid bare, and Mr. Batchel's chief purpose achieved. How the stones were carefully arranged, and set up in other parts of the garden, is well known, and need not concern us now.

One detail, however, must not be omitted. A large and stout stake of yew, evidently of considerable age, but nevertheless quite sound, stood exposed after the clearing of the bank. There was no obvious reason for its presence, but it had been well driven in, so well that the strength of the gardener, or, if it made any difference, of the gardener and Mr. Batchel together, failed even to shake it. It was not unsightly, and might have remained where it was, had not the gardener exclaimed, "This is the very thing we want for the pump." It was so obviously "the very thing" that its removal was then and there decided upon.

The pump referred to was a small iron pump used to draw water from the lode. It had been affixed to many posts in turn, and defied them all to hold it. Not that the pump was at fault. It was a trifling affair enough. But the pumpers were usually garden-boys, whose impatient energy had never failed, before many days, to wriggle the pump away from its supports. When the gardener had, upon one occasion, spent half a day in attaching it firmly to a post, they had at once shaken out the post itself. Since, therefore, the matter was causing daily inconvenience, and the gardener becoming daily more concerned for his reputation as a rough carpenter, it was natural for him to exclaim, "This is the very thing." It was a better stake than he had ever used, and as had just been made evident, a stake that the ground would hold.

"Yes!" said Mr. Batchel, "it is the very thing; but can we get it up?" The gardener always accepted this kind of query as a challenge, and replied only by taking up a pick and setting to work, Mr. Batchel, as usual, looking on, and making, every now and then, a fruitless suggestion. After a few minutes, however, he made somewhat more than a suggestion. He darted forward and laid his hand upon the pick. "Don't you see some copper?" he asked quickly.

Every man who digs knows what a hiding place there is in the earth. The monotony of spade work is always relieved by a hope of turning up something unexpected. Treasure lies dimly behind all these hopes, so that the gardener, having seen Mr. Batchel excited over so much that was precious from his own point of view, was quite ready to look for something of value to an ordinary reasonable man. Copper might lead to silver, and that, in turn, to gold. At Mr. Batchel's eager question, therefore, he peered into the hole he had made, and examined everything there that might suggest the rounded form of a coin.

He soon saw what had arrested Mr. Batchel. There was a lustrous scratch on the side of the stake, evidently made by the pick, and though the metal was copper, plainly enough, the gardener felt that he had been deceived, and would have gone on with his work. Copper of that sort gave him no sort of excitement, and only a feeble interest.

Mr. Batchel, however, was on his hands and knees. There was a small irregular plate of copper nailed to the stake; without any difficulty he tore it away from the nails, and soon scraped it clean with a shaving of wood; then, rising to his feet, he examined his find.

There was an inscription upon it, so legible as to need no deciphering. It had been roughly and effectually made with a hammer and nail, the letters being formed by series of holes punched deeply into the metal, and what he read was—

Move Not This
Stake, Nov. 1, 1702.

But to move the stake was what Mr. Batchel had determined upon, and the metal plate he held in his hand interested him chiefly as showing how long the post had been there. He had happened, as he supposed, upon an ancient landmark. The discovery, recorded elsewhere, of a well, near to the edge of his present lawn, had shown him that his premises had once been differently arranged. One of the minor antiquarian tasks he had set himself was to discover and record the old arrangement, and he felt that the position of this stake would help him. He felt no doubt of its being a point upon the western limit of the garden; not improbably marked in this way to show where the garden began, and where ended the ancient hauling-way, which had been secured to the public for purposes of navigation.

The gardener, meanwhile, was proceeding with his work. With no small difficulty he removed the rubble and clay which accounted for the firmness of the stake. It grew dark as the work went on, and a distant clock struck five before it was completed. Five was the hour at which the gardener usually went home; his day began early. He was not, however, a man to leave a small job unfinished, and he went on loosening the earth with his pick, and trying the effect, at intervals, upon the firmness of the stake. It naturally began to give, and could be moved from side to side through a space of some few inches. He lifted out the loosened stones, and loosened more. His pick struck iron, which, after loosening, proved to be links of a rusted chain. "They've buried a lot of rubbish in this hole," he remarked, as he went on loosening the chain, which, in the growing darkness, could hardly be seen. Mr. Batchel, meanwhile, occupied himself in a simpler task of working the stake to and fro, by way of loosening its hold. Ultimately it began to move with greater freedom. The gardener laid down his tool and grasped the stake, which his master was still holding; their combined efforts succeeded at once; the stake was lifted out.

It turned out to be furnished with an unusually long and sharp point, which explained the firmness of its hold upon the ground. The gardener carried it to the neighbourhood of the pump, in readiness for its next purpose, and made ready to go home. He would drive the stake to-morrow, he said, in the new place, and make the pump so secure that not even the boys could shake it. He also spoke of some designs he had upon the chain, should it prove to be of any considerable length. He was an ingenious man, and his skill in converting discarded articles to now uses was embarrassing to his master. Mr. Batchel, as has been said, was a prim gardener, and he had no liking for makeshift devices. He had that day seen his runner beans trained upon a length of old gas-piping, and had no intention of leaving the gardener in possession of such a treasure as a rusty chain. What he said, however, and said with truth, was that he wanted the chain for himself. He had no practical use for it, and hardly expected it to yield him any interest. But a chain buried in 1702 must be examined —nothing ancient comes amiss to a man of antiquarian tastes.

Mr. Batchel had noticed, whilst the gardener had been carrying away the stake, that the chain lay very loosely in the earth. The pick had worked well round it. He said, therefore, that the chain must be lifted out and brought to him upon the morrow, bade his gardener good night, and went in to his fireside.

This will appear to the reader to be a record of the merest trifles, but all readers will accept the reminder that there is no such thing as a trifle, and that what appears to be trivial has that appearance only so long as it stands alone. Regarded in the light of their consequences, those matters which have seemed to be least in importance, turn out, often enough, to be the greatest. And these trifling occupations, as we may call them for the last time, of Mr. Batchel and the gardener, had consequences which shall now be set down as Mr. Batchel himself narrated them. But we must take events in their order. At present Mr. Batchel is at his fireside, and his gardener at home with his family. The stake is removed, and the hole, in which lies some sort of an iron chain, is exposed.

Upon this particular evening Mr. Batchel was dining out. He was a good natured man, with certain mild powers of entertainment, and his presence as an occasional guest was not unacceptable at some of the more considerable houses of the neighbourhood. And let us hasten to observe that he was not a guest who made any great impression upon the larders or the cellars of his hosts. He liked port, but he liked it only of good quality, and in small quantity. When he returned from a dinner party, therefore, he was never either in a surfeited condition of body, or in any confusion of mind. Not uncommonly after his return upon such occasions did he perform accurate work. Unfinished contributions to sundry local journals were seldom absent from his desk. They were his means of recreation. There they awaited convenient intervals of leisure, and Mr. Batchel was accustomed to say that of these intervals he found none so productive as a late hour, or hour and a half, after a dinner party.

Upon the evening in question he returned, about an hour before midnight, from dining at the house of a retired officer residing in the neighbourhood, and the evening had been somewhat less enjoyable than usual. He had taken in to dinner a young lady who had too persistently assailed him with antiquarian questions. Now Mr. Batchel did not like talking what he regarded as "shop," and was not much at home with young ladies, to whom he knew that, in the nature of things, he could be but imperfectly acceptable. With infinite good will towards them, and a genuine liking for their presence, he felt that he had but little to offer them in exchange. There was so little in common between his life and theirs, he felt distinctly at his worst when he found himself treated as a mere scrap-book of information. It made him seem, as he would express it, de-humanised.

Upon this particular evening the young lady allotted to him, perhaps at her own request, had made a scrap-book of him, and he had returned home somewhat discontented, if also somewhat amused. His discontent arose from having been deprived of the general conversation he so greatly, but so rarely, enjoyed. His amusement was caused by the incongruity between a very light-hearted young lady and the subject upon which she had made him talk, for she had talked of nothing else but modes of burial.

He began to recall the conversation as he lit his pipe and dropped into his armchair. She had either been reflecting deeply upon the matter, or, as seemed to Mr. Batchel, more probable, had read something and half forgotten it. He recalled her questions, and the answers by which he had vainly tried to lead her to a more attractive topic. For example:

SHE: Will you tell me why people were buried at cross roads?
HE: Well, consecrated ground was so jealously guarded that a criminal would be held to have forfeited the right to

be buried amongst Christian folk. His friends would therefore choose cross roads where there was set a wayside cross, and make his grave at the foot of it. In some of my journeys in Scotland I have seen crosses...

But the young lady had refused to be led into Scotland. She had stuck to her subject.

SHE: Why have coffins come back into use? There is nothing in our Civil Service about a coffin.
HE: True, and the use of the coffin is due, in part, to an ignorant notion of confining the corpse, lest, like Hamlet's father, he should walk the earth. You will have noticed that the corpse is always carried out of the house feet foremost, to suggest a final exit, and that the grave is often covered with a heavy slab. Very curious epitaphs are to be found on these slabs...

But she was not to be drawn into the subject of epitaphs. She had made him tell of other devices for confining spirits to their prison, and securing the peace of the living, especially of those adopted in the case of violent and mischievous men. Altogether an unusual sort of young lady.

The conversation, however, had revived his memories of what was, after all, a matter of some interest, and he determined to look through his parish registers for records of exceptional burials. He was surprised at himself for never having done it. He dismissed the matter from his mind for the time being, and as it was a bright moonlight night he thought he would finish his pipe in the garden.

Therefore, although midnight was close at hand, he strolled complacently round his garden, enjoying the light of the moon no less than in the daytime he would have enjoyed the sun; and thus it was that he arrived at the scene of his labours upon the old rockery. There was more light than there had been at the end of the afternoon, and when he had walked up the bank, and stood over the hole we have already described, he could distinctly see the few exposed links of the iron chain. Should he remove it at once to a place of safety, out of the way of the gardener? It was about time for bed. The city clocks were then striking midnight. He would let the chain decide. If it came out easily he would remove it; otherwise, it should remain until morning.

The chain came out more than easily. It seemed to have a force within itself. He gave but a slight tug at the free end with a view of ascertaining what resistance he had to encounter, and immediately found himself lying upon his back with the chain in his hand. His back had fortunately turned towards an elm three feet away which broke his fall, but there had been violence enough to cause him no little surprise.

The effort he had made was so shift that he could not account for having lost his feet; and being a careful man, he was a little anxious about his evening coat, which he was still wearing. The chain, however, was in his hand, and he made haste to coil it into a portable shape, and to return to the house.

Some fifty yards from the spot was the northern boundary of the garden, a long wall with a narrow lane beyond. It was not unusual, even at this hour of the night, to hear footsteps there. The lane was used by rail-way men, who passed to and from their work at all hours, as also by some who returned late from entertainments in the neighbouring city.

But Mr. Batchel, as he turned back to the house, with his chain over one arm, heard more than footsteps. He heard for a few moments the unmistakable sound of a scuffle, and then a piercing cry, loud and sharp, and a noise of running. It was such a cry as could only have come from one in urgent need of help.

Mr. Batchel dropped his chain. The garden wall was some ten feet high and he had no means of scaling it. But he ran quickly into the house, passed out by the hall door into the street, and so towards the lane without a moment's loss of time.

Before he has gone many yards he sees a man running from the lane with his clothing in great disorder, and this man, at the sight of Mr. Batchel, darts across the road, runs along in the shadow of an opposite wall and attempts to escape.

The man is known well enough to Mr. Batchel. It is one Stephen Medd, a respectable and sensible man, by occupation a shunter, and Mr. Batchel at once calls out to ask what has happened. Stephen, however, makes no reply but continues to run along the shadow of the wall, whereupon Mr. Batchel crosses over and intercepts him, and again asks what is amiss. Stephen answers wildly and breathlessly, "I'm not going to stop here, let me go home."

As Mr. Batchel lays his hand upon the man's arm and draws him into the light of the moon, it is seen that his face is streaming with blood from a wound near the eye.

He is somewhat calmed by the familiar voice of Mr. Batchel, and is about to speak, when another scream is heard from the lane. The voice is that of a boy or woman, and no sooner does Stephen bear it than he frees himself violently from Mr. Batchel and makes away towards his home. With no less speed does Mr. Batchel make for the lane, and finds about half way down a boy lying on the ground wounded and terrified.

At first the boy clings to the ground, but he, too, is soon reassured by Mr. Batchel's voice, and allows himself to be lifted on to his feet. His wound is also in the face, and Mr. Batchel takes the boy into his house, bathes and plasters his wound, and soon restores him to something like calm. He is what is termed a call-boy, employed by the Railway Company to awaken drivers at all hours, and give them their instructions.

Mr. Batchel is naturally impatient for the moment he can question the boy about his assailant, who is presumably also the assailant of Stephen Medd. No one had been visible in the lane, though the moon shone upon it from end to end. At the first available moment, therefore, he asks the boy, "Who did this?"

The answer came, without any hesitation, "Nobody." "There was nobody there," he said, and all of a sudden somebody hit me with an iron thing."

Then Mr. Batchel asked, "Did you see Stephen Medd?" He was becoming greatly puzzled.

The boy replied that he had seen Mr. Medd "a good bit in front," with nobody near him, and that all of a sudden someone knocked him down.

Further questioning seemed useless. Mr. Batchel saw the boy to his home, left him at the door, and returned to bed, but not to sleep. He could not cease from thinking, and he could think of nothing but assaults from invisible hands. Morning seemed long in coming, but came at last.

Mr. Batchel was up betimes and made a very poor breakfast. Dallying with the morning paper, rather than reading it, his eye was arrested by a headline about "Mysterious assaults in Elmham." He felt that he had mysteries of his own to occupy him and was in no mood to be interested in more assaults. But he had some knowledge of Elmham, a small town ten miles distant from Stoneground, and he read the brief paragraph, which contained no more than the substance of a telegram. It said, however, that three persons had been victims of unaccountable assaults. Two of them had escaped with slight injuries, but the third, a young woman, was dangerously wounded, though still alive and conscious. She declared that she was quite alone in her house and had been suddenly struck with great violence by what felt like a piece of iron, and that she must have bled to death but for a neighbour who heard her cries. The neighbour had at once looked out and seen nobody, but had bravely gone to her friend's assistance.

Mr. Batchel laid down his newspaper considerably impressed, as was natural, by the resemblance of these tragedies to what he had witnessed himself. He was in no condition, after his excitement and his sleepless night, to do his usual work. His mind reverted to the conversation at the dinner party and the trifle of antiquarian research it had suggested. Such occupation had often served him when he found himself suffering from a cold, or otherwise indisposed for more serious work. He would get the registers and collect what entries there might be of irregular burial.

He found only one such entry, but that one was enough. There was a note dated All Hallows, 1702, to this effect:

> "This day did a vagrant from Elmham beat cruelly to death two poor men who had refused him alms, and upon a hue and cry being raised, took his

own life. He was buried in one Parson's Close with a stake through his body and his arms confined in chains, and stoutly covered in."

No further news came from Elmham. Either the effort had been exhausted, or its purpose achieved. But what could have led the young lady, a stranger to Mr. Batchel and to his garden, to hit upon so appropriate a topic? Mr. Batchel could not answer the question as he put it to himself again and again during the day. He only knew that she had given him a warning, by which, to his shame and regret, he had been too obtuse to profit.

The Indian Lamp-Shade

What has been already said of Mr. Batchel will have sufficed to inform the reader that he is a man of very settled habits. The conveniences of life, which have multiplied so fast of late, have never attracted him, even when he has heard of them. Inconveniences to which he is accustomed have always seemed to him preferable to conveniences with which he is unfamiliar. To this day, therefore, he writes with a quill, winds up his watch with a key, and will drink no soda-water but from a tumbling bottle with the cork wired to its neck.

The reader accordingly will learn without surprise that Mr. Batchel continues to use the reading-lamp he acquired 30 years ago as a Freshman in College. He still carries it from room to room as occasion requires, and ignores all other means of illumination. It is an inexpensive lamp of very poor appearance, and dates from a time when labour-saving was not yet a fine art. It cannot be lighted without the removal of several of its parts, and it is extinguished by the primitive device of blowing down the chimney. What has always shocked the womenfolk of the Batchel family, however, is the lamp's unworthiness of its surroundings. Mr. Batchel's house is furnished in dignified and comfortable style, but the handsome lamp, surmounting a fluted brazen column, which his relatives bestowed upon him at his institution, is still unpacked.

One of his younger and subtler relatives succeeded in damaging the old lamp, as she thought, irretrievably, by a well-planned accident, but found it still in use a year later, most atrociously repaired. The whole family, and some outsiders, had conspired to attack the offending lamp, and it had withstood them all.

The single victory achieved over Mr. Batchel in this matter is quite recent, and was generally unexpected. A cousin who had gone out to India as a bride, and that of Mr. Batchel's making, had sent him an Indian lamp-shade. The association was pleasing. The shade was decorated with Buddhist figures which excited Mr. Batchel's curiosity, and to the surprise of all his friends he set it on the lamp and there allowed it to remain. It was not, however, the figures which had reconciled him to this novel and somewhat incongruous addition to the old lamp. The singular colour of the material had really attracted him. It was a bright orange-red, like no colour he had ever seen, and the remarks of visitors whose experience of such things was greater than his own soon justified him in regarding it as unique. No one had seen the colour elsewhere; and of all the tints which have acquired distinctive names, none of the names could be applied without some further qualification. Mr. Batchel himself did not trouble about a name, but was quite certain that it was a colour that he liked; and more than that, a colour which had about it some indescribable fascination. When the lamp had been brought in, and the curtains drawn, he used to regard with singular pleasure the interiors of rooms with whose appearance he was unaccustomed to concern himself. The books in his study, and the old-fashioned solid furniture of his dining room, as reflected in the new light, seemed to assume a more friendly aspect, as if they had previously been rigidly frozen, and had now thawed into life. The lamp-shade seemed to bestow upon the light some active property, and gave to the rooms, as Mr. Batchel said, the appearance of being wide-awake.

These optical effects, as he called them, were especially noticeable in the dining room, where the convenience of a large table often induced him to spend the evening. Standing in a favourite attitude, with his elbow on the chimney-piece, Mr. Batchel found increasing pleasure in contemplating the interior of the room as he saw it reflected in a large old mirror above the fireplace. The great mahogany sideboard across the room, seemed, as he gazed upon it, to be penetrated by the light, and to acquire a softness of outline, and a sort of vivacity, which operated pleasantly upon its owner's imagination. He found himself playfully regretting, for example, that the mirror had no power of recording and reproducing the scenes enacted before it since the close of the 18th century, when it had become one of the fixtures of the house. The ruddy light of the lamp-shade had always a stimulating effect upon his fancy, and some of the verses which describe his visions before the mirror would delight the reader, but that the author's modesty forbids their reproduction. Had he been less firm in this matter we should have inserted here a poem in which Mr. Batchel audaciously ventured into the domain of Physics. He endowed his mirror with the power of retaining indefinitely the light which fell upon it, and of reflecting it only when excited by the appropriate stimulus. The passage beginning

> The mirror, whilst men pass upon their way,
> Treasures their image for a later day,

might be derided by students of optics. Mr. Batchel has often read it in after days, with amazement, for, when his idle fancies came to be so gravely substantiated, he found that in writing the verses he had stumbled upon a new fact—a fact based as soundly, as will soon appear, upon experiment, as those which the text-books use in arriving at the better-known properties of reflection.

He was seated in his dining room one frosty evening in January. His chair was drawn up to the fire, and the upper part of the space behind him was visible in the mirror. The brighter and clearer light thrown down by the shade was shining upon his book. It is the fate of most of us to receive visits when we should best like to be alone, and Mr. Batchel allowed an impatient exclamation to escape him, when, at nine o'clock on this evening, he heard the door-bell. A minute later, the boy announced "Mr. Mutcher," and Mr. Batchel, with such affability as he could hastily assume, rose to receive the caller. Mr. Mutcher was the Deputy Provincial Grand Master of the Ancient Order of Gleaners, and the formality of his manner accorded with the gravity of his title. Mr. Batchel soon became aware that the rest of the evening was doomed. The Deputy Provincial Grand Master had come to discuss the probable effect of the Insurance Act upon Friendly Societies, of which Mr. Batchel was an ardent supporter. He attended their meetings, in some cases kept their accounts, and was always apt to be consulted in their affairs. He seated Mr. Mutcher, therefore, in a chair on the opposite side of the fireplace, and gave him his somewhat reluctant attention.

"This," said Mr. Mutcher, as he looked round the room, "is a cosy nook on a cold night. I cordially appreciate your kindness, Reverend Sir, in affording me this interview, and the comfort of your apartment leads me to wish that it might be more protracted."

Mr. Batchel did his best not to dissent, and as he settled himself for a long half-hour, began to watch the rise and fall, between two lines upon the distant wall-paper of the shadow of Mr. Mutcher's side-whisker, as it seemed to beat time to his measured speech.

The D.P.G.M. (for these functionaries are usually designated by initials) was not a man to be hurried into brevity. His style had been studiously acquired at Lodge meetings, and Mr. Batchel knew it well enough to be prepared for a lengthy preamble.

"I have presumed," said Mr. Mutcher, as he looked straight before him into the mirror, "to trespass upon your Reverence's forbearance, because there are one or two points upon this new Insurance Act which seem calculated to damage our long-continued prosperity—I say long-continued prosperity," repeated Mr. Mutcher, as though Mr. Batchel had missed the phrase. "I had the favour of an interview yesterday," he went on, "with the Sub-Superintendent of the Perseverance Accident and General (these were household words in circles which Mr. Batchel frequented, so that he was at no loss to understand them), and he was unanimous with me in agreeing that the matter called for careful consideration. There are one or two of our rules which we know to be essential to the welfare of our Order, and yet which will have to go by the board—I say by the board—as from July next. Now we are not

Medes, nor yet Persians"—Mr. Mutcher was about to repeat "Persians" when he was observed to look hastily round the room and then to turn deadly pale. Mr. Batchel rose and hastened to his support; he was obviously unwell. The visitor, however, made a strong effort, rose from his chair at once, saying "Pray allow me to take leave," and hurried to the door even as he said the words. Mr. Batchel, with real concern, followed him with the offer of brandy, or whatever might afford relief. Mr. Mutcher did not so much as pause to reply. Before Mr. Batchel could reach him he had crossed the hall, and the door-knob was in his hand. He thereupon opened the door and passed into the street without another word. More unaccountably still, he went away at a run, such as ill became his somewhat majestic figure, and Mr. Batchel closed the door and returned to the dining-room in a state of bewilderment. He took up his book, and sat down again in his chair. He did not immediately begin to read, but set himself to review Mr. Mutcher's unaccountable behaviour, and as he raised his eyes to the mirror he saw an elderly man standing at the sideboard.

Mr. Batchel quickly turned round, and as he did so, recalled the similar movement of his late visitor. The room was empty. He turned again to the mirror, and the man was still there— evidently a servant—one would say without much hesitation, the butler. The cut-away coat, and white stock, the clean-shaven chin, and close-trimmed side-whiskers, the deftness and decorum of his movements were all characteristic of a respectable family servant, and he stood at the sideboard like a man who was at home there.

Another object, just visible above the frame of the mirror, caused Mr. Batchel to look round again, and again to see nothing unusual. But what he saw in the mirror was a square oaken box some few inches deep, which the butler was proceeding to unlock. And at this point Mr. Batchel had the presence of mind to make an experiment of extraordinary value. He removed, for a moment, the Indian shade from the lamp, and laid it upon the table, and thereupon the mirror showed nothing but empty space and the frigid lines of the furniture. The butler had disappeared, as also had the box, to re-appear the moment the shade was restored to its place.

As soon as the box was opened, the butler produced a bundled handkerchief which his left hand had been concealing under the tails of his coat. With his right hand he removed the contents of the handkerchief, hurriedly placed them in the box, closed the lid, and having done this, left the room at once. His later movements had been those of a man in fear of being disturbed. He did not even wait to lock the box. He seemed to have heard someone coming.

Mr. Batchel's interest in the box will subsequently be explained. As soon as the butler had left, he stood before the mirror and examined it carefully. More than once, as he felt the desire for a closer scrutiny, he turned to the sideboard itself, where of course no box was to be seen, and returned to the mirror unreasonably disappointed. At length, with the image of the box firmly impressed upon his memory, he sat down again in his chair, and reviewed the butler's conduct, or as he doubted he would have to call it, misconduct. Unfortunately for Mr. Batchel, the contents of the handkerchief had been indistinguishable. But for the butler's alarm, which caused him to be moving away from the box even whilst he was placing the thing within it, the mirror could not have shewn as much as it did. All that had been made evident was that the man had something to conceal, and that it was surreptitiously done.

"Is this all?" said Mr. Batchel to himself as he sat looking into the mirror, "or is it only the end of the first Act?" The question was, in a measure, answered by the presence of the box. That, at all events would have to disappear before the room could resume its ordinary aspect; and whether it was to fade out of sight or to be removed by the butler, Mr. Batchel did not intend to be looking another way at the time. He had not seen, although perhaps Mr. Matcher had, whether the butler had brought it in, but he was determined to see whether he took it out.

He had not gazed into the mirror for many minutes before he learned that there was to be a second Act. Quite suddenly, a woman was at the sideboard. She had darted to it, and the time taken in passing over half the length of the mirror had been altogether too brief to show what she was like. She now stood with her face to the sideboard, entirely concealing the box from view, and all Mr. Batchel could determine was that she was tall of stature, and that her hair was raven-black, and not in very good order. In his anxiety to see her face, he called aloud, "Turn round." Of course, he understood, when he saw that his cry had been absolutely without effect, that it had been a ridiculous thing to do. He turned his head again for a moment to assure himself that the room was empty, and to remind himself that the curtain had fallen, perhaps a century before, upon the drama—he began to think of it as a tragedy—that he was witnessing. The opportunity, however, of seeing the woman's features was not denied him. She turned her face full upon the mirror—this is to speak as if we described the object rather than the image—so that Mr. Batchel saw it plainly before him; it was a handsome, cruel-looking face, of waxen paleness, with fine, distended, lustrous, eyes. The woman looked hurriedly round the room, looked twice towards the door, and then opened the box.

"Our respectable friend was evidently observed," said Mr. Batchel. "If he has annexed anything belonging to this magnificent female, he is in for a bad quarter of an hour." He would have given a great deal, for once, to have had a sideboard backed by a looking glass, and lamented that the taste of the day had been too good to tolerate such a thing. He would have then been able to see what was going on at the oaken box. As it was, the operations were concealed by the figure of the woman. She was evidently busy with her fingers; her elbows, which shewed plainly enough, were vibrating with activity. In a few minutes there was a final movement of the elbows simultaneously away from her sides, and it shewed, as plainly as if the hands had been visible, that something had been plucked asunder. It was just such movement as accompanies the removal, after a struggle, of the close-fitting lid of a canister.

"What next?" said Mr. Batchel, as he observed the movement, and interpreted it as the end of the operation at the box. "Is this the end of the second Act?"

He was soon to learn that it was not the end, and that the drama of the mirror was indeed assuming the nature of tragedy. The woman closed the box and looked towards the door, as she had done before; then she made as if she would dart out of the room, and found her movement suddenly arrested. She stopped dead, and, in a moment, fell loosely to the ground. Obviously she had swooned away.

Mr. Batchel could then see nothing, except that the box remained in its place on the sideboard, so that he arose and stood close up to the mirror in order to obtain a view of the whole stage, as he called it. It showed him, in the wider view he now obtained, the woman lying in a heap upon the carpet, and a grey-wigged clergyman standing in the doorway of the room.

"The Vicar of Stoneground, without a doubt," said Mr. Batchel. "The household of my reverend predecessor is not doing well by him; to judge from the effect of his appearance upon this female, there's something serious afoot. Poor old man," he added, as the clergyman walked into the room.

This expression of pity was evoked by the Vicar's face. The marks of tears were upon his cheeks, and he looked weary and ill. He stood for a while looking down upon the woman who had swooned away, and then stooped down, and gently opened her hand.

Mr. Batchel would have given a great deal to know what the Vicar found there. He took something from her, stood erect for a moment with an expression of consternation upon his face; then his chin dropped, his eyes showed that he had lost consciousness, and he fell to the ground, very much as the woman had fallen.

The two lay, side by side, just visible in the space between the table and the sideboard. It was a curious and pathetic situation. As the clergyman was about to fall, Mr. Batchel had turned to save him, and felt a real distress of helplessness at being reminded again that it was but an image that he had looked upon. The two persons now lying upon the carpet had been for some hundred years beyond human aid. He could no more help them than he could help the wounded at Waterloo. He was tempted to relieve his distress by removing the shade of the lamp; he had even laid his hand upon it, but the feeling of curiosity was now become too strong, and he knew that he must see the matter to its end.

The woman first began to revive. It was to be expected, as she had been the first to go. Had not Mr. Batchel seen her face in the mirror, her first act of consciousness would have astounded him. Now it only revolted him. Before she had sufficiently recovered to raise herself upon her feet, she forced open the lifeless hands beside her and snatched away the contents of that which was not empty; and as she did this, Mr. Batchel saw the glitter of precious stones. The woman was soon upon her feet and making feebly for the door, at which she paused to leer at the prostrate figure of the clergyman before she disappeared into the hail. She appeared no more, and Mr. Batchel felt glad to be rid of her presence.

The old Vicar was long in coming to his senses; as he began to move, there stood in the doorway the welcome figure of the butler. With infinite gentleness he raised his master to his feet, and with a strong arm supported him out of the room, which at last, stood empty.

"That, at least," said Mr. Batchel, "is the end of the second Act. I doubt whether I could have borne much more. If that awful woman comes back I shall remove the shade and have done with it all. Otherwise, I shall hope to learn what becomes of the box, and whether my respectable friend who has just taken out his master is, or is not, a rascal." He had been genuinely moved by what he had seen, and was conscious of feeling something like exhaustion. He dare not, however, sit down, lest he should lose anything important of what remained. Neither the door nor the lower part of the room was visible from his chair, so that he remained standing at the chimney-piece, and there awaited the disappearance of the oaken box.

So intently were his eyes fixed upon the box, in which he was especially interested, that he all but missed the next incident. A velvet curtain which he could see through the half-closed door had suggested nothing of interest to him. He connected it indefinitely, as it was excusable to do, with the furniture of the house, and only by inadvertence looked at it a second time. When, however, it began to travel slowly along the hail, his curiosity was awakened in a new direction. The butler, helping his master out of the room ten minutes since, had left the door half open, but as the opening was not towards the mirror, only a strip of the hall beyond could be seen. Mr. Batchel went to open the door more widely, only to find, of course, that the vividness of the images had again betrayed him. The door of his dining-room was closed, as he had closed it after Mr. Mutcher, whose perturbation was now so much easier to understand.

The curtain continued to move across the narrow opening, and explained itself in doing so. It was a pall. The remains it so amply covered were being carried out of the house to their resting-place, and were followed by a long procession of mourners in long cloaks. The hats they held in their black-gloved hands were heavily banded with crêpe whose ends descended to the ground, and foremost among them was the old clergyman, refusing the support which two of the chief mourners were in the act of proffering. Mr. Batchel, full of sympathy, watched the whole procession pass the door, and not until it was evident that the funeral had left the house did he turn once more to the box. He felt sure that the closing scene of the tragedy was at hand, and it proved to be very near. It was brief and uneventful. The butler very deliberately entered the room, threw aside the window-curtains and drew up the blinds, and then went away at once, taking the box with him. Mr. Batchel thereupon blew out his lamp and went to bed, with a purpose of his own to be fulfilled upon the next day.

His purpose may be stated at once. He had recognised the oaken box, and knew that it was still in the house. Three large cupboards in the old library of Vicar Whitehead were filled with the papers of a great law-suit about tithe, dating from the close of the 18th century. Amongst these, in the last of the three cupboards, was the box of which so much has been said. It was filled, so far as Mr. Batchel remembered, with the assessments for poor's-rate of a large number of landholders concerned in the suit, and these Mr. Batchel had never thought it worth his while to disturb. He had gone to rest, however, on this night with the full intention of going carefully through the contents of the box. He scarcely hoped, after so long an interval, to discover any clue to the scenes he had witnessed, but he was determined at least to make the attempt. If he found nothing, he intended that the box should enshrine a faithful record of the transactions in the dining-room.

It was inevitable that a man who had so much of the material of a story should spend a wakeful hour in trying to piece it together. Mr. Batchel spent considerably more than an hour in connecting, in this way and that, the butler and his master, the gypsy-looking woman, the funeral, but could arrive at no connexion that satisfied him. Once asleep, he found the problem easier, and dreamed a solution so obvious as to make him wonder that the matter had over puzzled him. When he awoke in the morning, also, the defects of the solution were so obvious as to make him wonder that he had accepted it; so easily are we satisfied when reason is not there to criticise. But there was still the box, and this Mr. Batchel lifted down from the third cupboard, dusted with his towel, and when he was dressed, carried downstairs with him. His breakfast occupied but a small part of a large table, and upon the vacant area he was soon laying, as he examined them, one by one, the documents which the box contained. His recollection of them proved to be right. They were overseers' lists of parochial assessments, of which he soon had a score or more laid upon the table. They were of no interest in themselves, and did nothing to further the matter in hand. They would appear to have been thrust into the box by someone desiring to find a receptacle for them.

In a little while, however, the character of the papers changed. Mr. Batchel found himself reading something of another kind, written upon paper of another form and colour.

"Irish bacon to be had of Mr. Broadley, hop merchant in Southwark."

"Rasin wine is kept at the Wine and Brandy vaults in Catherine Street."

"The best hones at Mr. Forsters in Little Britain."

There followed a recipe for a "rhumatic mixture," a way of making a polish for mahogany, and other such matters. They were evidently the papers of the butler.

Mr. Batchel removed them one by one, as he had removed the others; household accounts followed, one or two private letters, and the advertisement of a lottery, and then he reached a closed compartment at the bottom of the box, occupying about half its area. The lid of the compartment was provided with a bone stud, and Mr. Batchel lifted it off and laid it upon the table amongst the papers. He saw at once what the butler had taken from his handkerchief. There was an open pocket-knife, with woeful-looking deposits upon its now rusty blade. There was a delicate human finger, now dry and yellow, and on the finger a gold ring.

Mr. Batchel took up this latter pitiful object and removed the ring, even now, not quite easily. He allowed the finger to drop back into the box, which he carried away at once into another room. His appetite for breakfast had left him, and he rang the bell to have the things cleared away, whilst he set himself, with the aid of a lens, to examine the ring.

There had been three large stones, all of which had been violently removed. The claws of their settings were, without exception, either bent outwards, or broken off. Within the ring was engraved, in graceful italic characters, the name *Amey Lee*, and on the broader part, behind the place of the stones

> She doth joy double,
> And halveth trouble.

This pathetic little love token Mr. Batchel continued to hold in his hand as he rehearsed the whole story to which it afforded the clue. He knew that the ring had been set with such stones as there was no mistaking: he remembered only too well how their discovery had affected the aged vicar. But never would he deny himself the satisfaction of hoping that the old man had been spared the distress of learning how the ring had been removed.

The name of Amey Lee was as familiar to Mr. Batchel as his own. Twice at least every Sunday during the past seven years had he read it at his feet, as he sat in the chancel, as well as the name of Robert Lee upon an adjacent slab, and he had wondered during the leisurely course of many a meandering hymn whether there was good precedent for the spelling of the name. He made another use now of his knowledge of the pavement. There was a row of tiles along the head of the slabs, and Mr. Batchel hastened to fulfil without delay, what he conceived to be his duty. He replaced the ring upon Amey Lee's finger and carried it into the church, and there, having raised one of the tiles with a chisel, gave it decent burial.

Whether the butler ever learned that he had been robbed in his turn, who shall say? His immediate dismissal, after the funeral, seemed inevitable, and his oaken box was evidently placed by him, or by another, where no man heeded it. It still occupies a place amongst the law papers and may lie undisturbed for another century; and when Mr. Batchel put it there, without the promised record of events, he returned to the dining room, removed the Indian shade from the lamp, and, having put a lighted match to the edge, watched it slowly burn away.

Only one thing remained. Mr. Batchel felt that it would give him some satisfaction to visit Mr. Mutcher. His address, as obtained from the District Miscellany of the Order of Gleaners, was 13, Albert Villas, Williamson Street, not a mile away from Stoneground.

Mr. Mutcher, fortunately, was at home when Mr. Batchel called, and indeed opened the door with a copious apology for being without his coat.

"I hope," said Mr. Batchel, "that you have overcome your indisposition of last Tuesday evening."

"Don't mention it, your Reverence," said Mr. Mutcher, "my wife gave me such a talking to when I came 'ome that I was quite ashamed of myself—I say ashamed of myself."

"She observed that you were unwell," said Mr. Batchel, "I am sure; but she could hardly blame you for that."

By this time the visitor had been shewn into the parlour, and Mrs. Mutcher had appeared to answer for herself.

"I really was ashamed, Sir," she said, "to think of the way Mutcher was talking, and a clergyman's 'ouse too. Mutcher is not a man, Sir, that takes anything, not so much as a drop; but he is wonderful partial to cold pork, which never does agree with him, and never did, at night in partic'lar."

"It was the cold pork, then, that made you unwell?" asked Mr. Batchel.

"It was, your Reverence, and it was not," Mr. Mutcher replied, "for internal discomfort there was none—I say none. But a little light-'eaded it did make me, and I could 'ave swore, your Reverence, saving your presence, that I saw an elderly gentleman carry a box into your room and put it down on the sheffoneer."

"There was no one there, of course," observed Mr. Batchel.

"No!" replied the D.P.G.M., "there was not; and the discrepancy was too much for me. I hope you will pardon the abruptness of my departure."

"Certainly," said Mr. Batchel, "discrepancies are always embarrassing."

"And you will allow me one day to resume our discourse upon the subject of National Insurance," he added, when he shewed his visitor to the door.

"I shall not have much leisure," said Mr. Batchel, audaciously, taking all risks, "until the Greek Kalends."

"Oh, I don't mind waiting till it does end," said Mr. Mutcher, "there is no immediate 'urry."

"It's rather a long time," remarked Mr. Batchel.

"Pray don't mention it," answered the Deputy Provincial Grand Master, in his best manner. "But when the time comes, perhaps you'll drop me a line."

The Place of Safety

"I thank my governors, teachers, spiritual pastors, and masters," said Wardle, as he lit a cigar after breakfast, "that I never acquired a taste for that sort of thing."

Wardle was a pragmatical and candid friend who paid Mr. Batchel occasional visits at Stoneground. He regarded antiquarian tastes as a form of insanity, and it annoyed him to see his host poring over registers, churchwardens' accounts, and documents which he contemptuously alluded to as "dirty papers." "If you would throw those things away, Batchel," he used to say, "and read the *Daily Mail*, you'd be a better man for it."

Mr. Batchel replied only with a tolerant smile, and, as his friend went out of doors with his cigar, continued to read the document before him, although it was one he had read twenty times before. It was an inventory of church goods, dated the 6th year of Edward VI.—to be exact, the 15th May, 1552. By a royal order of that year, all Church goods, saving only what sufficed for the barest necessities of Divine Service, were collected and deposited in safe hands, there to await further instructions. The instructions, which had not been long delayed, had consisted in a curt order for seizure. Everyone who cares for such matters, knows and laments the grievous spoliation of those times.

Mr. Batchel's document, however, proved that the Churchwardens of the day were not incapable of self-defence. They were less dumb than sheep before the shearers. For, on the copy of the inventory of which he had become possessed, was written the

Commissioners' Report that "at Stoneground did John Spayn and John Gounthropp, Churchwardens, declare upon their othes that two gilded senseres with candellstickes, old paynted clothes, and other implements, were contained in a chest which was robbed on St. Peter's Eve before the first inventorye made."

Mr. Batchel had a shrewd suspicion, which the reader will not improbably share, that John Spayne and his colleague knew more about the robbery than they chose to admit. He said to himself again and again, that the contents of the chest had been carefully concealed until times should mend. But from the point of view of the Churchwardens, times had not mended. There was evidence that Stoneground had been in no mood to tolerate censers in the reign of Mary, and it seemed unlikely that any later time could have re-admitted the ancient ritual. On this account, Mr. Batchel had never ceased to believe that the contents of the chest lay somewhere near at hand, nor to hope that it might be his lot to discover it.

Whenever there was any work of the nature of excavation or demolition within a hundred yards of the Church, Mr. Batchel was sure to be there. His presence was very distasteful in most cases, to the workmen engaged, whom it deprived of many intervals of leisure to which they were accustomed when left alone. During a long course of operations connected with the restoration of the Church, Mr. Batchel's vigilance had been of great advantage to the work, both in raising the standard of industry and in securing attention to details which the builders were quite prepared to overlook. It had, however, brought him no nearer to the censers and other contents of the chest, and when the work was completed, his hopes of discovery had become pitifully slender.

Mr. Wardle, notwithstanding his general contempt for antiquarian pursuits, was polite enough to give Mr. Batchel's hobbies an occasional place in their conversation, and in this way was informed of the "stolen" goods. The information, however, gave him no more than a very languid interest.

"Why can't you let the things alone?" he said, "what's the use of them?"

Mr. Batchel felt it all but impossible to answer a man who could say this; yet he made the attempt.

"The historic interest," he said seriously, "of censers that were used down to the days of Edward VI. is in itself sufficient to justify—"

"Etcetera," said his friend, interrupting the sentence which even Mr. Batchel was not sure of finishing to his satisfaction, "but it takes so little to justify you antiquarians, with your axes and hammers. What can you do with it when you get it, if you ever do get it?"

"There are two censers," Mr. Batchel mildly observed in correction, "and other things."

"All right," said Wardle; "tell me about one of them, and leave me to do the multiplication."

With this permission, Mr. Batchel entered upon a general description of such ancient thuribles as he knew of, and Wardle heard him with growing impatience.

"It seems to me," he burst in at length, "that what you are making all this pother about is a sort of silver cruet-stand, which was thin metal to begin with, and cleaned down to the thickness of egg-shell before the Commissioners heard of it. At this moment, if it exists, it is a handful of black scrap. If you found it, I wouldn't give a shilling for it; and if I would, it isn't yours to sell. Why can't you let the things alone?"

"But the interest of it," said Mr. Batchel, "is what attracts me."

"It's a pity you can't take an interest in something less uninteresting," said Wardle, petulantly; "but let me tell you what I think about your censers and all the rest of it. Your Churchwardens lied about them, but that's all right; I'd have done the same myself. If their things couldn't be used, they were not going to have them abused, so they put them safely out of the way, your's and everybody's else."

"I was not proposing to abuse them," interrupted Mr. Batchel.

"Were you proposing to use them?" rejoined Wardle. "It's one thing or the other, to my mind. There are people who dig out Bishops and steal their rings to put in glass cases, but I don't know how they square the police; and it's the same sort of thing you seem to be up to. Let the things alone. You're a Prayer Book man, and just the sort the Churchwardens couldn't stomach. You talk fast enough at the Dissenters because they want to collar your property now. Why can't you do as you would be done by?"

Mr. Batchel thought it useless to say any more to a man in so unsympathetic an attitude, or to enter upon any defence of the antiquarian researches to which his friend had so crudely referred. He did not much like, however, to be anticipated in a theory of the "robbery" which he felt to be reasonable and probable. He had hoped to propound the same theory himself, and to receive a suitable compliment upon his penetration. He began, therefore, somewhat irritably, to make the most of conjectures which, at various times, had occurred to him. "Men of that sort," he said, "would have disposed of the censers to some one who could go on using them, and in that case they are not here at all."

"Men of that sort," answered Wardle, "are as careful of their skins as men of any other sort, and besides that, your Stoneground men have a very good notion of sticking to what they have got. The things are here, I daresay, if they are anywhere; but they are not yours, and you have no business to meddle with them. If you would spend your time in something else than poking about after other people's things, you'd get better value for it."

This brief conversation, in which Mr. Batchel had scarcely been allowed the part to which he felt entitled, was in one respect satisfactory. It supported his belief that the censers lay somewhere within reach. In other respects, however, the attitude of Wardle was intolerable. He was evidently out of all sympathy with the quest upon which Mr. Batchel was set, and, for their different reasons, each was glad to drop the subject.

During the next two or three days, the matter of the censers was not referred to, if only for lack of opportunity. Wardle was a kind of visitor for whom there was always a welcome at Stoneground, and the welcome was in his case no less cordial on account of his brutal frankness of expression, which, on the whole, his host enjoyed. His pungent criticisms of other men were vastly entertaining to Mr. Batchel, who was not so unreasonable as to feel aggrieved at an occasional attack upon himself.

A guest of this unceremonious sort makes but small demands upon his host. Mr. Wardle used to occupy himself contentedly and unobtrusively in the house or in the garden whilst his host followed his usual avocations. The two men met at meals, and liked each other none the less because they were apart at most other times. A great part of Mr. Wardle's day was passed in the company of the gardener, to whose talk his own master was but an indifferent listener. The visitor and the gardener were both lovers of the soil, and taught each other a great deal as they worked side by side. Mr. Wardle found that sort of exercise wholesome, and, as the gardener expressed it, "was not frit to take his coat off."

The gardening operations at this time of year were such as Mr. Wardle liked. The over-crowded shrubberies were being thinned, and a score or so of young shrubs had to be moved into better quarters. Upon a certain morning, when Mr. Batchel was occupied in his study, some aucubas were being transplanted into a strip of ground in front of the house, and Wardle had undertaken the task of digging holes to receive them. It was this task that he suddenly interrupted in order to burst in upon his host in what seemed to the latter a repulsive state of dirt and perspiration.

"Talk of discoveries," he cried, "come and see what I've found."

"Not the censers, I suppose," said Mr. Batchel.

"Censers be hanged," said Wardle, "come and look."

Mr. Batchel laid down his pen, with a sigh, and followed Wardle to the front of the house. His guest had made three large holes, each about two feet square, and drawing Mr. Batchel to the nearest of them, said "Look there."

Mr. Batchel looked. He saw nothing, and said so.

"Nothing?" exclaimed Wardle with impatience. "You see the bottom of the hole, I suppose?"

This Mr. Batchel admitted.

"Then," said Wardle, "kindly look and see whether you cannot see something else."

"There is apparently a cylindrical object lying across the angle of your excavation," said Mr. Batchel.

"That," replied his guest, "is what you are pleased to call nothing. Let me inform you that the cylindrical object is a piece of thick lead pipe, and that the pipe runs along the whole front of your house."

"Gas-pipe, no doubt," said Mr. Batchel.

Is there any gas within a mile of this place?" asked Wardle.

Mr. Batchel admitted that there was not, and felt that he had made a needlessly foolish suggestion. He felt safer in the amended suggestion that the object was a water-pipe.

An ironical cross-examination by Mr. Wardle disposed of the amended suggestion as completely as he had disposed of the other, and his host began to grow restive. "If this sort of discovery pleases you," he said testily, "I will not grudge you your pleasure, but, to quote your own words, why can't you let it alone?"

"Have you any idea," said Mr. Wardle, "of the value of this length of piping, at the present price of lead?"

Even Mr. Wardle could hardly have suspected his host of knowing anything so preposterous as the price of lead, but he felt himself ill-used when Mr. Batchel disclaimed any interest in the matter, and returned to his study.

Wardle had a commercial mind, which elsewhere was the means of securing him a very satisfactory income, and on this account, his host, as he resumed his work indoors, excused what he regarded as a needless interruption.

He little suspected that his friend's commercial mind was to do him the great service of putting him in possession of the censers, and then to do him a disservice even greater.

Had any such connexion so much as suggested itself, Mr. Batchel would more willingly have answered to the summons which came an hour later, when the gardener appeared at the window of the study, evidently bursting with information. When he had succeeded in attracting his master's attention, and drawn him away from his desk, it was to say that the whole length of pipe had been uncovered, and found to issue from a well on the south side of the house.

The discovery was at least unexpected, and Mr. Batchel went out, even if somewhat grudgingly, to look at the place. He came upon the well, close by the window of his dining-room. It had been covered by a stone slab, now partially removed. The narrow trench which Wardle and the gardener had made in order to expose the pipe, extended eastwards to the corner of the house, and thence along the whole length of the front, probably to serve a pump on the north side, where lay the yard and stables. The pipe itself, Mr. Wardle's prize, had been withdrawn, and there remained only a rusted chain which passed from some anchorage beneath the soil, over the lip of the well. Mr. Batchel inferred that it had carried, and perhaps carried still, the bucket of former times, and stooped down to see whether he could draw it up. He heard, far below, the light splash of the soil disturbed by his hands; but before he could grasp the chain, he felt himself seized by the waist and held back.

The exaggerated attentions of his gardener had often annoyed Mr. Batchel. He was not allowed even to climb a short ladder without having to submit to absurd precautions for his safety, and he would have been much better pleased to have more respect paid to his intelligence, and less to his person. In the present instance, the precaution seemed so unnecessary that he turned about angrily to protest, both against the interference with his movements, and the unseemly force used.

It was at this point that he made a disquieting discovery. He was standing quite alone. The gardener and Mr. Wardle were both on the north side of the house, dealing with the only thing they cared about—the lead pipe. Mr. Batchel made no further attempt to move the chain; he was, in fact, in some bodily fear, and he returned to his study by the way he had come, in a disordered condition of mind.

Half an hour later, when the gong sounded for luncheon, he was slowly making his way into the dining-room, when he encountered his guest running downstairs from his room, in great spirits. "A trifle over two hundred-weight!" he exclaimed, as he reached the foot of the staircase, and seemed disappointed that Mr. Batchel did not immediately shake hands with him upon so fine a result of the morning's work. Mr. Batchel, needless to say, was occupied with other recollections.

"I suppose it is unnecessary to ask," said he to his guest as he proceeded to carve a chicken, "whether you believe in ghosts?"

"I do not," said Wardle promptly, "why should I?"

"Why not?" asked Mr. Batchel.

"Because I've had the advantage of a commercial education," was the reply, "instead of learning dead languages and soaking my mind in heathen fables."

Mr. Batchel winced at this disrespectful allusion to the University education of which he was justly proud. He wanted an opinion, however, and the conversation had to go on.

"Your commercial education," he continued, "allows you, I daresay, to know what is meant by a hypothetical case."

"Make it one," said Wardle.

"Assuming a ghost, then, would it be capable of exerting force upon a material body?"

"Whose?" asked Wardle.

"If you insist upon making it a personal matter," replied Mr. Batchel, "let us say mine."

"Let me have the particulars."

In reply to this, Mr. Batchel related his experience at the well.

Mr. Wardle merely said "Pass the salt, I need it."

Undeterred by the scepticism of his friend, Mr. Batchel pressed the point, and upon that, Mr. Wardle closed the conversation by observing that since, by hypothesis, ghosts could clank chains, and ring bells, he was bound to suppose them capable of doing any silly thing they chose. "A month in the City, Batchel," he gravely added, "would do you a world of good."

As soon as the meal was over, Mr. Wardle went back to his gardening, whilst his host betook himself to occupations more suited to his tranquil habits. The two did not meet again until dinner; and during that meal, and after it, the conversation turned wholly upon politics, Mr. Wardle being congenially occupied until bedtime in demonstrating that the politics of his host had been obsolete for three-quarters of a century. His outdoor exercise, followed by an excellent dinner, had disposed him to retire early; he rose from his chair soon after ten. "There is one thing," he pleasantly remarked to his host, "that I am bound to say in favour of a University education; it has given you a fine taste in victuals." With this compliment, he said "good-night," and went up to bed.

Mr. Batchel himself, as the reader knows, kept later hours. There were few nights upon which he omitted to take his walk round the garden when the world had grown quiet, even in unfavourable weather. It was far from favourable upon the present occasion; there was but little moon, and a light rain was falling. He determined, however, to take at least one turn round, and calling his terrier Punch from the kitchen, where he lay in his basket, Mr. Batchel went out, with the dog at his heel. He carried, as his custom was, a little electric lamp, by whose aid he liked to peep into birds' nests, and make raids upon slugs and other pests.

They had hardly set out upon their walk when Punch began to show signs of uneasiness. Instead of running to and fro, with his nose to the ground, as he ordinarily did, the terrier remained whining in the rear. Shortly, they came upon a hedgehog lying coiled up in the path; it was a find which the dog was wont to regard as a rare piece of luck, and to assail with delirious enjoyment. Now, for some reason, Punch refused to notice it, and, when it was illuminated for his especial benefit, turned his back upon it and looked up, in a dejected attitude, at his master. The behaviour of the dog was altogether unnatural, and Mr. Batchel occupied himself, as they passed on, in trying to account for it, with the animal still whining at his heel. They soon reached the head of the little path which descended to the Lode, and there Mr. Batchel found a much harder problem awaiting him, for at the other end of the path he distinctly saw the outline of a boat.

There had been no boat on the Lode for twenty years. Just so long ago the drainage of the district had required that the main sewer should cross the stream at a point some hundred yards below the Vicar's boundary fence. There, ever since, a great pipe three feet in diameter had obstructed the passage. It lay just at the level of the water, and effectually closed it to all traffic. Mr. Batchel knew that no boat could pass the place, and that none survived in the parts above it. Yet here was a boat drawn up at the edge of his garden. He looked at it intently for a minute or so, and had no difficulty in making out the form of such a boat as was in common use all over the Fen country—a wide flat-bottomed boat, lying low in the water. The "sprit" used for punting it along lay projecting over the stern. There was no accounting for such a boat being there: Mr. Batchel did not understand how it possibly could be there, and for a while was disposed to doubt whether it actually was. The great drain-pipe was so perfect a defence against intrusion of the kind that no boat had ever passed it. The Lode, when its water was low enough to let a boat go under the pipe, was not deep enough to float it, or wide enough to contain it. Upon this occasion the water was high, and the pipe half submerged, forming an insuperable obstacle. Yet there lay, unmistakeably, a boat, within ten yards of the place where Mr. Batchel stood trying to account for it.

These ten yards, unfortunately, were impassable. The slope down to the water's edge had to be warily trodden even in dry weather. It was steep and treacherous. After rain it afforded no foothold whatever, and to attempt a descent in the darkness would have been to court disaster. After examining the boat again, therefore, by the light of his little lamp, Mr. Batchel proceeded upon his walk, leaving the matter to be investigated by daylight.

The events of this memorable night, however, were but beginning. As he turned from the boat his eye was caught by a white streak upon the ground before him, which extended itself into the darkness and disappeared. It was Punch, in veritable panic, making for home, across flower-beds and other places he well knew to be out of bounds. The whistle he had been trained to obey had no effect upon his flight; he made a lightning dash for the house. Mr. Batchel could not help regretting that Wardle was not there to see. His friend held the coursing powers of Punch in great contempt, and was wont to criticise the dog in sporting jargon, whose terms lay beyond the limits of Mr. Batchel's vocabulary, but whose general drift was as obvious as it was irritating. The present performance, nevertheless, was so exceptional that it soon began to connect itself in Mr. Batchel's mind with the unnatural conduct to which we have already alluded. It was somehow proving to be an uncomfortable night, and as Mr. Batchel felt the rain increasing to a steady drizzle he decided to abandon his walk and to return to the house by the way he had come.

He had already passed some little distance beyond the little path which descended to the Lode. The main path by which he had come was of course behind him, until he turned about to retrace his steps.

It was at the moment of turning that he had ocular demonstration of the fact that the boat had brought passengers. Not twenty yards in front of him, making their way to the water, were two men carrying some kind of burden. They had reached an open space in the path, and their forms were quite distinct: they were unusually tall men; one of them was gigantic. Mr. Batchel had little doubt of their being garden thieves. Burglars, if there had been anything in the house to attract them, could have found much easier ways of removing it.

No man, even if deficient in physical courage, can see his property carried away before his eyes and make no effort to detain it. Mr. Batchel was annoyed at the desertion of his terrier, who might at least have embarrassed the thieves' retreat; meanwhile he called loudly upon the men to stand, and turned upon them the feeble light of his lamp. In so doing he threw a new light not only upon the trespassers, but upon the whole transaction. No response was made to his challenge, but the men turned away their faces as if to avoid recognition, and Mr. Batchel saw that the nearest of them, a burly, square-headed man in a cassock, was wearing the tonsure. He described it as looking, in the dim, steely light of the lamp, like a crown-piece on a door-mat. Both the men, when they found themselves intercepted, hastened to deposit their burden upon the ground, and made for the boat. The burden fell upon the ground with a thud, but the bearers made no sound. They skimmed down to the Lode without seeming to tread, entered the boat in perfect silence, and shoved it off without sound or splash. It has already been explained that Mr. Batchel was unable to descend to the water's edge. He ran, however, to a point of the garden which the boat must inevitably pass, and reached it just in time. The boat was moving swiftly away, and still in perfect silence. The beams of the pocket-lamp just sufficed to reach it, and afforded a parting glimpse of the tonsured giant as he gave a long shove with the sprit, and carried the boat out of sight. It shot towards the drain-pipe, then not forty yards ahead, but the men were travelling as men who knew their way to be clear.

It was by this time evident, of course, that these were no garden-thieves. The aspect of the men, and the manner of their disappearance, had given a new complexion to the adventure. Mr. Batchel's heart was in his mouth, but his mind was back in the 16th century; and having stood still for some minutes in order to regain his composure, he returned to the path, with a view of finding out what the men had left behind.

The burden lay in the middle of the path, and the lamp was once more brought into requisition. It revealed a wooden box, covered in most parts with moss, and all glistening with moisture. The wood was so far decayed that Mr. Batchel had hopes of forcing open the box with his hands; so wet and slimy was it, however, that he could obtain no hold, and he hastened to the house to procure some kind of tool. Near to the cupboard in which such things were kept was the sleeping-basket of the dog, who was closely curled inside it, and shivering violently. His master made an attempt to take him back into the garden; it would be useful, he thought, to have warning in case the boat should return. The prospect of being surprised by these large, noiseless men was not one to be regarded with comfort. Punch, however, who was usually so eager for an excursion, was now in such distress at being summoned that his master felt it cruel to persist. Having found a chisel, therefore, he returned to the garden alone. The box lay undisturbed where he had left it, and in two minutes was standing open.

The reader will hardly need to be told what it contained. At the bottom lay some heavy articles which Mr. Batchel did not disturb. He saw the bases of two candlesticks. He had tried to lift the box, as it lay, by means of a chain passing through two handles in the sides, but had found it too heavy. It was by this chain that the men had been carrying it. The heavier articles, therefore, he determined to leave where they were until morning. His interest in them was small compared with that which the other contents of the box had excited, for on the top of these articles was folded "a paynted cloth," and upon this lay the two gilded censers.

It was the discovery Mr. Batchel had dreamed of for years. His excitement hardly allowed him to think of the strange manner in which it had been made. He glanced nervously around him to see whether there might be any sign of the occupants of the boat, and seeing nothing, he placed his broad-brimmed hat upon the ground, carefully laid in it the two censers, closed the box again, and carried his treasure delicately into the house. The occurrences of the last hour have not occupied long in the telling; they occupied much longer in the happening. It was now past midnight, and Mr. Batchel, after making fast the house, went at once upstairs, carrying with him the hat and its precious contents, just as he had brought it from the garden. The censers were not exactly "blackscrap," as Mr. Wardle had anticipated, or pretended to anticipate, but they were much discoloured, and very fragile. He spread a clean handkerchief upon the chest of drawers in his bedroom, and, removing the vessels with the utmost care, laid them upon it. Then after spending some minutes in admiration of their singularly beautiful form and workmanship, he could not deny himself the pleasure of calling Wardle to look.

The guest-room was close at hand. Mr. Wardle, having been already disturbed by the locking up of the house, was fully awakened by the entrance of his host into the room with a candle in his hand. The look of excitement on Mr. Batchel's face could not escape the observation even of a man still yawning, and Mr. Wardle at once exclaimed "What's up?"

"I have got them," said Mr. Batchel, in a hushed voice.

His guest, who had forgotten all about the censers, began by interpreting "them" to mean a nervous disorder that is plural by nature, and so was full of sympathy and counsel. When, however, his host had made him understand the facts, he became merely impatient.

"Won't you come and look?" said Mr. Batchel.

"Not I," said Wardle, "I shall do where I am."

"They are in excellent preservation," said Mr. Batchel.

"Then they will keep till morning," was the answer.

"But just come and tell me what you think of them," said Mr. Batchel, making a last attempt.

"I could tell you what I think of them," answered Wardle, "without leaving my bed, which I have no intention of leaving; but I have to leave Stoneground to-morrow, and I don't want to hurt your feelings, so 'Good-night.'" Upon this, he turned over in bed and gave a loud snore, which Mr. Batchel accepted as a manifesto. He has never ceased to regret that he did not compel his guest to see the censers, but he did not then foresee the sore need he would have of a witness. He answered his friend's good-night, and returned to his own room. Once more he admired the two censers as their graceful outlines stood out, sharp and clear, against the white handkerchief, and having done this, he was soon in bed and asleep. To the men in the boat he had not given another thought, since he became possessed of the box they had left behind; of the other contents of the box he had thought as little, since he had secured the chief treasures of which he had been so long in search.

Now, Mr. Wardle, when he arose in the morning, felt somewhat ashamed of his surliness of the preceding night. His repudiation of all interest in the censers had not been quite sincere, for beneath his affectation of unconcern there lay a genuine curiosity about his friend's discovery. Before he had finished dressing, therefore, he crossed over into Mr. Batchel's room. The censers, to his surprise, were nowhere to be seen. His host, less to his surprise, was still fast asleep. Mr. Wardle opened the drawers, one by one, in search of the censers, but the drawers proved to be all quite full of clothing. He looked with no more success into every other place where they might have been bestowed. His mind was always ready with a grotesque idea, "Blest if he hasn't taken them to bed with him," he said aloud, and at the sound of his voice Mr. Batchel awoke.

His eyes, as soon as they were open, turned to the chest of drawers; and what he saw there, or rather, what he failed to see, caused him, without more ado, to leap out of bed.

"What have you done with them?" he cried out.

The serious alarm of Mr. Batchel was so evident as to check the facetious reply which Wardle was about to frame. He contented himself with saying that he had not touched or seen the things.

"Where are they?" again cried Mr. Batchel, ignoring the disclaimer. "You ought not to have touched them, they will not bear handling. Where are they?"

Mr. Wardle turned away in disgust. "I expect," he said, "they're where they've been this three hundred and fifty years." Upon that he returned to his room, and went on with his dressing.

Mr. Batchel immediately followed him, and looked eagerly round the room. He proceeded to open drawers, and to search, in a frenzied manner, in every possible, and in many an impossible, place of concealment. His distress was so patent that his friend soon ceased to trifle with it. By a few minutes serious conversation he made it clear that there had been no practical joking, and Mr. Batchel returned to his room in tears. "Look here, Batchel," said Mr. Wardle as he left, "you want a holiday."

Within a few minutes Mr. Batchel returned fully dressed. "You seem to think, Wardle," he said, "that I have been dreaming about these censers. Come out into the garden and let me show you the box and the other things."

Mr. Wardle was quite willing to assent to anything, if only out of pity, and the two went together into the garden, Mr. Batchel leading the way. Going at a great pace, they soon came to the path upon which the box had lain. The marks it had left upon the soft gravel were plain enough, and Mr. Batchel eagerly appealed to his friend to notice them. Of the box and its contents, however, there was no other trace. The whole adventure was described—the strange behaviour and subsequent flight of the terrier—the men with averted faces—the boat—and the opening of the box. Mr.

Batchel tried to shake the obvious incredulity of his guest by pointing to the chisel which still lay beside the path. Mr. Wardle only replied, "You want a holiday, Batchel! Let's go in to breakfast."

Breakfast on that morning was not the cheerful meal it was wont to be. During the few minutes of waiting for it Mr. Batchel stood at the window of his dining-room looking out upon the site of the well which the gardener had now covered in. He rehearsed the whole of the adventure from first to last, wondering whether the new place of safety would ever be discovered. But he said no more to his guest; his heart was too full.

The two breakfasted almost in silence, and the meal was scarcely over when the cab arrived to take Mr. Wardle to his train. Mr. Batchel bade him farewell, and saw him depart with genuine regret; he was returning sadly into the house when he heard his name called. It was Wardle, leaning out of the window of his cab as it drove away, and waving his hand, "Batchel," he cried again, "mind you take a holiday."

The Kirk Spook

Before many years have passed it will be hard to find a person who has ever seen a parish clerk.

The parish clerk is all but extinct. Our grandfathers knew him well—an oldish, clean-shaven man, who looked as if he had never been young, who dressed in rusty black, bestowed upon him, as often as not, by the rector, and who usually wore a white tie on Sundays, out of respect for the seriousness of his office. He it was who laid out the rector's robes, and helped him to put them on; who found the places in the large Bible and Prayer Book, and indicated them by means of decorous silken book-markers; who lighted and snuffed the candles in the pulpit and desk, and attended to the little stove in the squire's pew; who ran busily about, in short, during the quarter-hour which preceded Divine Service, doing a hundred little things, with all the activity, and much of the appearance, of a beetle.

Just such a one was Caleb Dean, who was clerk of Stoneground in the days of William IV. Small in stature, he possessed a voice which Nature seemed to have meant for a giant, and in the discharge of his duties he had a dignity of manner disproportionate even to his voice. No one was afraid to sing when he led the Psalm, so certain was it that no other voice could be noticed, and the gracious condescension with which he received his meagre fees would have been ample acknowledgement of double their amount.

Man, however, cannot live by dignity alone, and Caleb was glad enough to be sexton as well as clerk, and to undertake any other duties by which he might add to his modest income. He kept the churchyard tidy, trimmed the lamps, chimed the bells, taught the choir their simple tunes, turned the barrel of the organ, and managed the stoves.

It was this last duty in particular, which took him into church "last thing", as he used to call it, on Saturday night. There were people in those days, and may be some in these, whom nothing would induce to enter a church at midnight; Caleb, however, was so much at home there that all hours were alike to him. He was never an early man on Saturdays. His wife, who insisted upon sitting up for him, would often knit her way into Sunday before he appeared, and even then would find it hard to get him to bed. Caleb, in fact, when off duty, was a genial little fellow; he had many friends, and on Saturday evenings he knew where to find them.

It was not, therefore, until the evening was spent that he went to make up his fires; and his voice, which served for other singing than that of Psalms, could usually be heard, within a little of midnight, beguiling the way to church with snatches of convivial songs. Many a belated traveller, homeward bound, would envy him his spirits, but no one envied him his duties. Even such as walked with him to the neighbourhood of the churchyard would bid him "Goodnight" whilst still a long way from the gate. They would see him disappear into the gloom amongst the graves, and shudder as they turned homewards.

Caleb, meanwhile, was perfectly content. He knew every stone in the path; long practice enabled him, even on the darkest night, to thrust his huge key into the lock at the first attempt, and on the night we are about to describe—it had come to Mr Batchel from an old man who heard it from Caleb's lips—he did it with a feeling of unusual cheerfulness and contentment.

Caleb always locked himself in. A prank had once been played upon him, which had greatly wounded his dignity; and though it had been no midnight prank, he had taken care, ever since, to have the church to himself. He locked the door, therefore, as usual, on the night we speak of, and made his way to the stove. He used no candle. He opened the little iron door of the stove, and obtained sufficient light to show him the fuel he had laid in readiness; then, when he had made up his fire, he closed this door again, and left the church in darkness. He never could say what induced him upon this occasion to remain there after his task was done. He knew that his wife was sitting up, as usual, and that, as usual, he would have to hear what she had to say. Yet, instead of making his way home, he sat down in the corner of the nearest seat. He supposed that he must have felt tired, but had no distinct recollection of it.

The church was not absolutely dark. Caleb remembered that he could make out the outlines of the windows, and that through the window nearest to him he saw a few stars. After his eyes had grown accustomed to the gloom he could see the lines of the seats taking shape in the darkness, and he had not long sat there before he could dimly see everything there was. At last he began to distinguish where books lay upon the shelf in front of him. And then he closed his eyes. He does not admit having fallen asleep, even for a moment. But the seat was restful, the neighbouring stove was growing warm, he had been through a long and joyous evening, and it was natural that he should at least close his eyes.

He insisted that it was only for a moment. Something, he could not say what, caused him to open his eyes again immediately. The closing of them seemed to have improved what may be called his dark sight. He saw everything in the church quite distinctly, in a sort of grey light. The pulpit stood out, large and bulky, in front. Beyond that, he passed his eyes along the four windows on the north side of the church. He looked again at the stars, still visible through the nearest window on his left hand as he was sitting. From that, his eyes fell to the further end of the seat in front of him, where he could even see a faint gleam of polished wood. He traced this gleam to the middle of the seat, until it disappeared in black shadow, and upon that his eye passed on to the seat he was in, and there he saw a man sitting beside him.

Caleb described the man very clearly. He was, he said, a pale, old-fashioned looking man, with something very churchy about him. Reasoning also with great clearness, he said that the stranger had not come into the church either with him or after him, and that therefore he must have been there before him. And in that case, seeing that the church had been locked since two in the afternoon, the stranger must have been there for a considerable time.

Caleb was puzzled; turning therefore, to the stranger, he asked "How long have you been here?"

The stranger answered at once "Six hundred years."

"Oh! come!" said Caleb.

"Come where?" said the stranger.

"Well, if you come to that, come out," said Caleb.

"I wish I could," said the stranger, and heaved a great sigh.

"What's to prevent you?" said Caleb. "There's the door, and here's the key."

"That's it," said the other.

"Of course it is," said Caleb. "Come along."

With that he proceeded to take the stranger by the sleeve, and then it was that he says you might have knocked him down with a feather. His hand went right into the place where the sleeve seemed to be, and Caleb distinctly saw two of the stranger's buttons on the top of his own knuckles.

He hastily withdrew his hand, which began to feel icy cold, and sat still, not knowing what to say next. He found that the stranger was gently chuckling with laughter, and this annoyed him.

"What are you laughing at?" he enquired peevishly.

"It's not funny enough for two," answered the other.

"Who are you, anyhow?" said Caleb.

"I am the kirk spook," was the reply.

Now Caleb had not the least notion what a "kirk spook" was. He was not willing to admit his ignorance, but his curiosity was too much for his pride, and he asked for information.

"Every church has a spook," said the stranger, "and I am the spook of this one."

"Oh," said Caleb, "I've been about this church a many years, but I've never seen you before."

"That," said the spook, "is because you've always been moving about. I'm flimsy—very flimsy indeed—and I can only keep myself together when everything is quite still."

"Well," said Caleb, "you've got your chance now. What are you going to do with it?"

"I want to go out," said the spook, "I'm tired of this church, and I've been alone for six hundred years. It's a long time."

"It does seem rather a long time," said Caleb, "but why don't you go if you want to? There's three doors."

"That's just it," said the spook, "They keep me in."

"What?" said Caleb, "when they're open?"

"Open or shut," said the spook, "it's all one."

"Well, then," said Caleb, "what about the windows?"

"Every bit as bad," said the spook, "They're all pointed." Caleb felt out of his depth. Open doors and windows that kept a person in—if it was a person—seemed to want a little understanding. And the flimsier the person, too, the easier it ought to be for him to go where he wanted. Also, what could it matter whether they were pointed to not?

The latter question was the one which Caleb asked first.

"Six hundred years ago," said the Spook, "all arches were made round, and when these pointed things came in I cursed them. I hate new-fangled things."

"That wouldn't hurt them much," said Caleb.

"I said I would never go under one of them," said the spook.

"That would matter more to you than to them," said Caleb.

"It does," said the spook, with another great sigh.

"But you could easily change your mind," said Caleb.

"I was tied to it," said the spook, "I was told that I never more should go under one of them, whether I would or not."

"Some people will tell you anything," answered Caleb.

"It was a Bishop," explained the spook.

"Ah!" said Caleb, "that's different, of course."

The spook told Caleb how often he had tried to go under the pointed arches, sometimes of the doors, sometimes of the windows, and how a stream of wind always struck him from the point of the arch, and drifted him back into the church. He had long given up trying.

"You should have been outside," said Caleb, "before they built the last door."

"It was my church," said the spook, "and I was too proud to leave."

Caleb began to sympathize with the spook. He had a pride in the church himself, and disliked even to hear another person say Amen before him. He also began to be a little jealous of this stranger who had been six hundred years in possession of the church in which Caleb had believed himself, under the vicar, to be master. And he began to plot.

"Why do you want to get out?" he asked. "I'm no use here," was the reply, "I don't get enough to do to keep myself warm. And I know there are scores of churches now without any kirk-spooks at all. I can hear their cheap little bells dinging every Sunday."

"There's very few bells hereabouts," said Caleb.

"There's no hereabouts for spooks," said the other. "We can hear any distance you like."

"But what good are you at all?" said Caleb.

"Good!" said the spook. "Don't we secure proper respect for churches, especially after dark? A church would be like any other place if it wasn't for us. You must know that."

"Well, then," said Caleb, "you're no good here. This church is all right. What will you give me to let you out?"

"Can you do it?" asked the spook.

"What will you give me?" said Caleb.

"I'll say a good word for you amongst the spooks," said the other.

"What good will that do me?" said Caleb.

"A good word never did anybody any harm yet," answered the spook.

"Very well then, come along," said Caleb.

"Gently then," said the spook; "don't make a draught."

"Not yet," said Caleb, and he drew the spook very carefully (as one takes a vessel quite full of water) from the seat.

"I can't go under pointed arches," cried the spook, as Caleb moved off.

"Nobody wants you to," said Caleb. "Keep close to me."

He led the spook down the aisle to the angle of the wall where a small iron shutter covered an opening into the flue. It was used by the chimney sweep alone, but Caleb had another use for it now. Calling to the spook to keep close, he suddenly removed the shutter.

The fires were by this time burning briskly. There was a strong up-draught as the shutter was removed. Caleb felt something rush across his face, and heard a cheerful laugh away up in the chimney. Then he knew that he was alone. He replaced the shutter, gave another look at his stoves, took the keys, and made his way home.

He found his wife asleep in her chair, sat down and took off his boots, and awakened her by throwing them across the kitchen.

"I've been wondering when you'd wake," he said.

"What?" she said, "Have you been in long?"

"Look at the clock," said Caleb. "Half after twelve."

"My gracious," said his wife. "Let's be off to bed."

"Did you tell her about the spook?" he was naturally asked.

"Not I," said Caleb. "You knew what she'd say. Same as she always does of a Saturday night."

* * * * * *

This fable Mr Batchel related with reluctance. His attitude towards it was wholly deprecatory. Psychic phenomena, he said, lay outside the province of the mere humourist, and the levity with which they had been treated was largely responsible for the presumptuous materialism of the age.

He said more, as he warmed to the subject, than can here be repeated. The reader of the foregoing tales, however, will be interested to know that Mr Batchel's own attitude was one of humble curiosity. He refused even to guess why the *revenant* was sometimes invisible, and at other times partly or wholly visible; sometimes capable of using physical force, and at other times powerless. He knew that they had their periods, and that was all.

There is room, he said, for the romancer in these matters; but for the humourist, none. Romance was the play of intelligence about the confines of truth. The invisible world, like the visible, must have its romancers, its explorers, and its interpreters; but the time of the last was not yet come.

Criticism, he observed in conclusion, was wholesome and necessary. But of the idle and mischievous remarks which were wont to pose as criticism, he held none in so much contempt as the cheap and irrational *pooh-pooh*.

Tedious Brief Tales of Granta and Gramarye

"INGULPHUS"

(ARTHUR GRAY, MASTER OF JESUS COLLEGE)

ILLUSTRATIONS BY

E. JOYCE SHILLINGTON SCALES

(1919)

Entrance Gateway,
Jesus College.

To Two Cambridge Magicians

In London lanes, uncanonized, untold
By letter'd brass or stone, apart they lie,
Dead and unreck'd of by the passer-by.
Here still they seem together, as of old,
To breathe our air, to walk our Cambridge ground,
Here still to after learners to impart
Hints of the magic that gave Faustus art
To make blind Homer sing "with ravishing sound
To his melodious harp" of Oenon, dead
For Alexander's love; that framed the spell
Of him who, in the Friar's "secret cell,"
Made the great marvel of the Brazen Head.
Marlowe and Greene, on you a Cambridge hand
Sprinkles these pious particles of sand.

The Everlasting Club

There is a chamber in Jesus College the existence of which is probably known to few who are now resident, and fewer still have penetrated into it or even seen its interior. It is on the right hand of the landing on the top floor of the precipitous staircase in the angle of the cloister next the Hall—a staircase which for some forgotten story connected with it is traditionally called "Cow Lane." The padlock which secures its massive oaken door is very rarely unfastened, for the room is bare and unfurnished. Once it served as a place of deposit for superfluous kitchen ware, but even that ignominious use has passed from it, and it is now left to undisturbed solitude and darkness. For I should say that it is entirely cut off from the light of the outer day by the walling up, some time in the eighteenth century, of its single window, and such light as ever reaches it comes from the door, when rare occasion causes it to be opened.

Yet at no extraordinarily remote day this chamber has evidently been tenanted, and, before it was given up to darkness, was comfortably fitted, according to the standard of comfort which was known in college in the days of George II. There is still a roomy fireplace before which legs have been stretched and wine and gossip have circulated in the days of wigs and brocade. For the room is spacious and, when it was lighted by the window looking eastward over the fields and common, it must have been a cheerful place for a sociable don.

Let me state in brief, prosaic outline the circumstances which account for the gloom and solitude in which this room has remained now for nearly a century and a half.

In the second quarter of the eighteenth century the University possessed a great variety of clubs of a social kind. There were clubs in college parlours and clubs in private rooms, or in inns and coffee-houses: clubs flavoured with politics, clubs clerical, clubs purporting to be learned and literary. Whatever their professed particularity, the aim of each was convivial. Some of them, which included undergraduates as well as seniors, were dissipated enough, and in their limited provincial way aped the profligacy of such clubs as the Hell Fire Club of London notoriety.

Among these last was one which was at once more select and of more evil fame than any of its fellows. By a singular accident, presently to be explained, the Minute Book of this Club, including the years from 1738 to 1766, came into the hands of a Master of Jesus College, and though, so far as I am aware, it is no longer extant, I have before me a transcript of it which, though it is in a recent handwriting, presents in a bald shape such a singular array of facts that I must ask you to accept them as veracious. The original book is described as a stout duodecimo volume bound in red leather and fastened with red silken strings. The writing in it occupied some 40 pages, and ended with the date November 2, 1766.

The Club in question was called the Everlasting Club—a name sufficiently explained by its rules, set forth in the pocket-book. Its number was limited to seven, and it would seem that its members were all young men, between 22 and 30. One of them was a Fellow-Commoner of Trinity: three of them were Fellows of Colleges, among whom I should specially mention a Fellow of Jesus, named Charles Bellasis: another was a landed proprietor in the county, and the sixth was a young Cambridge physician. The Founder and President of the Club was the Honourable Alan Dermot, who, as the son of an Irish peer, had obtained a nobleman's degree in the University, and lived in idleness in the town. Very little is known of his life and character, but that little is highly in his disfavour.

He was killed in a duel at Paris in the year 1743, under circumstances which I need not particularise, but which point to an exceptional degree of cruelty and wickedness in the slain man.

I will quote from the first pages of the Minute Book some of the laws of the Club, which will explain its constitution:—

> "1. This Society consisteth of seven Everlastings, who may be Corporeal or Incorporeal, as Destiny shall determine.
>
> 2. The rules of the Society, as herein written, are immutable and Everlasting.
>
> 3. None shall hereafter be chosen into the Society and none shall cease to be members.
>
> 4. The Honourable Alan Dermot is the Everlasting President of the Society.
>
> 5. The Senior Corporeal Everlasting, not being the President, shall be the Secretary of the Society, and in this Book of Minutes shall record its transactions, the date at which any Everlasting shall cease to be Corporeal, and all fines due to the Society. And when such Senior Everlasting shall cease to be Corporeal he shall, either in person or by some sure hand, deliver this Book of Minutes to him who shall be next Senior and at the time Corporeal, and he shall in like manner record the transactions therein and transmit it to the next Senior. The neglect of these provisions shall be visited by the President with fine or punishment according to his discretion.
>
> 6. On the second day of November in every year, being the Feast of All Souls, at ten o'clock *post meridiem*, the Everlastings shall meet at supper in the place of residence of that Corporeal member of the Society to whom it shall fall in order of rotation to entertain them, and they shall all subscribe in this Book of Minutes their names and present place of abode.

7. It shall be the obligation of every Everlasting to be present at the yearly entertainment of the Society, and none shall allege for excuse that he has not been invited thereto. If any Everlasting shall fail to attend the yearly meeting, or in his turn shall fail to provide entertainment for the Society, he shall be mulcted at the discretion of the President.

8. Nevertheless, if in any year, in the month of October and not less than seven days before the Feast of All Souls, the major part of the Society, that is to say, four at the least, shall meet and record in writing in these Minutes that it is their desire that no entertainment be given in that year, then, notwithstanding the two rules last rehearsed, there shall be no entertainment in that year, and no Everlasting shall be mulcted on the ground of his absence."

The rest of the rules are either too profane or too puerile to be quoted here. They indicate the extraordinary levity with which the members entered on their preposterous obligations. In particular, to the omission of any regulation as to the transmission of the Minute Book after the last Everlasting ceased to be "Corporeal," we owe the accident that it fell into the hands of one who was not a member of the society, and the consequent preservation of its contents to the present day.

Low as was the standard of morals in all classes of the University in the first half of the eighteenth century, the flagrant defiance of public decorum by the members of the Everlasting Society brought upon it the stern censure of the authorities, and after a few years it was practically dissolved and its members banished from the University. Charles Bellasis, for instance, was obliged to leave the college, and, though he retained his fellowship, he remained absent from it for nearly twenty years. But the minutes of the society reveal a more terrible reason for its virtual extinction.

Between the years 1738 and 1743 the minutes record many meetings of the Club, for it met on other occasions besides that of

Doorway, Cow Lane.

All Souls Day. Apart from a great deal of impious jocularity on the part of the writers, they are limited to the formal record of the attendance of the members, fines inflicted, and so forth. The meeting on November 2nd in the latter year is the first about which there is any departure from the stereotyped forms. The supper was given in the house of the physician. One member, Henry Davenport, the former Fellow-Commoner of Trinity, was absent from the entertainment, as he was then serving in Germany, in the Dettingen campaign. The minutes contain an entry, "Mulctatus propter absentiam per Presidentem, Hen. Davenport." An entry on the next page of the book runs, "Henry Davenport by a Cannon-shot became an Incorporeal Member, November 3, 1743."

The minutes give in their own handwriting, under date November 2, the names and addresses of the six other members. First in the list, in a large bold hand, is the autograph of "Alan Dermot, President, at the Court of His Royal Highness." Now in October Dermot had certainly been in attendance on the Young Pretender at Paris, and doubtless the address which he gave was understood at the time by the other Everlastings to refer to the fact. But on October 28, five days *before* the meeting of the Club, he was killed, as I have already mentioned, in a duel. The news of his death cannot have reached Cambridge on November 2, for the Secretary's record of it is placed below that of Davenport, and with the date November 10: " this day was reported that the President was become an Incorporeal by the hands of a french chevalier." And in a sudden ebullition, which is in glaring contrast with his previous profanities, he has dashed down "The Good God shield us from ill."

The tidings of the President's death scattered the Everlastings like a thunderbolt. They left Cambridge and buried themselves in widely parted regions. But the Club did not cease to exist. The Secretary was still bound to his hateful records: the five survivors did not dare to neglect their fatal obligations. Horror of the presence of the President made the November gathering once and for ever impossible: but horror, too, forbade them to neglect the precaution of meeting in October of every year to put in writing their objection to the celebration. For five years five names are appended to that entry in the minutes, and that is all the business of the Club. Then another member died, who was not the Secretary.

For eighteen more years four miserable men met once each year to deliver the same formal protest. During those years we gather from the signatures that Charles Bellasis returned to Cambridge, now, to appearance, chastened and decorous. He occupied the rooms which I have described on the staircase in the corner of the cloister.

Then in 1766 comes a new handwriting and an altered minute: "Jan. 27, on this, day Francis Witherington, Secretary, became an Incorporeal Member. The same day this Book was delivered to me, James Harvey." Harvey lived only a month, and a similar entry on March 7 states that the book has descended, with the same mysterious celerity, to William Catherston. Then, on May 18, Charles Bellasis writes that on that day, being the date of Catherston's decease, the Minute Book has come to him as the last surviving Corporeal of the Club.

As it is my purpose to record fact only I shall not attempt to describe the feelings of the unhappy Secretary when he penned that fatal record. When Witherington died it must have come home to the three survivors that after twenty-three years' intermission the ghastly entertainment must be annually renewed, with the addition of fresh incorporeal guests, or that they must undergo the pitiless censure of the President. I think it likely that the terror of the alternative, coupled with the mysterious delivery of the Minute Book, was answerable for the speedy decease of the two first successors to the Secretaryship. Now that the alternative was offered to Bellasis alone, he was firmly resolved to bear the consequences, whatever they might be, of an infringement of the Club rules.

The graceless days of George II. had passed away from the University. They were succeeded by times of outward respectability, when religion and morals were no longer publicly challenged. With Bellasis, too, the petulance of youth had passed: he was discreet, perhaps exemplary. The scandal of his early conduct was unknown to most of the new generation, condoned by the few survivors who had witnessed it.

On the night of November 2nd, 1766, a terrible event revived in the older inhabitants of the College the memory of those evil days. From ten o'clock to midnight a hideous uproar went on in the chamber of Bellasis. Who were his companions none knew. Blasphemous outcries and ribald songs, such as had not been heard for twenty years past, aroused from sleep or study the occupants of the court; but among the voices was not that of Bellasis. At twelve a sudden silence fell upon the cloisters. But the Master lay awake all night, troubled at the relapse of a respected colleague and the horrible example of libertinism set to his pupils.

In the morning all remained quiet about Bellasis' chamber. When his door was opened, soon after daybreak, the early light creeping through the drawn curtains revealed a strange scene. About the table were drawn seven chairs, but some of them had been overthrown, and the furniture was in chaotic disorder, as after some wild orgy. In the chair at the foot of the table sat the lifeless figure of the Secretary, his head bent over his folded arms, as though he would shield his eyes from some horrible sight. Before him on the table lay pen, ink and the red Minute Book. On the last inscribed page, under the date of November 2nd, were written, for the first time since 1742, the autographs of the seven members of the Everlasting Club, but without address. In the same strong hand in which the President's name was written there was appended below the signatures the note, "Mulctatus per Presidentem propter neglectum obsonii, Car. Bellasis."

The Minute Book was secured by the Master of the College, and I believe that he alone was acquainted with the nature of its contents. The scandal reflected on the College by the circumstances revealed in it caused him to keep the knowledge rigidly to himself. But some suspicion of the nature of the occurrences must have percolated to students and servants, for there was a long-abiding belief in the College that annually on the night of November 2 sounds of unholy revelry were heard to issue from the chamber of Bellasis. I cannot learn that the occupants of the adjoining rooms have ever been disturbed by them. Indeed, it is plain from the minutes that owing to their improvident drafting no provision was made for the perpetuation of the All Souls entertainment after the last Everlasting ceased to be Corporeal. Such superstitious belief must be treated with contemptuous incredulity. But whether for that cause or another the rooms were shut up, and have remained tenantless from that day to this.

The Treasure of John Badcoke

As this narrative of an occurrence in the history of Jesus College may appear to verge on the domain of romance, I think it proper to state by way of preface, that for some of its details I am indebted to documentary evidence which is accessible and veracious. Other portions of the story are supplied from sources the credibility of which my readers will be able to estimate.

On the 8th of November, 1538, the Priory of St. Giles and St. Andrew, Barnwell, was surrendered to King Henry VIII. by John Badcoke, the Prior, and the convent of that house. The surrender was sealed with the common seal, subscribed by the Prior and six canons, and acknowledged on the same day in the Chapter House of the Priory, before Thomas Legh, Doctor of Laws.[1]

Dr. Legh and his fellows, who had been deputed by Cromwell to visit the monasteries, had too frequent occasion to deplore the frowardness of religious households in opposing the King's will in the matter of their dissolution. Among many such reports I need only cite the case of the Prior of Christ Church, Canterbury, mentioned in a letter to Cromwell from one of his agents, Christopher Leyghton.[2] He tells Cromwell that in an inventory exhibited by the Prior to Dr. Leyghton, the King's visitor, the Prior had "wilfullye left owte a remembraunce of certayne parcells of silver, gold and stone to the value of thowsandys of poundys"; that it was not to be

---

[1] Cooper, *Annals*, I., p. 393.
[2] *The Suppression of the Monasteries* (Camden Society's Publications), p. 90.

doubted that he would "eloyne owt of the same howse into the handys of his secret fryndys thowsandes of poundes, which is well knowne he hathe, to hys comfort hereafter"; and that it was common report in the monastery that any monk who should open the matter to the King's advisers "shalbe poysenyde or murtheryde, as he hath murthredde diverse others."

Far different from the truculent attitude of this murderous Prior was the conduct on the like occasion of Prior John Badcoke. Dr. Legh reported him to be "honest and conformable." He furnished an exact inventory of the possessions of his house, and quietly retired on the pittance allowed to him by the King. He prevailed upon the other canons to shew the same submission to the royal will, and they peaceably dispersed, some to country incumbencies, others to resume in the Colleges the studies commenced in earlier life.

John Badcoke settled in Jesus College. The Bursar's Rental of 1538-39 shows that his residence there began in the autumn of the earlier year, immediately after the surrender of the monastery. Divorced from the Priory he was still attached to Barnwell, and took up the duties of Vicar of the small parish church of St. Andrew, which stood close to the Priory gate. So long as Henry VIII. lived, and the rites of the old religion were tolerated, he seems to have ministered faithfully to the spiritual needs of his parishioners, unsuspected and unmolested.

More than twelve months elapsed before the demolition of the canons' house was taken in hand, and, for so long, in the empty church the Prior still offered mass on ceremonial days for the repose of the souls of the Peverels and Peches who had built and endowed the house in long bygone days, and were buried beside the High Altar. In the porter's lodge remained the only occupant of the monastery—a former servant of the house, who, from the circumstance that in his secular profession he was a mason, had the name of Adam Waller. Occasional intruders on the solitude of the cloister or the monastic garden sometimes lighted on the ex-Prior pacing the grass-grown walks, as of old, and generally in company with a younger priest.

Oriel Window of Hall & Entrance to "K" Staircase

This companion was named Richard Harrison. He was not one of the dispossessed canons, but came from the Priory of Christ Church, Canterbury, of which mention has been made. He was the youngest and latest professed of the monks there, a nephew of the Prior, as also of John Badcoke. He had not been present at the time of Dr. Leyghton's visitation, as he happened then to be visiting his uncle at Barnwell. As the Canterbury monks were ejected in his absence he had remained at Barnwell, and there he shared his uncle's parochial duties. He, too, became a resident at Jesus; and he occupied rooms in the College immediately beneath those of Badcoke.

Late in the year 1539 the demolition of Barnwell Priory was begun. Adam Waller was engaged in the work. One incident, which apparently passed almost unnoticed at the time, may be mentioned in connection with this business. The keys of the church were in the keeping of Waller, who had been in the habit of surrendering them to the two ecclesiastics whenever they performed the divine offices there. On the morning when the demolition was to begin, it was found that the stone covering the altar-tomb of Pain Peverel, crusader and founder of the Priory, had been dislodged, and that the earth within it had been recently disturbed. Waller professed to know nothing of the matter:

The account rolls of the College Bursars in the reigns of Henry VIII. and Edward VI. fortunately tell us exactly the situation of the rooms occupied by Badcoke and Harrison, and as, for the proper understanding of subsequent events, it is necessary that we should realise their condition and relation to the rest of the College, I shall not scruple to be particular. They were on the left-hand side of the staircase now called K, in the eastern range of the College, and at the northern end of what had once been the dormitory of the Nuns of St. Radegund. Badcoke's chamber, which was on the highest floor, was one of the largest in the College, and for that reason the Statutes prescribed that it should be reserved "for more venerable persons resorting to the College"; and Badcoke, being neither a Fellow nor a graduate, was regarded as belonging to this class. Below his chamber was that of Harrison, and on the ground-floor was the "cool-house," where the College fuel was kept. Between this ground-floor room and L staircase—which did not then exist—there is seen at the present day a rarely opened door. Inside the door a flight of some half-dozen steps descends to a narrow space, which might be deemed a passage, save that it has no outlet at the farther end. On either side it is flanked, to the height of two floors of K staircase, by walls of ancient monastic masonry; the third and highest floor is carried over it. Here, in the times of Henry VIII. and the Nunnery days before them, ran or stagnated a Stygian stream, known as "the kytchynge sinke ditch," foul with scum from the College offices. Northward from Badcoke's staircase was "the wood-yard," on the site of the present L staircase. It communicated by a door in its outward, eastern wall with a green close which in the old days had been the Nunnery graveyard. In Badcoke's times it was still uneven with the hillocks which marked the resting-places of nameless, unrecorded Nuns. The old graveyard was intersected by a cart-track leading from Jesus Lane to the wood-yard door. The Bursar's books show that Badcoke controlled the wood-yard and coal-house, perhaps in the capacity of Promus, or Steward.

Now when Badcoke and Harrison came to occupy their chambers on K staircase, Jesus, like other Colleges in those troublous times, had fallen on evil days. Its occupants comprised only the Master, some eight Fellows, a few servants, and about half-a-dozen "disciples." Nearly half the rooms in College were empty, and the records show that many were tenantless, *propter defectum reparacionis*; that is, because walls, roofs and floors were decayed and ruinous. Badcoke, being a man of means, paid a handsome rent for his chambers, not less than ten shillings by the year, in consideration of which the College put it in tenantable repair; and, as a circumstance which has some significance in relation to this narrative, it is to be noted that the Bursar—the accounts of the year are no longer extant—recorded that in 1539 he paid a sum of three shillings and fourpence "to Adam Waller for layyinge of new brick in ye cupboard of Mr. Badcoke's chamber." The cupboard in question was seemingly a small recessed space, still recognisable in a gyp-room belonging to the chambers which were Badcoke's. The rooms on the side of the staircase opposite to those of Badcoke and Harrison were evidently unoccupied; the Bursar took no rent from them. The other inmates of the College dwelt in the cloister court.

In this comparative isolation Badcoke and Harrison lived until the death of Henry VIII. in 1546. In course of time Harrison became a Fellow of the College; but Badcoke preferred to retain the exceptional status of its honoured guest. To the Master, Dr. Reston, and the Fellows, whose religious sympathies were with the old order of things, their company was inoffensive and even welcome. But trouble came upon the College in 1549, when it was visited by King Edward's Protestant Commissioners. It stands on record, that on May 26th "they commanded six altars to be pulled down in the church," and in a chamber, which may have been Badcoke's, "caused certayn images to be broken." Mr. Badcoke "had an excommunicacion sette uppe for him," and was dismissed from the office, whatever it was, that he held in the College. Worse still for his happiness, his companion of many years, Richard Harrison, was "expulsed his felowshippe" on some supposition of trafficking with the court of Rome.[1] He went overseas, as it was understood, to the Catholic University of Louvain in Flanders.

In 1549 Badcoke must have been, as age went in the sixteenth century, an old man. His deprivation of office, the loss of his friend, and the abandonment of long treasured hopes for the restitution of the religious system to which his life had been devoted, plunged him in a settled despondency. The Fellows, who showed for him such sympathy as they dared, understood that between him and Harrison there passed a secret correspondence. But in course of years this source of consolation dried up. Harrison was dead, or he had travelled away from Louvain. With the other members of the College Badcoke wholly parted company, and lived a recluse in his unneighboured room. By the wood-yard gate, of which he still had a key, he could let himself out beyond the College walls, and

---

[1] Cooper, *Annals*, II. p. 29.

sometimes by day, oftener after nightfall, he was to be seen wandering beneath his window in the Nuns' graveyard, his old feet, like Friar Laurence's, "stumbling at graves." An occasional visitor, who was known to be his pensioner, was Adam Waller. But, though Waller was still at times employed in the service of the College, his character and condition had deteriorated with years. He was a sturdy beggar, a drunkard, sullen and dangerous in his cups, and Badcoke was heard to hint some terror of his presence. At last the Master learnt from the ex-Prior that he was about to quit the College, and none doubted that he would follow Harrison to Louvain.

Shortly after this became known, Badcoke disappeared from College. He had lived in such seclusion that for a day or two it was not noticed that his door remained closed, and that he had not been seen in his customary walks. When the door was at last forced it was discovered that he had indeed gone, but, strangely, he had left behind him the whole of his effects. Adam Waller was the last person who was known to have entered his chamber, and, being questioned, he said that Badcoke had informed him of his intention to depart three days previously, but, for some unexplained reason, had desired him to keep his purpose secret, and had not imparted his destination. Badcoke's life of seclusion, and his known connection with English Catholics beyond sea, gave colour to Waller's story, and, so far as I am aware, no enquiries were made as to the subsequent fate of the ex-Prior. But a strange fact was commented on—that the floor of the so-called cupboard was strewn with bricks, and that in the place from which they had been dislodged was an arched recess of considerable size, which must have been made during Badcoke's tenancy of the room. There was nothing in the recess. Another circumstance there was which called for no notice in the then dilapidated state of half the College rooms. Two boards were loose in the floor of the larger chamber. Thirty feet below the gap which their removal exposed, lay the dark impurities of the "kytchynge sinke ditch."

Adam Waller died a beggar as he had lived.

A century after these occurrences—in the year 1642—the attention of the College was drawn by a severe visitation of plague to a much-needed sanitary reform. The black ditch which ran under K staircase was "cast," that is, its bed was effectually cleaned out, and its channel was stopped; and so it came about that from that day to this it has presented a clean and dry floor of gravel. Beneath the settled slime of centuries was discovered a complete skeleton. How it came there nobody knew, and nobody enquired. Probably it was guessed to be a relic of some dim and grim monastic mystery.

Now whether Adam Waller knew or suspected the existence of a treasure hidden in the wall-recess of Badcoke's chamber, and murdered the ex-Prior when he was about to remove it to Louvain, I cannot say. One thing is certain—that he did not find the treasure there. When Badcoke disappeared he left his will, with his other belongings, in his chamber. After a decent interval, when it seemed improbable that he would return, probate was obtained by the Master and Fellows, to whom he had bequeathed the chief part of his effects. In 1858 the wills proved in the University court were removed to Peterborough, and there, for aught I know, his will may yet be seen. The property bequeathed consisted principally of books of theology. Among them was Stephanus' Latin Vulgate Bible of 1528 in two volumes folio. This he devised "of my heartie good wylle to my trustie felow and frynde, Richard Harrison, if he shal returne to Cambrege aftyr the tyme of my decesse." Richard Harrison never returned to Cambridge, and the Bible, with the other books, found its way to the College Library.

Now there are still in the Library two volumes of this Vulgate Bible. There is nothing in either of them to identify them with the books mentioned in Badcoke's will, for they have lost the fly-leaves which might have revealed the owner's autograph. Here and there in the margins are annotations in a sixteenth-century handwriting; and in the same handwriting on one of the lost leaves was a curious inscription, which suggests that the writer's mind was running on some treasure which was not spiritual. First at the top of the page, in clear and large letters, was copied a passage from Psalm 55: "Cor meum conturbatum est in me: et formido mortis cecidit super me. Et dixi, Quis dabit pennas mihi sicut columbae, et volabo

Old Hall, Master's Lodge.

et requiescam." (My heart is disquieted within me: and the fear of death is fallen upon me. And I said, O that I had wings like a dove: for then would I fly away, and be at rest.) Then, in lettering of the same kind, came a portion of Deuteronomy xxviii. 12: "Aperiet dominus thesaurum suum, benedicetque cunctis operibus tuis." (The Lord will disclose his treasure, and will bless all the works of thy hands.) Under this, in smaller letters, were the words, "Vide super hoc Ezechielis cap. xl."

If in the same volume the chapter in question is referred to, a singular fact discloses itself. Certain words in the text are underscored in red pencil, and fingers, inked in the margin, are directed to the lines in which they occur. Taken in their consecutive order these words run: "Ecce murus forinsecus . . . ad portam quae respiciebat viam orientalem . . . mensus est a facie portae extrinsecus ad orientem et aquilonem quinque cubitorum . . . hoc est gazophylacium." This may be taken to mean, "Look at the outside wall . . . at the gate facing towards the eastern road . . . he measured from the gate outwards five cubits (7½ feet) towards the north-east . . . there is the treasure."

The outer wall of the College, the wood-yard gate and the road through the Nuns' cemetery must at once have suggested themselves to Richard Harrison, had he lived to see his friend's bequest, and he must have taken it as an instruction from the testator that a treasure known to both parties was hidden in the spot indicated, close to Badcoke's chamber. And the first text cited must have conveyed to him that his friend, in some deadly terror, had transferred the treasure thither from the place where the two friends had originally laid it. But the message never reached Harrison, and it is quite certain that no treasure has been sought or found in that spot. If the Canterbury or any other treasure was deposited there by Badcoke it rests there still.

To those who are curious to know more of this matter I would say: first, ascertain minutely from Loggan's seventeenth-century plan of the College the position of the wood-yard gate; and, secondly, which indeed should be firstly, make absolutely certain that John Badcoke was not mystifying posterity by an elaborate jest.

The True History of Anthony Ffryar

The world, it is said, knows nothing of its greatest men. In our Cambridge microcosm it may be doubted whether we are better informed concerning some of the departed great ones who once walked the confines of our Colleges. Which of us has heard of Anthony Ffryar of Jesus? History is dumb respecting him. Yet but for the unhappy event recorded in this unadorned chronicle his fame might have stood with that of Bacon of Trinity, or Harvey of Caius. *They* lived to be old men: Ffryar died before he was thirty—his work unfinished, his fame unknown even to his contemporaries.

So meagre is the record of his life's work that it is contained in a few bare notices in the College Bursar's Books, in the Grace Books which date his matriculation and degrees, and in the entry of his burial in the register of All Saints' Parish. These simple annals I have ventured to supplement with details of a more or less hypothetical character which will serve to show what humanity lost by his early death. Readers will be able to judge for themselves the degree of care which I have taken not to import into the story anything which may savour of the improbable or romantic.

Anthony Ffryar matriculated in the year 1541-2, his age being then probably 15 or 16. He took his B.A. degree in 1545, his M.A. in 1548. He became a Fellow about the end of 1547, and died in the summer of 1551. Such are the documentary facts relating to him. Dr. Reston was Master of the College during the whole of his tenure of a Fellowship and died in the same year as Ffryar. The chamber which Ffryar occupied as a Fellow was on the first floor

North West Corner of Cloisters.

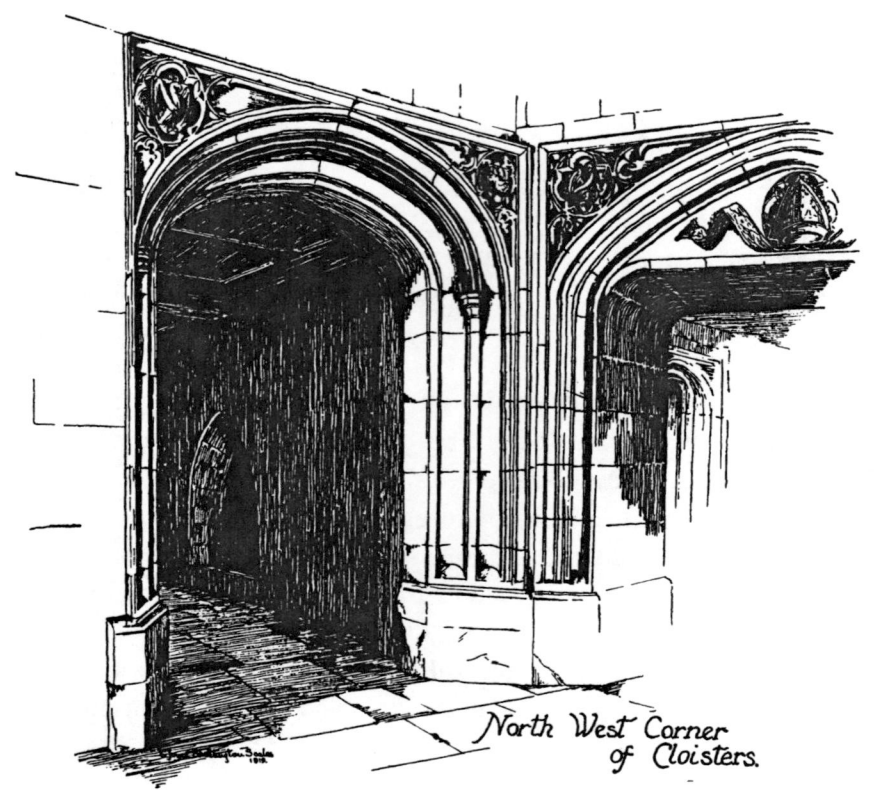

of the staircase at the west end of the Chapel. The staircase has since been absorbed in the Master's Lodge, but the doorway through which it was approached from the cloister may still be seen. At the time when Ffryar lived there the nave of the Chapel was used as a parish church, and his windows overlooked the graveyard, then called "Jesus churchyard," which is now a part of the Master's garden.

Ffryar was of course a priest, as were nearly all the Fellows in his day. But I do not gather that he was a theologian, or complied more than formally with the obligation of his orders. He came to Cambridge when the Six Articles and the suppression of the monasteries were of fresh and burning import: he became a Fellow in the harsh Protestant days of Protector Somerset: and in all his time the Master and the Fellows were in scarcely disavowed sympathy with the rites and beliefs of the Old Religion. Yet in the battle of creeds I imagine that he took no part and no interest. I should suppose that he was a somewhat solitary man, an insatiable student of Nature, and that his sympathies with humanity were starved by his absorption in the New Science which dawned on Cambridge at the Reformation.

When I say that he was an alchemist do not suppose that in the middle of the sixteenth century the name of alchemy carried with it any associations with credulity or, imposture. It was a real science and a subject of University study then, as its god-children, Physics and Chemistry, are now. If the aims of its professors were transcendental its methods were genuinely based on research. Ffryar was no visionary, but a man of sense, hard and practical. To the study of alchemy he was drawn by no hopes of gain, not even of fame, and still less by any desire to benefit mankind. He was actuated solely by an unquenchable passion for enquiry, a passion sterilizing to all other feeling. To the somnambulisms of the less scientific disciples of his school, such as the philosopher's stone and the elixir of life, he showed himself a chill agnostic. All his thought and energies were concentrated on the discovery of the *magisterium*, the master-cure of all human ailments.

For four years in his laboratory in the cloister he had toiled at this pursuit. More than once, when it had seemed most near, it had eluded his grasp; more than once he had been tempted to abandon it as a mystery insoluble. In the summer of 1551 the discovery waited at his door. He was sure, certain of success, which only experiment could prove. And with the certainty arose a new passion in his heart—to make the name of Ffryar glorious in the healing profession as that of Galen or Hippocrates. In a few days, even within a few hours, the fame of his discovery would go out into all the world.

The summer of 1551 was a sad time in Cambridge. It was marked by a more than usually fatal outbreak of the epidemic called "the sweat," when, as Fuller says, "patients ended or mended in twenty-four hours." It had smouldered some time in the town before it appeared with sudden and dreadful violence in Jesus College. The first to go was little Gregory Graunge, schoolboy and chorister, who was lodged in the College school in the outer court. He was barely thirteen years old, and known by sight to Anthony Ffryar. He died on July 31, and was buried the same day in Jesus churchyard. The service for his burial was held in the Chapel and at night, as was customary in those days. Funerals in College were no uncommon events in the sixteenth century. But in the death of the poor child, among strangers, there was something to move even the cold heart of Ffryar. And not the pity of it only impressed him. The dim Chapel, the Master and Fellows obscurely ranged in their stalls and shrouded in their hoods, the long-drawn miserable chanting and the childish trebles of the boys who had been Gregory's fellows struck a chill into him which was not to be shaken off.

Three days passed and another chorister died. The College gates were barred and guarded, and, except by a selected messenger, communication with the town was cut off. The precaution was unavailing, and the boys' usher, Mr. Stevenson, died on August 5. One of the junior Fellows, sir Stayner— "sir" being the equivalent of B.A.—followed on August 7. The Master, Dr. Reston, died the next day. A gaunt, severe man was Dr. Reston, whom his Fellows feared. The death of a Master of Arts on August 9 for a time completed the melancholy list.

Before this the frightened Fellows had taken action. The scholars were dismissed to their homes on August 6. Some of the Fellows abandoned the College at the same time. The rest—a terrified conclave—met on August 8 and decreed that the College should be closed until the pestilence should have abated. Until that time it was to be occupied by a certain Robert Laycock, who was a College servant, and his only communication with the outside world was to be through his son, who lived in Jesus Lane. The decree was perhaps the result of the Master's death, for he was not present at the meeting;

Goodman Laycock, as he was commonly called, might have been the sole tenant of the College but for the unalterable decision of Ffryar to remain there. At all hazards his research, now on the eve

The Master's Stall.

of realisation, must proceed; without the aid of his laboratory in College it would miserably hang fire. Besides, he had an absolute assurance of his own immunity if the experiment answered his confident expectations, and his fancy was elated with the thought of standing, like another Aaron, between the living and the dead, and staying the pestilence with the potent *magisterium*. Until then he would bar his door even against Laycock, and his supplies of food should be left on the staircase landing. Solitude for him was neither unfamiliar nor terrible.

So for three days Ffryar and Laycock inhabited the cloister, solitary and separate. For three days, in the absorption of his research, Ffryar forgot fear, forgot the pestilence-stricken world beyond the gate, almost forgot to consume the daily dole of food laid outside his door. August 12 was the day, so fateful to humanity, when his labours were to be crowned with victory: before midnight the secret of the *magisterium* would be solved.

Evening began to close in before he could begin the experiment which was to be his last. It must of necessity be a labour of some hours, and, before it began, he bethought him that he had not tasted food since early morning. He unbarred his door and looked for the expected portion. It was not there. Vexed at the remissness of Laycock he waited for a while and listened for his approaching footsteps. At last he took courage and descended to the cloister. He called for Laycock, but heard no response. He resolved to go as far as the Buttery door and knock. Laycock lived and slept in the Buttery.

At the Buttery door he beat and cried on Laycock; but in answer he heard only the sound of scurrying rats. He went to the window, by the hatch, where he knew that the old man's bed lay, and called to him again. Still there was silence. At last he resolved to force himself through the unglazed window and take what food he could find. In the deep gloom within he stumbled and almost fell over a low object, which he made out to be a truckle-bed. There was light enough from the window to distinguish, stretched upon it, the form of Goodman Laycock, stark and dead.

Sickened and alarmed Ffryar hurried back to his chamber. More than ever he must hasten the great experiment. When it was ended his danger would be past, and he could go out into the town to call the buryers for the old man. With trembling hands he lit the brazier which he used for his experiments, laid it on his hearth and placed thereon the alembic which was to distil the *magisterium*.

Then he sat down to wait. Gradually the darkness thickened and the sole illuminant of the chamber was the wavering flame of the brazier. He felt feverish and possessed with a nameless uneasiness which, for all his assurance, he was glad to construe as fear: better that than sickness. In the college and the town without was a deathly silence, stirred only by the sweltering of the distilment, and, as the hours struck, by the beating of the Chapel clock, last wound by Laycock. It was as though the dead man spoke. But the repetition of the hours told him that the time of his emancipation was drawing close.

Whether he slept I do not know. He was aroused to vivid consciousness by the clock sounding *one*. The time when his experiment should have ended was ten, and he started up with a horrible fear that it had been ruined by his neglect. But it was not so. The fire burnt, the liquid simmered quietly, and so far all was well.

Again the College bell boomed a solitary stroke: then a pause and another. He opened, or seemed to open, his door and listened. Again the knell was repeated. His mind went back to the night when he had attended the obsequies of the boy-chorister. This must be a funeral tolling. For whom? He thought with a shudder of the dead man in the Buttery.

He groped his way cautiously down the stairs. It was a still, windless night, and the cloister was dark as death. Arrived at the further side of the court he turned towards the Chapel. Its panes were faintly lighted from within. The door stood open and he entered.

In the place familiar to him at the chancel door one candle flickered on a bracket. Close to it—his face cast in deep shade by the light from behind—stood the ringer, in a gown of black, silent and absorbed in his melancholy task. Fear had almost given way to wonder in the heart of Ffryar, and, as he passed the sombre figure on his way to the chancel door, he looked him resolutely in the face. The ringer was Goodman Laycock.

Ffryar passed into the choir and quietly made his way to his accustomed stall. Four candles burnt in the central walk about a figure laid on trestles and draped in a pall of black. Two choristers—one on either side—stood by it. In the dimness he could distinguish four figures, erect in the stalls on either side of the Chapel. Their faces were concealed by their hoods, but in the tall form which occupied the Master's seat it was not difficult to recognise Dr. Reston.

The bell ceased and the service began. With some faint wonder Ffryar noted that it was the proscribed Roman Mass for the Dead. The solemn introit was uttered in the tones of Reston, and in the deep responses of the nearest cowled figure he recognised the voice of Stevenson, the usher. None of the mourners seemed to notice Ffryar's presence.

The dreary ceremony drew to a close. The four occupants of the stalls descended and gathered round the palled figure in the aisle. With a mechanical impulse, devoid of fear or curiosity, and with a half-prescience of what he should see, Anthony Ffryar drew near and uncovered the dead man's face. He saw—himself.

At the same moment the last wailing notes of the office for the dead broke from the band of mourners, and, one by one, the choristers extinguished the four tapers.

"Requiem aeternam dona ei, Domine," chanted the hooded four: and one candle went out

"Et lux perpetua luceat ei," was the shrill response of the two choristers: and a second was extinguished.

"Cum sanctis tuis in aeternum," answered the four: and one taper only remained.

The Master threw back his hood, and turned his dreadful eyes straight upon the living Anthony Ffryar: he threw his hand across the bier and held him tight. "Cras tu eris mecum,"[1] he muttered, as if in antiphonal reply to the dirge-chanters.

[1] Samuel xxvii. 19.

With a hiss and a sputter the last candle expired.

* * * * * *

The hiss and the sputter and a sudden sense of gloom recalled Ffryar to the waking world. Alas for labouring science, alas for the fame of Ffryar, alas for humanity, dying and doomed to die! The vessel containing the wonderful brew which should have redeemed the world had fallen over and dislodged its contents on the fire below. An accident reparable, surely, within a few hours; but not by Anthony Ffryar. How the night passed with him no mortal can tell. All that is known further of him is written in the register of All Saints' parish. If you can discover the ancient volume containing the records of the year 1551—and I am not positive that it now exists—you will find it written:

"Die Augusti xiii
    Buryalls in Jhesus churchyarde
        Goodman Laycock ⎱
        Anthony Ffryar ⎰ of ye sicknesse

Whether he really died of "the sweat" I cannot say. But that the living man was sung to his grave by the dead, who were his sole companions in Jesus College, on the night of August 12, 1551, is as certain and indisputable as any other of the facts which are here set forth in the history of Anthony Ffryar.

The Necromancer

This is a story of Jesus College, and it relates to the year 1643. In that year Cambridge town was garrisoned for the Parliament by Colonel Cromwell and the troops of the Eastern Counties' Association. Soldiers were billeted in all the colleges, and contemporary records testify to their violent behaviour and the damage which they committed in the chambers which they occupied. In the previous year the Master of Jesus College, Doctor Sterne, was arrested by Cromwell when he was leaving the chapel, conveyed to London, and there imprisoned in the Tower. Before the summer of 1643 fourteen of the sixteen Fellows were expelled, and during the whole of that year there were, besides the soldiers, only some ten or twelve occupants of the college. The names of the two Fellows who were not ejected were John Boyleston and Thomas Allen.

With Mr. Boyleston this history is only concerned for the part which he took on the occasion of the visit to the college of the notorious fanatic, William Dowsing. Dowsing came to Cambridge in December, 1642, armed with powers to put in execution the ordinance of Parliament for the reformation of churches and chapels. Among the devastations committed by this ignorant clown, and faithfully recorded by him in his diary, it stands on record that on December 28, in the presence and perhaps with the approval of John Boyleston, he "digg'd up the steps (*i.e.* of the altar) and brake down Superstitions and Angels, 120 at the least." Dowsing's account of his proceedings is supplemented by the Latin History of the college, written in the reign of Charles II. by one of the

Fellows, a certain Doctor John Sherman. Sherman records, but Dowsing does not, that there was a second witness of the desecration—Thomas Allen. Of the two he somewhat enigmatically remarks: "The one (*i.e.* Boyleston) stood behind a curtain to witness the evil work: the other, afflicted to behold the exequies of his Alma Mater, made his life a filial offering at her grave, and, to escape the hands of wicked rebels, laid violent hands on himself."

That Thomas Allen committed suicide seems a fairly certain fact: and that remorse for the part which he had unwillingly taken in the sacrilege of December 28 prompted his act we may accept on the testimony of Sherman. But there is something more to tell which Sherman either did not know or did not think fit to record. His book deals only with the college and its society. He had no occasion to remember Adoniram Byfield.

Byfield was a chaplain attached to the Parliamentary forces in Cambridge, and quarters were assigned to him in Jesus College, in the first floor room above the gate of entrance. Below his chamber was the Porter's lodge, which at that time served as the armoury of the troopers who occupied the college. Above it, on the highest floor of the gate-tower "kept" Thomas Allen. These were the only rooms on the staircase. At the beginning of the Long Vacation of 1643 Allen was the only member of the college who continued to reside.

Some light is thrown on the character of Byfield and his connection with this story by a pudgy volume of old sermons of the Commonwealth period which is contained in the library of the college. Among the sermons which are bound up in it is one which bears the date 1643 and is designated on the title page:

> A Faithful Admonicion of the Baalite sin of Enchanters & Stargazers, preacht to the Colonel Cromwell's Souldiers in Saint Pulcher's (*i.e.* Saint Sepulchre's) church, in Cambridge, by the fruitfull Minister, *Adoniram Byfield*, late departed unto God, in the yeare 1643, touching that of *Acts* the seventh, verse 43, *Ye took up the Tabernacle of Moloch, the Star of your god Remphan, figures which ye made*

to worship them; & I will carrie you away beyond Babylon.

The discourse, in its title as in its contents, reveals its author as one of the fanatics who wrought on the ignorance and prejudice against "carnal" learning which actuated the Cromwellian soldiers in their brutal usage of the University "scholars" in 1643. All Byfield's learning was contained in one book—*the* Book. For him the revelation which gave it sufficed for its interpretation. What needed Greek to the man who spoke mysteries in unknown tongues, or the light of comment to him who was carried in the spirit into the radiance of the third heaven?

Now Allen, too, was an enthusiast, lost in mystic speculation. His speculation was in the then novel science of mathematics and astronomy. Even to minds not darkened by the religious mania that possessed Byfield that science was clouded with suspicion in the middle of the seventeenth century. Anglican, Puritan, and Catholic were agreed in regarding its great exponent, Descartes, as an atheist. Mathematicians were looked upon as necromancers, and Thomas Hobbes says that in his days at Oxford the study was considered to be "smutched with the black art," and fathers, from an apprehension of its malign influence, refrained from sending their sons to that University. How deep the prejudice had sunk into the soul of Adoniram his sermon shows. The occasion which suggested it was this. A pious cornet, leaving a prayer-meeting at night, fell down one of the steep, unlighted staircases of the college and broke his neck. Two or three of the troopers were taken with a dangerous attack of dysentery. There was talk of these misadventures among the soldiers, who somehow connected them with Allen and his studies. The floating gossip gathered into a settled conviction in the mind of Adoniram.

For Allen was a mysterious person. Whether it was because he was engrossed in his studies, or that he shrank from exposing himself to the insults of the soldiers, he seldom showed himself outside his chamber. Perhaps he was tied to it by the melancholy to which Sherman ascribed his violent end. In his three months'

Main Gateway
& Porter's Lodge

sojourn on Allen's staircase Byfield had not seen him a dozen times, and the mystery of his closed door awakened the most fantastic speculations in the chaplain's mind. For hours together, in the room above, he could hear the mumbled tones of Allen's voice, rising and falling in ceaseless flow. No answer came, and no word that the listener could catch conveyed to his mind any intelligible sense. Once the voice was raised in a high key and Byfield distinctly heard the ominous ejaculation, "Avaunt, Sathanas, avaunt!" Once through his partly open door he had caught sight of him standing before a board chalked with figures and symbols which the imagination of Byfield interpreted as magical. At night, from the court below, he would watch the astrologer's lighted window, and when Allen turned his perspective glass upon the stars the conviction became rooted in his watcher's mind that he was living in perilous neighbourhood to one of the peeping and muttering wizards of whom the Holy Book spoke.

An unusual occurrence strengthened the suspicions of Byfield. One night he heard Allen creep softly down the staircase past his room; and, opening his door, he saw him disappear round the staircase foot, candle in hand. Silently, in the dark, Byfield followed him and saw him pass into the Porter's lodge. The soldiers were in bed and the armoury was unguarded. Through the lighted pane he saw Allen take down a horse-pistol from a rack on the wall. He examined it closely, tried the lock, poised it as if to take aim, then replaced it and, leaving the lodge, disappeared up the staircase with his candle. A world of suspicions rushed on Byfield's mind, and they were not allayed when the soldiers reported in the morning that the pistols were intact. But one of the sick soldiers died that week.

Brooding on this incident Adoniram became more than ever convinced of the Satanic purposes and powers of his neighbour, and his suspicions were confirmed by another mysterious circumstance. As the weeks passed he became aware that at a late hour of night Allen's door was quietly opened. There followed a patter of scampering feet down the staircase, succeeded by silence. In an hour or two the sound came back. The patter went up the stairs to

Allen's chamber, and then the door was closed. To lie awake waiting for this ghostly sound became a horror to Byfield's diseased imagination. In his bed he prayed and sang psalms to be relieved of it. Then he abandoned thoughts of sleep and would sit up waiting if he might surprise and detect this walking terror of the night. At first in the darkness of the stairs it eluded him. One night, light in hand, he managed to get a glimpse of it as it disappeared at the foot of the stairs. It was shaped like a large black cat.

Far from allaying his terrors, the discovery awakened new questionings in the heart of Byfield. Quietly he made his way up to Allen's door. It stood open and a candle burnt within. From where he stood he could see each corner of the room. There was the board scribbled with hieroglyphs: there were the magical books open on the table: there were the necromancer's instruments of unknown purpose. But there was no live thing in the room, and no sound save the rustling of papers disturbed by the night air from the open window.

A horrible certitude seized on the chaplain's mind. This Thing that he had caught sight of was no cat. It was the Evil One himself, or it was the wizard translated into animal shape. On what foul errand was he bent? Who was to be his new victim? With a flash there came upon his mind the story how Phinehas had executed judgment on the men that were joined to Baal-peor, and had stayed the plague from the congregation of Israel. He would be the minister of the Lord's vengeance on the wicked one, and it should be counted unto him for righteousness unto all generations for evermore.

He went down to the armoury in the Porter's lodge. Six pistols, he knew, were in the rack on the wall. Strange that to-night there were only five—a fresh proof of the justice of his fears. One of the five he selected, primed, loaded and cocked it in readiness for the

On 'O' Staircase

wizard's return. He took his stand in the shadow of the wall, at the entrance of the staircase. That his aim might be surer he left his candle burning at the stair-foot.

In solemn stillness the minutes drew themselves out into hours while Adoniram waited and prayed to himself. Then in the poring darkness he became sensible of a moving presence, noiseless and unseen. For a moment it appeared in the light of the candle, not two paces distant. It was the returning cat. A triumphant exclamation sprang to Byfield's lips, "God shall shoot at them, suddenly shall they be wounded"—and he fired.

With the report of the pistol there rang through the court a dismal outcry, not human nor animal, but resembling, as it seemed to the excited imagination of the chaplain, that of a lost soul in torment. With a scurry the creature disappeared in the darkness of the court, and Byfield did not pursue it. The deed was done—that he felt sure of—and as he replaced the pistol in the rack a gush of religious exaltation filled his heart. That night there was no return of the pattering steps outside his door, and he slept well.

* * * * * *

Next day the body of Thomas Allen was discovered in the grove which girds the college—his breast pierced by a bullet. It was surmised that he had dragged himself thither from the court. There were tracks of blood from the staircase foot, where it was conjectured that he had shot himself, and a pistol was missing from the armoury. Some of the inmates of the court had been aroused by the discharge of the weapon. The general conclusion was that recorded by Sherman—that the fatal act was prompted by brooding melancholy.

Of his part in the night's transactions Byfield said nothing. The grim intelligence, succeeding the religious excitation of the night, brought to him questioning, dread, horror. Whatever others might surmise, he was fatally convinced that it was by his hand that Allen had died. Pity for the dead man had no place in the dark cabin of his soul. But how was it with himself? How should his action be weighed before the awful Throne? His lurid thought pictured the Great Judgment as already begun, the Book opened, the Accuser of the Brethren standing to resist him, and the dreadful sentence of Cain pronounced upon him, "Now art thou cursed from the earth."

In the evening he heard them bring the dead man to the chamber above his own. They laid him on his bed, and, closing the door, left him and descended the stairs. The sound of their footsteps died away and left a dreadful silence. As the darkness grew the horror of the stillness became insupportable. How he yearned that he might hear again the familiar muffled voice in the room above! And in an access of fervour he prayed aloud that the terrible present might pass from him, that the hours might go back, as on the dial of Ahaz, and all might be as yesterday.

Suddenly, as the prayer died on his lips, the silence was broken. He could not be mistaken. Very quietly he heard Allen's door open, and the old, pattering steps crept softly down the stairs. They passed his door. They were gone before he could rise from his knees to open it. A momentary flash lighted the gloom in Byfield's soul. What if his prayer was heard, if Allen was not dead, if the events of the past twenty-four hours were only a dream and a delusion of the Wicked One? Then the horror returned intensified. Allen was assuredly dead. This creeping Thing—what might it be?

For an hour in his room Byfield sat in agonised dread. Most the thought of the open door possessed him like a nightmare. Somehow it must be closed before the foul Thing returned. Somehow the mangled shape within must be barred up from the wicked powers that might possess it. The fancy gripped and stuck to his delirious mind. It was horrible, but it must be done. In a cold terror he opened his door and looked out.

A flickering light played on the landing above. Byfield hesitated. But the thought that the cat might return at any moment gave him a desperate courage. He mounted the stairs to Allen's door. Precisely as yesternight it stood wide open. Inside the room the books, the instruments, the magical figures were unchanged, and a candle, exposed to the night wind from the casement, threw wavering shadows on the walls and floor. At a glance he saw it all, and he saw the bed where, a few hours ago, the poor remains of Allen had been laid. The coverlet lay smooth upon it. The dead necromancer was not there.

Then as he stood, footbound, at the door a wandering breath from the window caught the taper, and with a gasp the flame went out. In the black silence he became conscious of a moving sound. Nearer, up the stairs, they drew—the soft creeping steps—and in panic he shrank backwards into Allen's room before their advance.

Already they were on the last flight of the stairs; and then in the doorway the darkness parted and Byfield saw. In a ring of pallid light that seemed to emanate from its body he beheld the cat—horrible, gory, its foreparts hanging in ragged collops from its neck. Slowly it crept into the room, and its eyes, smoking with dull malevolence, were fastened on Byfield. Further he backed into the room, to the corner where the bed was laid. The creature followed. It crouched to spring upon him. He dropped in a sitting posture on the bed and as he saw it launch itself upon him, he closed his eyes and found speech in a gush of prayer, "O my God, make haste for my help." In an agony he collapsed upon the couch and clutched its covering with both hands. Beneath it he gripped the stiffened limbs of the dead necromancer, and, when he opened his eyes, the darkness had returned and the spectral cat was gone.

Brother John's Bequest

On a certain morning in the summer of the year 1510 John Eccleston, Doctor in Divinity and Master of Jesus College in Cambridge, stood at the door of his lodge looking into the cloister court. There was a faint odour of extinguished candles in the air, and a bell automatically clanked in unison with its bearer's step. It was carried by a young acolyte, who lagged in the rear of a small band of white-robed figures who were just disappearing from sight at the corner of the passage leading to the entrance court. They were the five Fellows of the newly-constituted College.

As they disappeared, the Master, with much deliberation, spat into the cloister walk.

To spit behind a man's back might be accounted a mark of disgust, contempt, malice—at least of disapproval. Such were not the feelings of Dr. Eccleston.

It is a fact known all over the world, Christian and heathen, that visitants from the unseen realm cannot endure to be spat at. The Master's action was prophylactic. For supernatural visitings of the transitory, curable kind the rites of the Church are, no doubt, efficacious. In inveterate cases it is well to leave no remedy untried.

With bell, book and candle the Master and Fellows had just completed a lustration of the lodge. The bell had clanked in the Founder's Chamber and in the Master's oratory. The Master's bedchamber had been well soused with holy water. The candle had explored dark places in cupboards and under the stairs. If It was there before it was almost inconceivable that It remained there now. But one cannot be too careful.

Two days previously a funeral had taken place in the College. It was a shabby affair. The deceased, John Baldwin, late a brother of the dissolved Hospital of Saint John, was put away in an obscure part of the College churchyard—now the Master's garden—behind some elder bushes which grew in the corner bounded by the street and the "chimney." The mourners were the gravedigger, the sexton and the parson of All Saints' Church. Though brother John had died in a college chamber the society of Jesus marked its reprobation of his manner of living by absenting themselves from his obsequies.

Brother John had been a disappointment: uncharitable persons might say he was a fraud. He had got into the College by false pretences. In life he had disgraced it by his excesses, and, when he was dead, he had perpetrated a mean practical joke on the society. It is not well for a man in religious orders to joke when he is dead.

How did it come that brother John Baldwin, late Granger of the Augustinian Hospital of Saint John, died in Jesus College?

The Hospital of Saint John was dissolved in the year 1510, to make room for the new college designed by the Lady Margaret. Bishops of Ely for three centuries and more had been its patrons and visitors, and dissolute James Stanley, bishop in 1510, fought stoutly for its maintenance. But circumstances were too strong for the bishop. The ancient Hospital was hopelessly bankrupt. The buildings were ruinous: there was not a doit in the treasury chest: the household goods were pawned to creditors in the town. The Master, William Tomlyn, had disappeared, none knew whither, and only two brethren were left in the place. One of them was John Baldwin: the other was the Infirmarer, a certain Bartholomew Aspelon.

On the eve of the dissolution, bishop Stanley wrote a letter to the Master and Fellows of the other Cambridge society of which he was visitor, namely, Jesus College. He commended to their charitable care brother John Baldwin, an aged man of godly conversation who was disposed to bestow his worldly goods for the comfort and sustenance of the Master and Fellows in consideration of their maintenance of him in College during the remaining years of his earthly pilgrimage. It was a not uncommon practice in those days for monasteries and colleges to accept as inmates persons, clerical or lay, who wished to withdraw from the world and were willing, either during life or by testamentary arrangements, to guarantee their hosts against pecuniary loss.

Report said that, though the Hospital was penniless, brother John in his private circumstances was well-to-do and even affluent. It did not befit the Master and Fellows to enquire how he had come by his wealth. They were wretchedly poor, and the bishop's certificate of character was all that could be desired. They thanked the bishop for his prudent care for their interests and covenanted to give the religious man a domicile in the College with allowance for victuals, barber, laundress, wine, wax and all other things necessary for celebrating Divine service, as to any Fellow of the College. Brother John promptly transferred himself to his new quarters, which were in a room called "the loft," on the top floor above the Founder's Chamber in the Master's lodge.

The Master and Fellows were disappointed in brother John's luggage. It consisted simply of two brass-hound boxes, heavy but unquestionably small, even for a man of religion. An encouraging feature about them was that they bore the monogram of Saint John's Hospital. Brother John and his former co-mate of the Hospital, Bartholomew Aspelon, constantly affirmed that the missing Master, William Tomlyn, had decamped with the contents of the Hospital treasury. But the society of Jesus hoped that they were not telling the truth. Brother John kept the two boxes under his bed. They were always carefully locked, but brother John threw out vague hints that their contents were destined for a princely benefaction to his hospitable entertainers.

In other respects brother John's equipment was not such as would betoken a man of wealth. Rather it savoured of monastical austerity. His only suit of clothing was ancient, and even greasy. It was never changed, night or day. Brother John was apparently under a religious obligation to abstain from washing.

As a man of godly conversation brother John was unfortunate in his personal appearance. It was presumably a stroke of paralysis which had drawn up one side of his face and correspondingly depressed the other. His mouth was a diagonal compromise with the rest of his features. One eye was closed, and the other was bleared and watery. His nose was red, but the rest of his face was of a parchment colour.

Brother John was an elderly person, and continued ill health unfortunately confined him to his chamber, above the Master's. He expressed a deep regret that he could not share the society of the Fellows in the Hall at their meals of oatmeal porridge, salt fish, and thin ale. His distressing ailments necessitated a sustaining diet of capons and oysters, supplied to him in his chamber by the College. He was equally debarred from attending services in the Chapel, but the wine with which the society had covenanted to supply him was punctually consumed at the private offices which he performed in his chamber. A suitable pecuniary compensation was made to him on the ground that his domestic arrangements rendered the services of the College laundress unnecessary.

Bartholomew Aspelon, who lodged in an alehouse in the town, was the constant and affectionate attendant at brother John's sick bed: for, indeed, he seldom got out of it. From a neighbouring tavern he brought to him abundant supplies of the ypocras and malmsey wine which were requisite for the maintenance of the invalid's failing strength. Brother Bartholomew was an individual of a merry countenance and gifted with cheerful song. In the sick room the Fellows would often hear him trolling a drinking catch, to which the invalid joined a quavering note. So constant and familiar was the lay that John Bale, one of the Fellows, remembered it thirty years afterwards, and put it in the mouth of a roystering monk whom he introduced as one of the characters in his play, *King Johan*. The words ran thus:

> Wassayle, wassayle, out of the mylke payle,
> Wassayle, wassayle, as whyte as my nayle,
> Wassayle, wassayle, in snow, frost and hayle,

Wassayle, wassayle, with partriche and rayle,
Wassayle, wassayle, that much doth avayle,
Wassayle, wassayle, that never wyll fayle.

The invasion of the college silences by this unusual concert was marked by the Fellows with growing disapproval: and they were not comforted when they discovered that the new robe which they had contracted to supply to their guest had been pledged to the host of the Sarazin's Head in part payment of an account rendered. But they possessed their souls in patience as they noted that the health of their venerable guest was declining with obvious rapidity. With some insistence they pointed out to the Master the desirability of having a prompt and clear understanding about brother John's testamentary dispositions. Dr. Eccleston was entirely of the Fellows' mind in the matter.

Fireplace in Master's Lodge.

One evening in June, some three months after brother John had begun his residence in the College, it seemed to Dr. Eccleston that the time had come to sound him about his intentions. The patient was very low, and brother Bartholomew was much depressed. With inkhorn and pen the Master went upstairs to the sick man's chamber. Nuncupatory wills were in those days accepted as legal obligations, and the Master was minded that he would not leave brother John until he had obtained, from his dictation, a statement of his intentions as to the disposal of his goods.

Obviously brother John's mind was wandering when the Master entered the room, for he greeted his arrival with a snatch of the old scurvy tune,

> Wassayle, wassayle, that never wyll fayle,

and feebly added "Art there, bully Bartholomew? Bear me thy hand to the bottle, for I am dry."

"Brother John, brother John," said the Master, "bestir thee, and think of thy state. It is time for thee to consider of thy world's gear and how thou wilt bestow it according to thy promise to our poor company, for their tendance of thee." Brother John raised himself in his bed and opened his serviceable eye. Something like a grin puckered up his sloping mouth. "Art thou of that counsel, goodman Doctor?" said he: "then have with thee. I were a knave if I did not thank you for your kindness, and, trust me, ye shall not be the losers for your pains. Take quill and write. I will dictate my will in two fillings of thy pen. Write": and the Master wrote.

"To the Master and Fellows of Jesus College I give and bequeath that chest that lieth beneath my bed and is marked with a great letter A, and all that is in it. To brother Bartholomew Aspelon, late of the Hospital of Saint John, in like manner I bequeath that other chest that is marked B."

"Is that all?" asked the Master. "Gogswouns, it is all I have," said brother John. "Yet stay, good Master. Nothing for nothing is a safe text. Thou shalt write it as a condition, on pain of forfeiting my bequest, that ye shall bury me in the aisle of your church, immediately before the High Altar: that ye shall keep my obit, or anniversary, with *placebo* and *dirige* and mass of requiem; and that once each week a Fellow that is a priest shall pray and sing for the soul of John Baldwin, the benefactor of the College. Is it rehearsed, master doctor?" "It is written," said the Master. "*Ite, missa est,*" said the invalid, "and fetch me a stoup of small ale, good Master."

A few days later John Baldwin made his unimproving, unregretted end. Brother Bartholomew carried off his portion of the legacy. The other chest was deposited on the table in the Founder's Chamber and opened by the Master before the assembled Fellows.

It contained half a dozen bricks, a fair quantity of straw and shavings, and nothing else—nothing except a small scrap of torn and dirty paper at the bottom of the box. With one voice the Master and Fellows decreed that their unworthy guest should be buried in the least respectable portion of the churchyard. Which thing was done, as I have already mentioned.

Of course the dirty paper under the straw was scrutinized by the Master and Fellows. But it was of no importance. It looked like a deed or a will, in which the deceased, in return for nursing in sickness, proposed to give some unspecified property to his disreputable friend, Aspelon, and apparently stipulated that he should be buried in the choir of the Hospital chapel. But it was not witnessed: it had obviously been torn up, and all that was left of it was the part on the scribe's right hand. It ran thus:

> ego Johannes Baldewyn nuper frat
> rigiam do lego et confirmo domino
> u pro mea in egritudine relevaci
> domino Bartolomeo Aspelon confrat
> ne quod habeat uter prior invener
> am in tumulo sepultus subter quen
> parte chori in sacello Hospitalis
> theshede

The last word, if rightly read, was unintelligible.

But the College had by no means done with brother John. On the evening after his burial, as the Master and Fellows were leaving the Chapel, their steps were suddenly arrested as they heard the familiar Wassail stave raised in a thin and tuneless voice. It came from the open window of the deceased brother, and unquestionably the voice was not Aspelon's. In consternation they listened till it died ineffectually away in an attempted chorus strain.

After brief deliberation they resolved to visit the "loft" in a body—Master, Fellows, "disciples" and servants—and see what this thing might mean. They found the place as blank and silent as it remained when the deceased had been taken out to his burial. But before they reached the stair-foot in their descent the thin piping strain fell on their ears again, and this time none were bold enough to go back. After that, at all times of night and day, the interminable ditty was fitfully renewed, and panic held the College. At night the "disciples" huddled in one room, and the Fellows lay two in a bed.

Unfortunately for Dr. Eccleston, he was condemned to the solitude of the lodge, deserted even by his *famulus*, the sizar who attended him. He sat up all night and studied works of divinity, in the hope that theology, if it did not put the songster to rout, would at least distract his own thoughts from the devilish roundelay in the garret above his head. On the second night he began to congratulate himself on the success of his experiment, for the singer relapsed into silence. In his exhaustion he might even have slept, but that the door of his study had a gusty habit of flying open unexpectedly and closing with a bang. He had actually begun to drowse over his folio when a sharp pressure on his right shoulder aroused him. Hastily turning his head he saw the papery countenance of the dead brother gazing on him with all the affection that one eye could testify, the chin planted on the Master's shoulder, and the mouth slewed into a simulation of innocent mirth. Dr. Eccleston read no more divinity that night.

Early next morning a College meeting was summoned by the Master. It was resolved by the unanimous voice of the society that brother John's remains should be exhumed and re-interred in the middle of the chancel aisle, in accordance with the stipulation of the deceased: and there was no delay in carrying the resolution into effect. The Master also insisted that the whole society should help in the purgation of his lodge and the loft above it, in accordance with the ritual of the Church in that case applying and this too was incontinently done, as I have already described. The consideration of the performance of the rest of the contract entered into by the Master with the late brother was deferred until it should be ascertained how far the deceased was satisfied with the measures already adopted.

Whether John Baldwin acquiesced in this somewhat lame execution of his wishes, or whether his perturbed spirit was laid to rest by the rites of exorcism it is impossible to say. It is quite certain that he troubled the College no more.

But in the afternoon following his re-interment an incident happened which possibly had some connection with the placation of his shade. Bartholomew Aspelon had not attended brother John's funeral in the churchyard. In truth, he was filled with a moral resentment at his late friend's lack of feeling and good taste which was only equalled by that of the society of Jesus: and the motive was the same. On opening the treasure chest bequeathed to him he had found it filled with bricks and straw, just like the other. If the Fellows were indignant Bartholomew was more so: for, from private sources of information which he possessed as a member of the dissolved Hospital, he was assured that brother John had prospered in its service to the extent of £200, at the least, and he was profoundly convinced that the whole sum had gone into the treasury of Jesus College. Under the straw he had found a morsel of paper, which was, indeed, too fragmentary to give any connected clue to its drift, but which, nevertheless, rather plainly indicated on the part of the deceased an intention of bequeathing to the College a certain treasure, the whereabouts of which, owing to the imperfection of the document, were not stated. He was confirmed in his interpretation of the manuscript by the honourable interment given to brother John's remains in the Chapel.

Filled with resentment at the ingratitude of the patient whom he had so tenderly nursed and at the duplicity of the "dons" who had robbed him of the reward of his devoted service, Bartholomew sought the Master's lodge. He used no language of studied courtesy in representing to Dr. Eccleston the nature of his grievance and the Master, whose temper was severely tried by want of sleep and the disagreeable nature of the interment ceremony in which he had just unwillingly participated, replied with equal vehemence.

"Ye are robbers all," cried Bartholomew: "you cheated him in his weakness into signing his property away from the friend who smoothed his pillow in his dying hours."

"Thou naughty knave," retorted the Master, "talk not to me of bricks and straw. It was gold that was contained in thy box, and the devil knows by what scurvy arts thou didst cozen us of our promised reward. His own paper convicts thee of the fraudulent attempt to get him to will his goods to thee. See what he left in the bottom of our box." And the Master threw the scrap above-transcribed upon the table. "Take it and never let me see thy rogue's face again."

Brother Bartholomew leaped in his skin as he grabbed the document. He made no ceremony of leave-taking, but bolted down the stairs. When he got into the cloister outside he took from his pouch a dingy scrap of paper, which was the fellow of that which the Master had thrown to him. What he read on it was this:

> Sciant omnes presentes et futuri quod
> er Hospitalis Divi Johannis apud Canteb
> doctori Eccleston et sociis Collegii Jes
> one equaliter inter so dividendum aut
> ri meo in antedicto Hospitali ea racio
> it totum thesaurum meum ita ut extat cl
> dam lapidem iacentem in septentrionali
> eiusdem cuius istud signum extat a dea

Then brother Bartholomew put the two pieces together, and it was thus that he translated the continuous lines:

Know all men present and to come that |
   I, John Baldwin, late a broth
er of the Hospital of Saint John at Cam |
   ridge, give, grant and bequeath to master
doctor Eccleston and the fellows of the College of Jes |
   u for my relief during sick
ness, equally to be divided among them, or |
   to master Bartholomew Aspelon, a brother
of mine in the aforesaid Hospital, provid |
   ed that he shall have it who is first fin
der, all my treasure as it now lies pri |
   vily buried in a tomb under a cer
tain stone lying on the northern |
   side of the choir in the chapel of the Hospital
aforesaid, of which this is the sign, a dea |
   th's head.

Of what further pertains to brother John Baldwin and his bequest I have no more to say than that his name is not included in the Form for the Commemoration of Benefactors of Jesus College. Also that for twenty years after the events here recorded a cheerful individual, in a lay habit, might be seen, seated of custom on the ale-bench at the Sarazin's Head. He drank of the best, paid in cash and never lacked for money. He could tell a good tale and he sang a good song. His Wassail song was always in request at the Sarazin's Head.

The Burden of Dead Books

By its air of reverend quiet, its redolence of dusty death, in the marshalled lines of its sleeping occupants, and in the labels that briefly name the dead author and his work, an ancient repository of books, such as a college library, suggests the, perhaps, hackneyed similitude of a great cemetery. Here and there, among the vast majority of the undistinguished dead, we detect names that are still familiar. Here and there are the monuments of men who have at least been the ancestors of a surviving family of scholars and scientists. Some names will awake memories, not for the individual achievement of their bearers, but for the cause in which they worked. Royalist and Republican, Anglican, Romanist and Puritan here have laid down the arms which they bore against each other, and together sleep the sleep from which there is no rising. Though the issues for which these men fought are dead things now, their spirit is with us and their works follow them. But with the majority it is not so. Outnumbering all others are the hand-labourers of whose names the catalogue has no record. Their daywork, paid or unpaid, was commanded by more ambitious masters, who absorbed whatever temporary measure of credit attended the collaboration. Over the ashes of these unnamed toilers we waste no regrets: they sleep well. It is the fallen ambitions, the wasted energies, the mistaken aims of the master-craftsmen in letters that are food for ironical contemplation.

I do not know that in such a cemetery of small and great, the servant and his master, a more dismal corner exists than that which is reserved for the stillborn. They are a great host, and they are mostly of the family of Theology. Of one such product of fruitless travail I have to speak. It has rested undisturbed in the library of Jesus College for over 300 years, and in all that time, perhaps, no human being, except the official who transcribed its title in the catalogue, has ever had occasion to recall its existence. Its author was one Matthew Makepeace, S.T.P., a Fellow of the College in the last quarter of the sixteenth century. Its elaborate title is: "Speculum Archimagiae, sive Straguli Babyloniaci Direptio, necnon Offuciarum et Praestigiarum Romano-papisticarum Apocalypsis liberrima": from which I conclude that the Pope received some hard knocks in it, and that the Babylonian lady of the Book of Revelation was left in pitiful disarray by the learned doctor's assault. The title-page informs us that the book was printed at London by Melchisedeck Bradwell, for John Bill, in the year 1604: furthermore, that it had been "perused and approved by publike authoritie." That it was ever perused I do not believe. Only in the most cursory way I have perused it myself, and I do not think that any other man has done as much. To our patient ancestors a book was a book, let it be ever so dull. They glossed it, annotated it, added their approving or inimical comments. But nobody has been at the pains to add his marginal notes to the text of Matthew Makepeace. Its cover is unworn, its pages as clean as on the day when it first saw light. This only: on a loose scrap of paper, contained between its pages, I have discovered a name written in Greek characters and a short Greek quotation.

Let me get done with this dull book as fast as I can. It is, of course, written in Latin, and its style does not suggest that the author had a facile Latinity. The extensive list of authors cited indicates that he had read widely, but digested little of what he read, in Patristic and Rabbinical literature. The purpose of the book is to discredit the claim of the Roman Church to the possession of supernatural gifts. The subjects dealt with are naturally the Roman sacraments and hagiology. The learned author arrives at the conclusion, on grounds which I have not had the patience to investigate, that the human exercise of miraculous powers ceased at the precise date, A.D. 430.

Of the writer, Doctor Makepeace, I can find little more information than is supplied in the History of Jesus College, written by John Sherman in the reign of Charles II. This work, composed in the fulsome Latin which was esteemed elegant in the seventeenth century, gives brief biographical notes of each of the Fellows from the date of the foundation of the College. There are various manuscript versions of the History, some ampler than others, and if you wish to read the original Latin, of which I subjoin a translation, you must search out the single copy which contains the full note of his life and work. It may be rendered:

> "Matthew Makepeace, S.T.P., of the county of Northumberland, succeeded to a fellowship in 1565: a most learned investigator of theological matters (*rei theologicae indagator*), especially of the writings of the Fathers: a chastiser of the Pope (*Papomastix*): he illuminated by his knowledge the College and the University, most fearlessly attacking the unclean practices of the Babylonian harlot. He had one much-loved pupil, Marmaduke Dacre, first-born son of the lord baron Dacre, of the county of Cumberland. The same having disappeared from the College in a fashion as yet unknown (*modo adhuc inscibili*) the old man, seized with a phrenetic malady, gradually declined (*contabuit*), often asserting that he was that same pupil whom he had lost. Dying at the age of sixty years, he was buried in the chapel, September 8th, 1604."

To the information given by Sherman I can only add the evidence of a blue flagstone—unhappily removed in the course of chapel restoration, in 1863—which lay in the floor of the south transept. Its simple inscription was: "*Matthaeus Makepeace, S.T.P., decessit,* 1604."

With the evidence as to the date of the death of Dr. Makepeace, furnished by Sherman and the old gravestone, it is difficult to reconcile a curious entry in the register of burials in All Saints' Parish Churchyard. The entry is dated April 13, 1654, and it runs:—

> "Matthew Makepeace, an oldman y^t lodged with ye widow Pearson in Jesus Lane, of ye age of about three score years and ten. He was burried in Poorman's Corner, by ye parish."

The date, the age of the deceased, the place of burial, the fact that this Makepeace was evidently a pauper and a stranger to Cambridge, all would seem to make it certain that he could not be the same man who is mentioned by Sherman. Nevertheless, I have my doubts, and the story which I have to unfold will explain the reason.

The story begins on August 16th, 1604, the very day on which the learned *Speculum* made its first appearance, bound and complete, on the table of Matthew Makepeace. The doctor's chamber was on an upper floor of the staircase at the western end of the chapel nave, and it overlooked what was then called Fair Yard, a plot of ground since annexed to the Master's garden. August 16th happened to be the last of the three days of Garlick Fair, the ancient fair which, since the days of King Stephen, had been associated with the Church of Saint Radegund, and took place under the chapel walls.

Matthew Makepeace was alone. It was Long Vacation, and his sole pupil, Marmaduke Dacre, who shared his chamber, had been allowed a day's outing. Heavy books of divinity lined the walls of the chamber, which had little of comfort about it and no elegance. The doctor's high bed, with curtains of faded say, the pupil's truckle-bed, a hanging cupboard for clothes, a rough deal stand on which was set an ewer and basin of coarse earthenware, a chair, two stools and a large oaken table in the middle of the room—these were the doctor's principal household effects. There was but one window, of bottle-green glass, and its lattice was open to admit the air and sunlight of the August afternoon.

A Corner of the Library.

On the table lay the doctor's new book, brave in its stamped leather and gilded label but it was unopened. It was the outcome of five and twenty years of incessant study, and the single offspring of Matthew's lucubration. And now that it was brought to birth he was in a mood to stifle it. It had been begun in the white heat of the controversies with Rome and Spain, and it lingered in parturition until the fire had burnt low, and the readers who should have applauded it were in their graves. Its author was not very sure that its contentions were true, and he was very sure that they were addressed to deaf ears. Had he gone out into the world he might have learnt what the world was interested in—what battles remained to fight, what causes were already finished. But Matthew's world consisted of books, and his books were out of date. Of recent political developments, of the growth of scientific knowledge, of the blossoming of a native literature he had no more knowledge than a child. The work which had been begun with enthusiasm had been completed in mechanical drudgery, and too late he was conscious of the fact.

How well he recollected the enthusiasms of 1579! How ardent his friends were that his immense learning should signalise itself in the great national strife with the powers of darkness! If he could only live his life again with the old enthusiasm and the added knowledge of a life that should combine learning and action! The boy, Dacre, blessed with genius, wealth, high birth and noble aspirations—how wide the horizon that opened before him! For Matthew Makepeace it rested only to be forgotten before he died.

It was a strange bird of passage that had dropped the seed from which Matthew's book grew. Alessandro Galiani was a medical doctor of Padua University when he came to Cambridge, and for a few months resided in Jesus College. Why he came nobody precisely knew; but he claimed to be a Protestant refugee, and he was certainly profoundly learned in many languages, as well as in medicine. He brought letters of introduction from the Chancellor, Lord Burleigh, and it was surmised that he was an agent of the Government, engaged to report on the University. But his talk and conduct were so equivocal that the suspicion presently arose that his

Protestantism was simulated, and that he was a papal spy. The sentiments to which he gave expression were certainly Macchiavellian in the highest degree—intolerable to English ears. Wherefore his sojourn at Cambridge ended abruptly after a few months, and he passed away into the same mysterious spaces from which he had come. He was a man of extraordinary powers of observation and suggestion, and from a chance hint that he once let fall Makepeace got the idea of writing his book. It was Galiani who directed his attention to the Jewish and Arabic authors whom he consulted. But how little of the force and insight of the Italian entered into the completed book, Makepeace knew only too well.

So the book lay on the table and Matthew had no heart to open it. Through the window came sounds of merriment from the Fair Yard without. Regularly as August came round Makepeace had heard those sounds for forty years past, but until to-day he had regarded them only as a troublesome distraction, and closed his casement against them. To-day a profound lassitude made him draw his stool from the table, where lay the slighted volume, to the open window. His attention was especially drawn by a strident voice which came from near his chamber. Looking out on the Fair Yard he saw a platform of a few planks, mounted on casks, immediately beneath his window. On it a vagabond charlatan was loudly advertising to a group of gaping rustics the merits of a wonderful heal-all.

"Come buy, my masters, come buy," he cried. "Buy the infallible salve of the famous doctor Pinchbeck, the ointment that heals the ague, the rheum, the palsy, the serpigo. Let him that goes on one leg but buy, and with thrice laying on he shall go on two. Let him that goes with crutches buy, and he shall dance home in a coranto. One groat only for the learned doctor's ointment that shall quit you of the cramp, the gout, the quotidian and the tertian. An it rid you not in two days come again and Pinchbeck shall restore you fourfold."

From time to time an ague-ridden swain mounted the platform, haggled with the quack, reluctantly parted with his groat and departed, dubious of his purchase. On the whole, Dr. Pinchbeck seemed to be doing a fair trade, when, late in the afternoon, an old man, bent double with rheumatism, raised a loud expostulation. He affirmed that he had purchased a box of the ointment on the first day of the fair, and had applied it thrice without the promised result.

He demanded the fourfold restitution of his money, and the mountebank stoutly resisted the claim. Angry cries arose from the bystanders, and it might have gone ill with the empiric, had not a diversion been effected by one of the crowd. This was a tall middle-aged man of somewhat dark complexion and foreign appearance, whose dress distinguished him as a gentleman and possibly a practiser of medicine. He stepped on the platform, spoke a few words to the ointment-vendor, and then, beckoning the old man to him, made him sit on a stool. He gazed fixedly for a few moments in the patient's eyes, made some mysterious motions of the hands before his face, whispered in his ear, and then, with a few more passes of his hands, bade him stand. The old fellow stood erect without effort; then, at the stranger's bidding, walked a few easy steps, and with a pleased and puzzled look descended to join his friends in the crowd. Loud applause greeted the wonderful cure, and patients crowded to receive the stranger's ministrations. The same operations in each case were attended with the same result. Never had there been seen such a wonder at the fair.

Most of all it wrought wonder in Matthew Makepeace. This unknown individual—was he possessed of those miraculous gifts of healing which Makepeace in 400 quarto pages had proved to be extinct? He would accost him and, if possible, learn from his lips whether what he had seen were the operation of nature or of the magic art. Descending in the majesty of his doctor's robes he mingled in the crowd, and mildly laid his hand on the stranger's arm. "Pardon, learned sir," said he, "the curiosity of a scholar—alas too ignorant of books and all unskilled in the manual acts of healing. I would fain question with you of these same cures that by chance I have witnessed from my chamber." The stranger was engaged in giving parting words of counsel to some of his patients. He turned at the touch of the doctor's hand, surveyed him up and down for a moment, and said, "Anon, Master Makepeace, anon: I will be with you presently."

Dr. Makepeace started to hear his name and threw a sharp look on the speaker. No; he was a complete stranger, and his accent betrayed him as a foreigner. Dr. Makepeace had certainly never seen him in his life before. He began to explain where his chamber was to be found.

"I know it," interrupted the stranger, "I know it. Bear with me for a moment and I will seek you there."

Makepeace was a little ruffled that the speaker, knowing his name, did not give him his academic title. "*Doctor* Makepeace," he said; "ask for *Doctor* Makepeace."

"Surely, surely," replied the stranger carelessly: "yet *Master* Makepeace, methinks, served you then."

More than ever perplexed the doctor sought his room. Only a few minutes had passed when he heard his visitor mounting with no faltering step to his door, and Makepeace opened to him before he knocked. The stranger glanced rapidly round. He seemed to find something familiar in each article of furniture. He ran his eye, with a look of some amused contempt, over the array of worn volumes that lined the walls. "Old books, doctor Makepeace," he said, "old books. I think you have not changed one these thirty years."

"Old books are old friends," said the doctor with a touch of resentment at his tone: "I would not change them."

"Old friends die, doctor," observed the stranger, "they die, and then we have no use for them but to bury them."

"Sir," said the doctor with a quick reminiscence of his wasted studies, "I *have* buried my friends: but I love them still. But," he went on, "it is not of old notions that I have to speak with you. You have shown me this afternoon something newer and," he added sadly, "it may be, something better than all that old books tell. I ask you to impart to me no secret that might hurt you by the telling. Until now I have maintained that nothing exists in this present world that is not of natural course. If it be an honest mystery that you exercise, tell me, the humblest and poorest of scholars, whether

Chapel Doorway in Master's Garden.

it be the miraculous working of God's power in human hands or simply the exercise of human art."

The stranger seated himself, uninvited, in the doctor's chair, and the doctor took a stool. "Everything," said the stranger, "is miracle to him who does not know."

"Great heavens," cried Makepeace, "that is the beginning of my quotation from the learned Theodorus Gazophylacius. I never heard of the great Gazophylacius until Galiani told me of him: nobody that I know had heard of him. A marvellous scholar, truly, was Gazophylacius, but a pagan at heart, albeit a Byzantine Christian—and sadly drowned in superstition. Shall I show you the passage in the original Greek." And he feverishly turned the pages of the *Speculum* to find it.

"You may spare yourself that trouble," said the stranger composedly. "Shall I finish the quotation? Shall I write it for you?" And he unceremoniously tore a corner from one of the immaculate leaves, took a quill and wrote. "There," said he, "there, I have written in Greek what follows in your quotation, and I have added my name that you may remember the writer." The doctor took it and read the delicate Greek characters: "Demetrius Commagenus. All things are possible to him who knows and wills with earnestness."

Makepeace was stupified. "Commagenus," he said: "that is a Greek name, I take it. And yet I would have sworn that the handwriting was Galiani's, and Galiani was an Italian. Besides, Galiani is dead, or he is sixty years old, less or more, by now: and you—I cannot think that you are past forty."

Indifferently the self-styled Commagenus replied: "Galiani or Commagenus—what matters? What I wrote then I write now and always I am your humble servant and the poor scholar who drew wisdom from the lips of the divine Gazophylacius."

"We talk in dreams," said Matthew: "Galiani told me—*you* told me, if you are he—that Gazophylacius died at Rome, ten years after the Turks entered Constantinople: and that was a hundred and fifty years ago."

"Yes," answered Commagenus, "he died—the more is the pity; for he might have lived, had he chosen to use his own wisdom. Instead of that he imparted it on his death-bed to me. What care had he to live, an outcast in strange lands? But this world lost its wisest man; for I am no Gazophylacius. Only I am always learning."

"Why, this is as strange a maze as ever man trod," cried Makepeace. "You tell me that your master died a hundred and forty years ago, and that you, Galiani, were with him at the time."

"Not Galiani, but Commagenus," said the stranger in complacent amusement at the doctor's bewilderment: "that was my name then. I was a youth, twenty years old, when I first came to Constantinople from the country which gave me my name—three years before the siege. There I became the favourite pupil of the great student of natural and medical science, Theodorus Gazophylacius."

"Why, that makes you a hundred and seventy years old," feebly remonstrated Makepeace. "Are you then the Wandering Jew?"

"Doctor, I am shocked," said Commagenus. "Are such fables the stuff of which the *Speculum* is made? I tell you there is nothing in this world that is not natural. That was my master's constant teaching: also that to know and to will makes man master of nature. That much I learnt from him while he taught at Constantinople, and it was in my noviciate that I gathered from him the art to work such simple cures as you saw this afternoon. To prolong mere existence by keeping disease at bay—that he esteemed a vulgar art. To live long and die old, feeble and foolish—what gain is that to the man or his fellow-men? To live always, always to be young, always eager, always to be growing in wisdom and power—that was the secret for which he spent a lifetime's search, and with his dying breath he told me that he had sought it in vain. Death, the last disease, is incurable: there is a stronger will than man's. But he told me of a door of escape. In his last moments he was possessed with a dread that his discovery would perish in the general eclipse of learning which he foresaw as the result of the disappearance of the Byzantine schools, and, with solemn admonition as to its use, he imparted it to me. Death, the mere accident of the flesh, is transferable with the flesh. With will and knowledge, the spirit—all that you call character, intelligence, consciousness, memory—may pass from form to form, unchanged in the transition and always capable of growth and ripening. Alas, that I have not made better use of my master's prescriptions! But it has been my evil fate. Another might do better."

"These are heathen imaginings—snares and delusions of Satan," cried Makepeace. "What talk is this of tampering with the divine in us? Man, are you a Christian?"

"I am what I am," replied Commagenus: "but that this is waking fact and no delusion my history shall show you. After my beloved master's death I set up in medical practice in a certain city of Dalmatia. The fame of my unusual healing powers spread in all the neighbourhood. Unfortunately it reached the ears of the bishop of the diocese. He was a sincere, well-meaning man, kind in all his relations with the laity of his diocese, but a trifle superstitious. He concluded that I was a necromancer and condemned me to be burnt alive. Until the moment when I found myself in a dungeon and on the eve of execution I had never thought to avail myself of the secret communicated to me by my master, and had even questioned its efficacy. The prospect of burning was so extremely repugnant to my feelings that I resolved to make practical trial of it. Shall I show you how it is done? No, you need not shrink from me. I have no wish to pass into simple old Matthew Makepeace. I can do better. Be assured that the will goes not with the act."

Commagenus rose and fastened his gaze on Matthew. As he did so it seemed to the doctor that he grew and grew to a bulk and stature ineffable and dim. But that, he reasoned with himself, was an illusion of the sense, and for the moments when the fascinating glare was fixed on him he retained his consciousness. Slowly, deliberately, that Matthew might follow every movement in succession, he moved his hands and arms in gyrations and waves more intricate than any that Matthew had witnessed when the Greek stood on the mountebank's platform that afternoon. Then he stooped over the table, and with extraordinary distinctness of articulation whispered in his ear one word. What that word was I do not know. Matthew Makepeace remembered it once, and forgot it for all the years that he lived afterwards.

The Greek took up his tale again. "My excellent master had informed me that, whether the subject were waking or asleep, the will and the word had equal effect. My gaoler slept in the condemned cell with me and the occasion seemed to me a particularly happy one for testing the accuracy of my master's conclusions. Though I did not doubt the intensity of my will, in prospect of such an undesirable event as being burnt alive, I confess that I was surprised and more than gratified by the issue of the experiment. I had the satisfaction of leading my gaoler to the stake on the following morning."

"What" cried Makepeace: "do you tell me that the man was burnt? True," he added, as a mitigating consideration suggested itself to his bewildered brain, "he was a papist. But, after all, what were you?"

Commagenus answered with the resignation of a parent satisfying an inquisitive child. "Yes, Matthew Makepeace, when your raiment is past your own use you make a gift of it to some humble dependent. When *he* has worn it threadbare, what happens? It is burnt. You do not burn it: I did not burn him. Besides, this common man in ages to come will be held in reverence—in another name, I admit—as a martyr to medical science. Nevertheless I was little pleased, as you may think, with the integument which my brutal gaoler had left me. In my new and humble sphere of life I had few opportunities of self-improvement, and, taking the first that offered, I installed myself in the person of a Dominican friar. I am disposed to doubt whether I really bettered myself by my change of profession. I found that it required much ingenuity to sustain the part of crass ignorance which was associated with my new character, and the man's companions were deplorable people. An accident, which had nearly proved fatal, relieved me of the disagreeable situation. In the course of my professional duties I was directed to take ship for Spain, where the Dominican order had an especial interest in the Office of the Holy Inquisition. On the voyage we fell in with a vessel belonging to a respectable merchant of

Marseilles. The merchant, who was likewise the ship's captain, was in the habit, when occasion offered, of diversifying the routine of commerce by piratical enterprise. With his crew he boarded and took possession of our vessel, informing us that we were his prisoners. As he had a reputation for probity to sustain at Marseilles, he judged it prudent to throw the whole of the crew and passengers of our vessel into the waves. However, learning that there was a clergyman on board, he seized the opportunity of making confession first and receiving plenary absolution from him of an outstanding balance of prior delinquencies. It was natural to avail myself of the opportunity for transferring myself into his person. It was pleasant to see him flounder in the sea with the rest, and I returned—if that is the right word—to Marseilles, in circumstances sufficiently ample to warrant retirement from a profession the ambiguous character of which offended my moral sense. But my experiences in the three careers of life which my destiny had recently forced upon me gave me an indelible prejudice against the Western Church. On the whole I am a Protestant.

"I need not detain you with my subsequent transmigrations. The merchant was elderly and so oppressively respectable that I was glad to exchange into the superior rank of a French marquisate. Since then, from Trebizond to Tarifa, I have studied men and manners in many capacities. Perhaps the time which was pleasantest to me, as a man of science, was spent in Peru with Pizarro, whom I attended as a captain of cavalry. But a fatal wound, inflicted by a poisoned arrow, compelled my return to Spain in the office of a ship's boatswain. After all my wanderings my conscience reproached me with my culpable neglect of the art in whose elements I had been grounded by the ever-revered Gazophylacius. I resumed the medical studies which I was convinced were best suited to my bent and upbringing, by adopting the features and the status of a freshman in the University of Padua. As the freshman, under no possible circumstances, could have passed his examinations you will see that I conferred on him no small obligation by the assistance which I rendered. In my first year I obtained advancement to the person and professorial chair of Galiani. I am grieved to tell you that I left him seriously unwell at Salerno, ten years ago; and his decease, which followed almost immediately after, proved to me how wise had been my course in transferring myself into the healthy frame of the brother professor who attended him in the earlier phases of his malady. Come, doctor, you have let me chatter on with these tiresome details till I see you are three parts asleep."

"Asleep!" roared Makepeace, who had been filled with rage, disgust and hatred by the shameless recital. "Asleep! Wretch, thief, assassin, defiler of the sanctuary of man! Begone, skirr, fly! Would that I could crush your basilisk head on the floor as I stand! But stay. I will fetch the University bedel. He shall clap you in the lowest hold of the Castle gaol."

"Marry, good words, master doctor," said the imperturbable stranger. "Your bedel, possibly, is a family man; and conscience forbids that, except in the last resort, I should lay a father of a family in a dungeon for crimes that, you are pleased to assert, are of my doing: and, except that I do not propose myself for the office of bedel, it were an easy thing for me to do so. But hearken, my honest friend. I wish you well—no man better. Getting old is a sad affair, sadder even than dying. I think that you are sixty, and I don't think that just now you are quite in your best health. Has the world gone very well with you? In five years, ten years, will it go better? You have written a silly book that nobody will read, and you are ashamed of it. You have wasted your years of manhood in twisting ropes of sand. And the solitude, Matthew! My heart bleed to think what your solitude will be. What friend have you to smooth the downhill course? Who cares for the friend of dead books? Altogether, you have very little use now for Matthew Makepeace. Who is it that should sleep in yonder bed?" he asked, pointing to the truckle used by Marmaduke Dacre. "Is he young? Is he comely? Has he friends to love him and be loved? Is he of a quick spirit and a high hope. Matthew Makepeace, you know the acts and the word. The door lies open to you. Take wisdom, and be young."

"The door lies open to *you*," shouted Makepeace, throwing it open as he spoke. "Pass out of it, and avoid the chamber of a

Christian man: and the foul fiend fly away with you and your abominable suggestions!"

"Doctor Makepeace, I wish you a very good evening," said his visitor.

* * * * * *

The night was far advanced, and Matthew Makepeace had no mind for bed. A dim rush candle, set on a stool in a corner of the apartment, cast flickering shadows on the walls and floor. In an opposite dark corner his pupil slept. But for the dread of awaking him, Makepeace would have paced the room in his perplexity. As it was, he sat bent double on the stool by the window.

One thing was clear enough. If what he had seen and heard was not a fiction or the delusion of his senses, the *Speculum* was a colossal stupidity. Even if the rejuvenations of Commagenus were as much in the course of nature as he affirmed them to be, did they not warrant the Pope's most arrogant pretensions? But it was with himself that he was most concerned. Was it not the fact that, as Commagenus had declared, his life had been most miserably wasted? And the mistake was past repair. If only his youth had known! And his mind went back to a short, happy time, just after he had taken his degree, when he had served as chaplain in his far-away northern country, at the ancestral castle of the Dacres. His pupil then had been the present Lord, Marmaduke's father; and the pupil had had so much to teach his master about hawks and horses and hounds that the master had little leisure to repay it in Greek and Latin. Those were happy days when they had roamed the Cumbrian fells together. And now this Lord Dacre was great in the councils of his sovereign, the wise and respected ruler of a barony that was almost a kingdom in itself. And in his trusting confidence he had committed his son to the care of his old master at Cambridge; and that son in course of years would naturally succeed to his father's station.

Had Commagenus indeed sat in that chamber, only a few hours since, and unfolded to him the secret of perpetual youth? Yes there was the evidence of the written scrap lying on the open page of the Speculum. True, Commagenus had made a detestable use of his wonderful power. But with Makepeace it would be different. He was conscious of his sobriety and virtue, and there were the noble traditions of the house of Dacre to keep him in the right way. He had abilities, if only he had youth and opportunity to use them, and the experience of sixty years was a better guarantee for their proper employment than any that a callow youth could offer. Clearer, louder than the voices of conscience or calculation there came back to him, like the drumming burden of an iterated song, the words "The door is open. Be young." Was it fancy that a door seemed to open in the dark book-press opposite, and that through it he looked out on a sunny haze enveloping blue hills and waters and the towers of Dacre Castle? And cool breaths from heathery heights took up the refrain, and whispered to him "Be young."

Matthew Makepeace crept quietly to the dark corner where his pupil lay. His will was intense as he had never known it before. He took care that his shadow should not fall on the sleeper's face and arouse him. He made the wonderful passes—with what extraordinary clearness they were printed on his recollection! He stooped and whispered in his pupil's ear the mysterious word.

If Matthew had expected a flash of lightning, the apparition of the Evil One, the jubilations of triumphant fiends on the success of his experiment, he was agreeably disappointed Nothing of the kind happened. Only in the dim light of the candle he saw a grey shadow of weary age steal over his pupil's face, and he felt the vigour and vitality of youth invade his own limbs as with the intoxication of wine. Then the wick suddenly flickered in the candle-socket and went out. He heard Marmaduke turn over in his bed with an uneasy sigh.

Then Makepeace woke to reason and a horrible dread. He dared not relight the candle for fear of rousing the sleeper. In the dark, before he was discovered, he must repeat the process which should restore each to his own person. In the dark, as nearly as he could, he went through the magical passes, and with extraordinary vehemence he willed himself back into Matthew Makepeace. But the word! Great heavens! It had passed from him as suddenly and completely as the light of the extinguished candle. In vain he racked his memory of every language, living or dead. It had no meaning in any language, living or dead: of that he felt sure, and he was sure of nothing else. For an hour, by his pupil's bedside, he tore his hair in desperate efforts to recall it. For an hour he alternately cursed Commagenus and prayed that he might return before day to give him the forgotten word. Then the grey morning light began to creep through the casement, and the birds woke and sang.

There could be no shadow of doubt about it. There lay Matthew Makepeace before him, and the old man was drowsily stirring his limbs as the light broadened into day. And young Dacre, in a doctor's gown, was looking down upon him, tortured with horrible thoughts. One thing was certain. He could never pass himself off as Marmaduke. Conscience, gratitude, affection forbade it. Besides, the thing was impossible. He, the torpid pedant, could never play the part of the young and chivalrous heir of the Dacres and there would be Marmaduke to convict the imposture. Before his pupil woke, before the discovery was made, he must disappear from Cambridge. Quietly and in haste he took down his pupil's clothes from the closet where they hung, and exchanged for them his doctor's robes. Then he descended his stairs and stepped out into the cool shadows of the August morning. The porter was just opening the gate. He nodded familiarly to young Dacre as he passed. That was the last which any soul in Jesus College saw of Matthew Makepeace.

Unless, indeed, it were that same Matthew Makepeace who, with the homing instinct of a dying animal, crept back to Cambridge in poverty and wretchedness, and died in widow Pearson's house in 1654. In any case the flagstone in the chapel transept told a lie: it was Marmaduke Dacre that lay beneath it.

One thing further I have to mention. When I first took down the *Speculum* from its shelf in the college library I found it in the same virgin condition in which it had lain on the table of Matthew Makepeace on that fatal afternoon in August, 1604. No living soul had disturbed its repose for over 300 years. It was evidently the same copy: perhaps no other was ever issued. As I turned its pages a scrap of paper fluttered to the floor. It had been torn from the bottom corner of pages 273-4. On it was written in minute Greek letters an inscription which I translate:

"Demetrius Commagenus. All things are possible to him who knows and wills with earnestness."

Thankfull Thomas

A passage in the lately edited *Diary of George Evans*, 1649-1658, has called my attention to a singular and, I believe, unrecorded episode in the history of Jesus College.

With Mr. Evans himself the story is not concerned. It is sufficient to say that he was appointed to a fellowship at Jesus in 1650 by the Committee for Reforming the Universities, in place of an expelled Presbyterian. He was, as his name suggests, a Welshman, of the county of Radnor, and, of course, an Independent. He vacated his fellowship, on his marriage, in 1654, and retired to the living of Marston Monceux, co. Salop. He held the incumbency until his death, in 1672, having conformed at the Restoration.

The portion of his diary which has awaked my interest relates to the date June 11, 1652. For its explanation it is necessary to state that ten years previously, just before the outbreak of the Civil War, the College had taken a quantity of its plate from the Treasury and delivered it to a certain Mr. John Poley, by him to be conveyed to His Majesty, who was then at Nottingham. As the whole society was under menace of expulsion before the end of 1642, they took the precaution, before quitting the College, of concealing the rest of the plate, as well as the chapel organ. This organ had been introduced in 1634 by the Master, Richard Sterne, who was Archbishop Laud's chaplain, and had actively promoted his plans for the re-organisation of church ritual in the University. It was a small chamber instrument, easily transportable. When the new society, consisting of Presbyterians introduced by the Earl of Manchester, entered the College in January, 1643, they noted in the Treasury Book that they could only discover three pieces of plate. Entries in the Bursar's Book in the year 1652 record that the rest of the plate was discovered in that year, and at a rather later date the organ was brought to light.

Some further notes respecting the Chapel in Commonwealth days will serve to explain certain points in the history which I have been able to unravel. The older of the two existing bells in the tower was cast by Christopher Gray in 1659. It took the place of another which was of pre-Reformation date and had probably served the Nunnery of Saint Radegund. This was a heavy tenor bell, and had apparently belonged to a set of four, named after the evangelists. It bore the emblem of Saint Mark, a lion, and the inscription in ancient lettering—

> Celorum Marce resonet tuus ympnus in Arce.

This bell, for many years previous to 1652, had been disused owing to the weakness of its frame and of the supporting floor.

The passage, above referred to, in George Evans' diary runs as follows:

> "June 11 [1652]. Present ye Master, Mr. Woodcocke and Mr. Machin, fellows, with Mr. Thomas Buck, Thankfull Thomas and Robert Hitchcock digging, we digged up ye treasury plate hidd in ye Masters orchard. In all were seventeen peeces (then follows a list). Searched till prayers. But Quaerendm whether there be not yit other peeces and ye treasure hidd by ye former societie. Thomas saith Mr. Germyn cld avouch for more."

On reading this extract, the name—for such it seemed to be—Thankfull Thomas, at once arrested my attention. It reminded me of a partially obliterated inscription on a flat gravestone which lies at the crossing of the transepts, close to the south-west pier of the tower—that one which is distinguished from the other piers by a dog-tooth moulding. The letters are so worn by treading that they can only be distinguished in certain lights, and indeed have altogether disappeared on the side of the stone which is furthest from the pier-base. What remains is to be read:—

nkfull
mas

followed by a date of which the figures 652 are legible.

I have searched the Register of the College for such a name, but, though it is complete for the years preceding 1652, I have been unable to find it. But in the College Order Book I have found, among other appointments of the year 1650, an entry, "Thomas constitutus est Custos Templi." From which it would seem that Thomas was the surname of the Independent official corresponding to a verger or chapel-clerk. It is singular that he should have been buried, among Masters and Fellows, in such a conspicuous place in the Chapel.

The discovery of the plate in the Master's orchard—brought about through the agency of Mr. Thomas Buck, of Catharine Hall, who was one of the Esquire Bedells—was matter for disappointment as much as congratulation to the Master and Fellows. They had a convinced belief that a much larger quantity of treasure remained concealed in some quarter of the College, and, as the passage in the diary shows, Thankfull Thomas suggested that Mr. Germyn probably knew something of the matter. Of him it is necessary to say a few words.

Gervase Germyn, of the county of Huntingdon, was admitted to the College in 1621, and in 1652 must have been a man of middle age. He was a Master of Arts, unmarried, and resided in Cambridge. He was not one of the expelled Fellows. He had acted as organist and choir-master in the mastership of Richard Sterne, and was passionately devoted to church music. After the removal of the organ and the installation of the new Master and Fellows, in 1643, his connection with the College ceased. He was miserably poor and supported himself by teaching music. His small, spare figure was ordinarily dressed in a thread-bare garb of semi-clerical appearance, and he had a quaintness of manner and speech which induced the belief that he was not of ordinary sanity.

Thankfull Thomas particularly disliked him. Gervase had a tone of superiority in addressing him which was the more galling because what he said was only remotely intelligible to the sexton and he had a disagreeable habit of meddling with what he considered to be the duties and prerogatives of his office. Germyn must have possessed a key to the Chapel, for he was constantly presenting himself there at unexpected times, often late in the evening. He had a distracting habit of roaming about the building, and, as Thomas thought, spying on his actions from unseen quarters. Thomas had seen him looking down on him from the Nuns' gallery in the north transept, or high up in the tower arcade.

Thomas took note of these circumstances and kept his knowledge to himself. His cupidity was aroused by the thought of the hidden treasure, and he was perfectly convinced that the clue to its discovery lay with Germyn. As it was useless to question him directly he resorted to a system of counter-espial.

His attention was particularly drawn to the Chapel tower, where he had more than once detected Germyn's presence. The arcaded storey beneath the belfry is reached by a dark, winding stair in the wall at the north-east angle of the north transept. The staircase emerges, at a considerable height, on a Norman gallery, which, at the time of which I am speaking, was not protected on the transept side by a railing. Thomas was a timid man, and he made this alarming passage clutching each pillar as he passed it. Then another stair in the tower pier led up to the arcaded gallery, and there the inner communication stopped. A door in the north arcade opened on the roof of the transept, from which a dizzy ladder ascended to the belfry window. The ladder gave Thomas pause. It was old, weather-worn and crazy, and, unless by the light figure of Germyn, had perhaps never been scaled for a generation. The silent belfry above, encompassed by wheeling jackdaws, was a terror to his weak nerves. Even from the floor below he could see the gaping rottenness of its rafters so he let it alone.

Secure on the Chapel floor he began his researches. In his vacant moments he roamed about chancel, transepts and nave, beating the walls and trampling the flags, if perchance he might light on some recess wherein the treasure was contained. At first his curiosity was excited by certain crosses graved on the nave floor. He did not know that they marked the processional path of the Saint Radegund nuns. But he could detect no sound of hollowness beneath them. Finally, he fastened his mind on a large, unmarked stone, next the south-west pier of the tower. Here; and in no other part of the Chapel, there was distinct evidence that a vault of some kind existed. Above it the disused bell-rope was attached to the pier.

Often, when the Chapel was closed after service hours, he scrutinised this stone. It had no mark of recent disturbance, but in ten years it was likely that any such indication had been obliterated. One summer evening in 1652 he was so engaged, and kneeling on the stone, when he was startled by the sudden falling of a shadow. He sprang to his feet and beheld Gervase Germyn.

"Good evening, friend," said Germyn. "You work late. I was visiting some old friends that lie under the stones here, having a word with him or him that I have known, a remembered jest with one, a snatch of old song with another—who knows what? And here are you at the like business. And who, pray, is your friend?"

"Master Germyn," replied Thomas stiffly, "an idle man may talk to dead men, if he will: a sexton has other business with them. How often am I to bid you not to meddle in my affairs?"

"You are very right," said Germyn, "and now I perceive this is no man's grave—yet. Perhaps the sexton is looking to make it one. And which, pray, of my friends, the new Fellows, has gone to his audit? Or is it to be mine, perhaps, or thine: and I think it be thine indeed, for I find thee lying on it. But you don't know the Prince of Denmark: else I should ask you the clown's riddle, 'What is he that builds stronger than either the mason, the shipwright, or the carpenter?' It is a pretty riddle to ask within walls that are five hundred years old."

Norman Gallery, North Transept.

"I make no graves," answered Thomas, "and I have no time or patience for your riddles. I only ask you to begone."

"Is the trade then so slack, friend Thomas, and is there none to give the sexton employment?—none of all that dig for death as for hid treasure, and some, perhaps, who dig for treasure and find death."

Thomas was startled at the hint that his purpose was detected. He looked dubiously on the speaker, and the thought dawned on him that perhaps Germyn was offering himself as a confederate.

"Treasure," he said slowly; "yes, if you talk of treasure there is more sense in you than I thought. I don't know but what we might find it together; and a poor man, such as you, might have his fair share, and none be the wiser."

"You are wholly mistaken," said Germyn, "if you think that I know anything of the treasure that you are looking for and, if I knew, God forbid that I should rob the dead of their trust. No, let them keep it until the day of restitution, when their friends claim it of them. You are a bold man, Thomas, to think of the dead as if they had no sense of what happens to-day. For my part, though we talk as old friends, I have a dreadful awe of them: they can do so much, and I can't hurt them, if I would. It is a marvel to me that you can walk and work at such an hour in a place that is so full of voices and presences. A holy man you should be! Do you know how Goodman Deane, the last man who held your office, died?"

"They tell me he died distracted. But I don't trouble myself with fancies."

"It was in August, two years since. What had he seen? What had he heard? They say that in his wanderings he often repeated 'I should have rung, I should have rung.' And I think I see his meaning. It is an old belief—God knows what of truth there is in it—that at the ringing of the church bell the congregations of the dead break up and give place to the living. Poor Deane! Mark could not speak for him: he has been dumb these twenty years, though one day, please God, he will speak again for his friends—of whom you are not one. And there is another old fancy that belongs to this church, and perhaps had something to do with Deane's matter. It used to be told among the old society, that are scattered or dead now, that the festival of the Name of Jesus was a great day with the old dead folk. Each year at midnight on that day, which is the seventh of August, they assemble—men or women, I know not which—herein the church to observe the hour of Lauds. It was said that you could hear them trooping down from their chambers outside by a stair that does not exist, and they came through the church wall by a door that is unseen. Then, each in order, they rank themselves on the crosses that mark this pavement, and go round the church in darkness, for they need no lights. Their singing has been often heard, but I do not know that living eye has seen their procession, unless it were Deane's, and, it seems, he did not live long after."

"It is a curious fancy, truly," said Thomas, "if one could credit it. But I don't know why you tell it me, as I never visit the church after nightfall. And little as I believe your tale, I believe you less when you tell me that you know nothing of this treasure. But I spoke of it at a venture, and it is none of my business. So I leave you to your ghosts."

* * * * * *

Thankfull Thomas was not courageous, but his fears were not of a sentimental order. He was more than ever convinced that Germyn knew the secret of the hidden treasure, and that his story was a device to prevent him from continuing his search for it; and he had made up his mind that it lay under the stone where Germyn had interrupted him. At night he would be secure from his interference, and would have time to lift the stone and replace it in such a manner as to leave no trace of its disturbance. And as the date which Germyn had mentioned had passed out of his mind, it so happened that August 7 was the night which he chose for his enterprise.

It was past eleven when he entered the church with lantern and tools. The stone was heavy, and it took a considerable time to dislodge and lift it. Beneath it he saw a vault, some five feet deep. He lowered his lamp into it. Great was his disappointment to find it blankly empty. He had so fastened his expectations on this particular spot that hardly yet could he think himself mistaken. He let himself down into the vault that he might explore for some recess in its walls or floor.

He was still groping in semi-gloom when, above his head, he caught the sound of quiet treading, and then a waft of strange music. He was too unskilled to tell what the instrument might be, but the sound of it was soft and pleasant. It rose, and died away, and rose again in fitful strains. Then it went on in a continuous melody and was taken up by a voice peculiarly sweet and clear—so clear that the words were plainly distinguishable. "When the Lord turned again the captivity of Sion then were we like unto them that dream."

Thomas listened in amazement till the psalm ended and silence returned. Then he heard the shuffling of descending steps, and with a sudden horror he remembered the story of the dead men's staircase and the phantom procession. He heard a door softly open in the dark transept, and he sprang wildly to the bell-rope above his head. One frightful clang: Mark spoke again after twenty years of

South West Pier
of Tower.

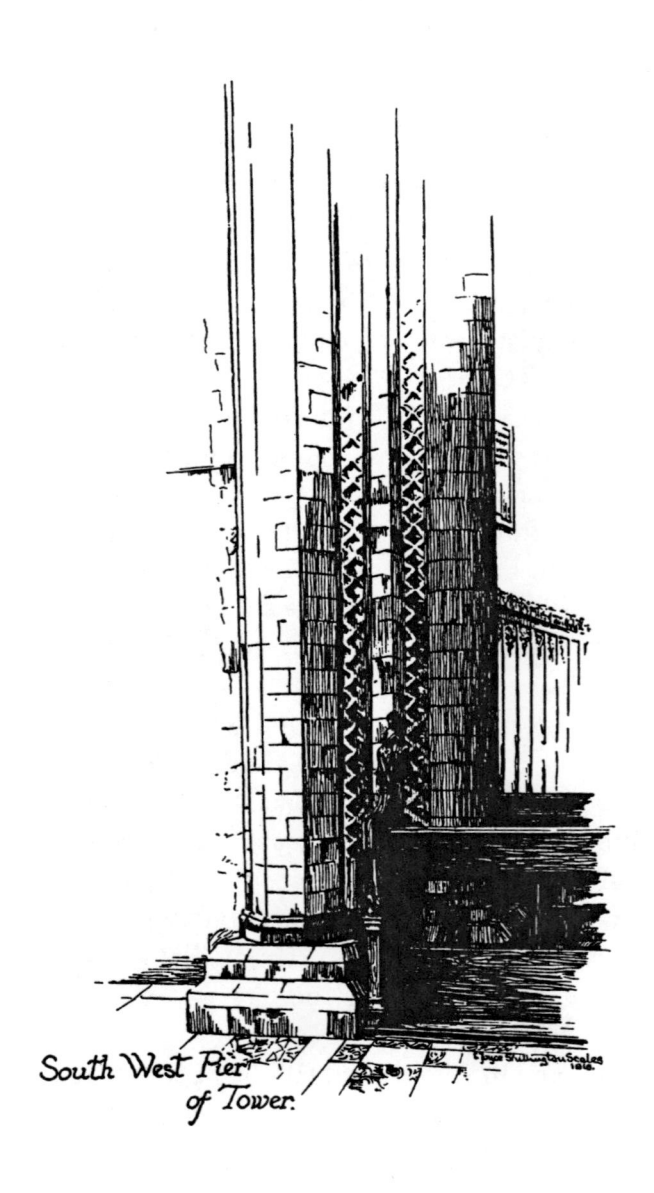

silence: a rumble and a roar: the heavy bell splintered itself on the floor beneath, and Thankfull Thomas, in a pool of blood, lay in the grave of his own making.

* * * * * *

In a corner of the belfry, where the floor was not broken by the falling bell, they discovered the organ, which had been hidden there since 1642.

The Palladium

On an unspecified morning in the year 1026, in the reign of Cnut, king, of happy memory, Aethelstan, abbat of Ramsey, delivered to the monks of his Benedictine household, in chapter assembled, an address which had notable consequences.

The reverend father took as the text of his discourse the verse, *in libro Regum Tertio*, which in our Authorised Version is expressed—Know ye not that Ramoth in Gilead is ours, and we be still, and take it not out of the hand of the King of Syria?

With the ghostly lessons to be drawn from this passage we need not concern ourselves: indeed they were but lightly touched upon by the abbat. He turned almost directly to practical matters.

He dwelt feelingly on the palpable evidences of the poverty of their household—the bell-tower of their church, which had fallen in sudden ruin, and which the means of their household did not permit them to rebuild: the indecent sordidness of their chapter-house, within whose mud-built walls they were then assembled the meagreness of the monastic diet, of which his brethren were the last to complain, but which reflected unfavourably on the coldness of Christian charity in the laity of the neighbourhood. And incidentally he contrasted these conditions with the splendour of the new temple, adorned with goodly stones and gifts, which their beloved friends at Ely had erected since the Danish wars had ended: the ephods of purple and scarlet affected by the ministers in Saint Etheldreda's church and the proverbial magnificence of Ely feasts.

He asked himself the cause of this contrast, and with humility he confessed that it lay in the remissness of himself and his venerable predecessors in the abbatial seat of Ramsey. He commended to the attention of his hearers a text, *in fine libri Josue*, in which it was recorded that the children of Israel had brought up the bones of Joseph with them from Egypt, and that the said bones had become the inheritance of the children of Joseph and he enlarged on the advantages, pecuniary as well as spiritual, which undoubtedly rewarded those children.

What had Ramsey done to emulate an example so worthy? Nothing, or next to nothing. At a cost relatively small they had, indeed, procured from an ignorant rustic, who had dug them up at the town of Slepe, some bones which competent authority declared to be those of the Persian bishop, Saint Yvo. But, whether or not the cause lay in some lack of orthodoxy in this oriental prelate, it must be confessed that his remains had not been so miraculously effectual in procuring the liberality of the laity as had been anticipated. He ventured to suggest that the relics of a local saint might be more successful. He casually drew their attention in this matter to the example of the holy brethren of Ely. Not content with their heritage of the bones of Saint Etheldreda and the virgins, her relatives, they had recently forcibly detained and appropriated a consignment of the remains of Aednoth, bishop of Dorchester, addressed to Ramsey Abbey and belonging of right to it. While he did not defend the methods of their Ely brethren, he must applaud their conspicuous and practical piety.

The abbat deplored the circumstance that the vicinity of their abbey had produced no saint of such eminent merits as to transmit to his remains the powers that should evoke the faith and the funds so necessary to their present needs. As an illustration of the spirit which he would like to find among his own brethren he again invited their attention to the religious activity of their friends at Ely, who had despatched a naval and military force as far as Dereham, in Norfolk, and with tumult of war had abstracted from the church there the shrine and body of Saint Withburga, virgin. In fact the pious solicitude of their friends had sometimes carried them to lengths which, making the widest allowance for the purity of their motives, the abbat could not regard as otherwise than regrettable. In the recent Danish troubles the brethren of Saint Alban's had committed to the safe keeping of the Ely monks the shrine containing the relics of the great Protomartyr of Britain. At the restoration of peace the Ely people had, indeed, returned the chest, but they afterwards maintained that they had substituted in it the remains of a less sacred person and had kept Saint Alban in their church. The Saint Alban's brotherhood on their part asserted that, from a conscientious regard for the sanctity of their trust, they had thought well not to part with the veritable person of their tutelar saint, but to employ the pardonable strategem of enclosing an inferior substitute in the shrine despatched to Ely. But the point in dispute was immaterial, inasmuch as the Ely relics, to whomsoever they had originally appertained, had contributed largely to the prosperity of that household, while the event proved that the proprietary interests of Saint Alban's had been in no degree prejudiced. Blind Isaac bestowed the same blessing of earth's fatness on supplanting Jacob and on first-born Esau. Charity and prudence alike dictated that, in the hearing of the giver, there should be no contention between brotherly households about a birth-right which, for all practical uses, each of them possessed in its integrity.

To what did the abbat's observations tend? At the obscure church of Soham, Cambs., unworthy receptacle of so divine a treasure, rested what had been mortal of Saint Felix, bishop and evangelist of the East Angles. The bishop of the diocese in which Ramsey was situated, at the abbat's instance, had procured royal letters patent authorising the Ramsey monks to transfer the sacred remains to their conventual church. Far be it from him to suggest such violent courses as had, in some measure, clouded the effulgent zeal of their Ely neighbours. The Soham folk, if properly approached, would, no doubt, show themselves compliant to the King's will, and would be eager to collaborate in a work so happily inspired. He requested the chapter to express its views as to the proper methods of attaining their pious object of putting the belltower in a condition of permanent stability.

Prior Alfwin rose and, protesting veneration for his Superior, ventured to offer some remarks which, he trusted, would not be regarded as derogating from the respect due to the abbatial chair. Fraternal affection had, in his opinion, betrayed the Lord Abbat into an estimate of the character of the Ely people which was not warranted by the facts. The prior regarded them as sons of Belial. By what instinct of the Devil the holy father, Saint Aethelwold, had induced King Edgar to endow their monastery with wealth so disproportioned to their merits it was not for him to surmise. Among the estates so granted was the manor of Soham. There could be no doubt that, if they got wind of the proposed translation of their saint, the Soham men would fight. It would ill become their sacred calling to employ the carnal weapons to which the Ely brigands had resorted. "Let us rather," said the prior, "attain our ends by friendly gifts and such arts as are permissible to our peaceful profession—wine, for instance, or beer." The rest of the prior's observations were directed to a discussion of the properties of poppy, mandragora and other soporific herbs.

After general discussion it was agreed that a letter should be despatched to the reeve of Soham, announcing the intention of the abbat and prior of paying their observance at the shrine of Saint Felix on an appointed day: that the abbey boat-earls should be in attendance to convey those officials thither from Erith hithe in the household barge: and that the cellarer should make such provision for the entertainment of the residents in Soham as might seem to his prudence expedient.

Brother Brihtmer, lately professed, added the observation that he knew a man or two—servants or tenants of the Abbey—Oswi, the miller, for instance, who carried off the ram for wrestling at Bury fair. With a few such at Erith he thought that he might be trusted to discuss the situation with the Ely men, if they got so far. He would also provide ten stout earls to row the barge from Erith to Soham and to undertake what else might be required of them at the latter place.

* * * * * *

It was a notable day in the annals of the little town of Soham when the Ramsey barge, propelled by ten rowers, five a side, clad in the abbey uniform of bare arms and legs and a loose gown of green falding, was sighted on the far side of Soham mere. Quite a considerable throng of the principal inhabitants watched it from the wooden jetty, to which were moored the cobbles of the Soham fishermen. The reeve, in a murrey coat and blue hood, was an important figure in the group, and was accompanied by a select party of the leading sokemen. The local clergy were in attendance with a hastily improvised band of thurifers and choristers. These, with some of the better class of artificers, smiled with conscious importance, as specially nominated guests at the feast which the Ramsey monks brought with them for their entertainment in the parish gild-hall. The rest of the crowd, consisting of mariners and farm churls, were curious rather than enthusiastic, and more suspicious than curious: for Ramsey is far from Soham, and ancient adage told them that *fýnd synt feorbúend*—far-dwellers are enemies. At the first landing of the venerable passengers a temporary disturbance was caused by Grim, the fisherman of Ely monastery, who provocatively bit his thumb at the starboard bow oar of the abbat's crew. When this difference had been adjusted by the intervention of the district hundred-man the procession was started for the church. At the tail of it, behind the boat-carls, stalked a black-avised monk of Ely, Peter by name, who pointedly withdrew from an official part in the ceremonies.

The banquet in the gild-hall was altogether a splendid affair. In the whole of their official experience the reeve, the hundred-man, and the local clergy had never received so warm a welcome or participated in such royal cheer. No thin English vintage this that was passed to them in the loving cup, fresh from dignified and consecrated lips, but rich old wine, warmed by Greek suns and cooled in the caverns of Ramsey cellars. The cottars who were admitted at the lower board had never known what it was to have so much ale, and so good, as the monastic vats supplied. Brother Peter of Ely looked on from the door, but took no part in the entertainment. He remarked that the Ramsey dignitaries were modest drinkers, and that the boat-carls looked at their blisters and passed the can to their Soham neighbours with the merest pretence of absorption.

As the liquor in the wassail bowls ebbed a gradual silence crept on the festal party. One after other, official and reverend heads declined upon the board rustic bodies dropped from their benches on the floor, and stertorous slumber filled the hail. Only the abbat and prior sat erect and looked about them with ferret eyes, and the boat-carls spat on their hands and inspected their blisters. Brother Peter withdrew to the mere-strand, and by the lapping waters mused on the weakness of human heads and the shocking aspect of intemperance in which one has not participated.

What is this spectacle which presents itself to Brother Peter, meditative on the muddy margin of Soham mere, at the grey hour when country cocks do crow and bells do toll? A procession, silent but solid, actual not ghostly, of ten men bearing a coffer strung upon poles. Two dignified figures, their heads wrapt from the raw air in their hoods, bring up the rear. So our friends are making an early and unannounced departure! This is no time to ask the wherefore. Brother Peter tucks up his frock and runs his fleetest to the church. When he looks back from the porch he sees a vessel launched on the shimmering lake, with a broadening track of broken water in its wake.

The abbat and his men are two miles away over the mere when a strange clamour reaches their ears. Horns are blown; a church bell clangs; cries of "Haro" echo over the water; lights flash upon the strand. The boat-carls rest upon their oars; the abbat smiles; the prior chuckles. "Two miles: impossible!" says he; "and, as lay-brother Oswald was so prudent as to hide the oars of the Ely boat in the church tower, they won't get started in a hurry."

The prior sits in the sternage and directs the vessel's course. Between him and the abbat Saint Felix reposes in his box. As they quit the mere and enter the narrow channel which connects it with the Ouse the abbat suggests a psalm and raises *Jubilate Deo*. The bow oars respond with a three-man glee in the fen-men's fashion.

Sleeping Barway they pass, well out of hearing of their pursuers, and then they take the right hand fork of the river, and follow the Ouse stream which we now call the West River. Here they find themselves in a maze of willow-fringed islets and wandering channels which quit and re-enter the main stream. The sopping, gurgling freshets that drain the shallow meres on either hand, as the tidal waters drop, warn them of the perils of a divergence from the river's course. But prior Alfwin knows what he is about, and holds on in the channel that in ten miles will bring them to Erith bank. Nevertheless their transit, impeded by snags and shallows and fallen trees, is of necessity slow. Under such circumstances one must think it an unwarranted security that induced some of the boat-carls to open a spare beer jar and beguile their toil with ill-timed refreshment. Three comatose bodies under the thwarts impose a severe addition of labour on the more self-respecting members of the crew.

It is the hour of prime, and alas! brother Alfwin, where are we now? Indubitably we are stuck in the mud, and the water is falling. We land on soggy banks, and with labour the boat-earls lift and pole the barge into deeper waters. The operation is repeated several times. Faint cries of "Haro" are borne by the breeze over the fens, and the Lord Abbat shudders with cold and fright. Praised be the saints, at last we are back in the main stream. But what is this? Is not this the identical snag on which we nearly wrecked ourselves the best part of an hour ago? *Deus in adjutorium!* Here is the black prow of the Ely barge rounding the corner, not a hundred yards away, and Monk Peter stands in the bows, raucously shouting and shaking his fist at us! Half-naked figures start up out of the fen and run, hopping from tuft to tuft, on the bank, cheering and waving as they run—friends, foes, or simple spectators, who knows?

The long sweeps of the boat-carls churn the water into oozy froth as they bend themselves with frenzied energy to their task. Foot by foot the Ely men gain upon their predecessors. The game is up unless, as the stroke oars suggest, they lighten ship by heaving Saint Felix into the river. Rather a muddy death than so! Courage! We are less than a mile from Erith.

Lauded be the good Saint Felix, who miraculously interposes for our salvation from the jaws of destruction. Sudden, mysterious, a blanket of white fog rises from the fens and envelopes the river banks. Blotted out are the runners: they cry and wave no more. The Ely prow is swallowed up in vacuous whiteness: the swish of the Ely oars is silenced, and Monk Peter's voice is raised in objurgation. They have run upon that willow that grows aslant the brook, and it is to be doubted that their bows are staved in. Were it not a Christian act to hail them with a loud *Benedicite* in parting? And here is Erith strand and Brother Brihtmer and the Ramsey men. Brother Alfwin, it will be proper for you to give direction to the kitchener for a suitable congratulation for the brethren at supper to-night. To-morrow we will deliberate on the matter of the bell-tower.

"Candid reader," says the Ramsey chronicler, "this is a queer tale. The authority for it is ancient but shaky—*fluctuans veterum nobis tradidit relatio*. I by no means require you to believe it, provided only that in any case you have unhesitating faith that the relics of Saint Felix were translated from the aforesaid town of Soham to Ramsey church, and that there the saint confers inestimable benefits on his worshippers." Ramsey abbey is gone: the shrine of Saint Felix is gone. The tale of the boat race remains. I ask you to believe it, if you can.

In the Fens

The Sacrist of Saint Radegund

On a certain day in mid June in the year 1431 the tolling of the bell in St Radegund's church tower announced to the neighbours of the Priory that a nun was to be buried that day.

In an interval between church services the nuns wander in the garden, which is also the graveyard of St Radegund's, and lies sequestered next the chancel walls. To-day they are drawn thither by a new-made empty grave; for a funeral is a mildly exciting incident in conventual routine. But three sisters sit in the cloister on the stone bench next the chapter door. Also a small novice is curled up on the paved floor with her back against the bench. The day is warm, and the church wall casts a grateful shadow where they sit. And, because labour and silence are enjoined in the cloister, they rest, and two of them gossip, and Agnes Senclowe, the novice, listens and lays to heart.

The two who gossip are Joan Sudbury, succentrix, and Elizabeth Daveys, who is older than Joan, and holds no office in the monastery. With them sits, and half dozes, Emma Denton, who is very old and very infirm. She does not gossip, for she has hardly spoken a word of sense these forty years past. She is a heavy affliction to the cloister society. She lives mainly in the infirmary, and does not attend church. She knows when it is the hour for a meal, and she knows very little else. If she speaks an intelligible word, it is about something that happened forty years ago. She remembers the great pestilence in 1390.

What ailed poor sister Emma to bring her to this sad pass? When she was young she was something of a religious enthusiast, and because enthusiasm was rare in the cloister, she was promoted by her sisters to high station. When they made her Sacrist she had her one and dearest wish. To have the charge of the beautiful church, of the books, vestments and jewels of the sanctuary, to live in the holy place, with holy thoughts for companions, and in the unfailing round of holy duties—was not that a happy lot? Dignified too the office was; for in the little cloister world the Prioress herself was scarcely a greater lady than the Sacrist. The Sacrist did not sleep with the other nuns in the dormitory; her constant duties did not allow her ordinarily to take her meals in the refectory. Like the Prioress, she had her own servant to attend her, her own house to dwell in. Her habitation was built against the northern chancel wall, and consisted of two chambers. From the upper room, through a hole pierced in the wall, she watched the never-dying light that hung before the High Altar.

But it was not good to be Sacrist for long. The unvarying routine of duty produces torpidity; holy thoughts uncommunicated end in cessation of thought; the solitude was deadly. The office was not coveted by the sisterhood, and was seldom held for more than a year or two together. Wherefore they rejoiced when Emma Denton held it for nine years. For nine years she trimmed the sacred lamp. During nine years her own light dwindled out, and at last the world became dark to sister Emma.

The crazy belfry rocked with the swaying of the bell, which, being cracked, was doubly dolorous. The sound of it roused old sister Emma to a dim consciousness of what was passing, and she spoke to nobody in particular.

"The bell," she said, "the bell again! Last week it tolled, and we buried two. Now there are two more in the dead-house."

"The saints protect us!" said sister Joan; "she is at her old talk of the pestilence year."

"It was Assumption Day," continued the old nun, "when we buried them. We had no Mass that day. To-day it is the cellaress and sister Margery Cailly—God pardon her for a sinful woman. No; Margery is sick, not dead; and I forget, I forget."

"Margery Cailly," cried Joan Sudbury, "what quoth she of Margery Cailly, that goes to her grave to-day? Margery Cailly, that has been our most religious Sacrist ever since yonder poor thing fell beside her wits."

"Religious you may call her," said Elizabeth Daveys, "but God knows, and sister Emma knows, that of her which we know not. Thirty years have I lived in St Radegund's, and I remember not the time when any but Margery was our Sacrist, and well I know that the sacristy has been her prison all those days. But I have heard sister Emma say in her dull way that Margery once knew the convent prison too."

"Well, twelve years I have spent here, and never had speech with the Sacrist. Once I was alone in the church when it was dark, and the daylight only lingered aloft in the roof, and of a sudden I lighted on her in the chancel, busied in her office. Her pale face in her black hood showed like a spirit's, and I thought it was the blessed Radegund that had come down from her window, and I was horribly afraid."

"I think that from the sacristy window her eye followed me about the garden as I walked there," said Elizabeth. "It follows me still, and it makes my flesh creep. What good woman would shun her sisters so? Heaven rest her soul, for be sure she has much to answer for. If she has confessed herself, it is not to our confessor or the Prioress, for I think she has hardly spoken these many years to any but Alice Portress that waits on her."

"Yes, Alice was with her at the end. It was Alice that dug the grave; Alice rings the knell; Alice laid her out in her Sacrist's chamber, and she has placed two white roses on the dead woman's breast."

"Roses?" said Elizabeth Daveys; "roses are not for dead nuns. Whence got she roses?"

"That I can tell you," said the novice, glad to take her part in the conversation, "for Alice told me herself. She got them from the churchyard of St Peter's on the hill."

* * * * * *

The office for the dead was said, the empty grave was filled, and Alice the Portress was closeted with the Prioress.

"To you, lady Prioress—not to the Nuns in Chapter—I confess the sin of my youth; not to them, nor yet to you while sister Margery lived. She is gone, and why should I remain? Forty years we shared the secret. She is past censure or forgiveness. On me let the blame rest. I ask no pardon, but only to be dismissed from the house of St Radegund, that I have so unworthily served.

"There is none but myself and poor sister Emma that remembers St Radegund's before the pestilence year. I was but a child then, and my mother was Portress before me. My mother often brought me to the lodge, and I used to play with the novices, or sit at the gate when my mother was away. Margery had but lately come to St Radegund's—seventeen, perhaps, or eighteen years of age she

Entrance to Chapter House.

was. Hers was a proud family—the Caillys of Trumpington, and they were rich, and good to St Radegund's. They are gone and forgotten now, but often have I heard old Thomas Key tell of them, for he was a Trumpington man, and he knew the De Freviles of Shelford too. There are De Freviles at Shelford yet, but I think that none there remembers young Nicholas De Frevile that was Sir Robert's son.

"I had a child's thought—that Margery was the most beautiful creature in the wide world—most beautiful and best. And because she was young and fair and gracious in speech even our hard sisters loved her, and thought it pity of the world when her fair tresses were shorn and she took the ugly veil. For Margery was not religious. God pardon me for my sinful words, but I think she was meant for better things than religion and a cloister. And though she was good and kind to all, Margery did not take to our sisters. There was some trouble—I know not what, for she never told—and for some family reason she was sent to St Radegund's, and ill she liked it. So she went about her work in cloister and church, grieving; and there was talk of her among the sisters. Some thought, some said, that they knew, but Margery said nothing.

"It is all forgotten now, for the pestilence wiped out the memory of those days. Scarcely twelve months had gone since she took the veil when Margery Cailly disappeared from the Priory. You may think what babble of tongues there was in our parlour—how they who were wisest had always known how it would be, and the rest rebuked them for not telling them beforehand. And so for another twelvemonth she was lost to us, and some sisters, who were kind, hoped that she would come back, and some who were kinder, hoped she would not.

"Then, one day in the year before the pestilence, comes an apparitor with our lost Margery, and a letter to the Prioress from the Lord Bishop of Ely. The letter is to say that the Archbishop of Canterbury, in his visitation of Lincoln diocese, has found Margery there, living a secular life; and because secular life is sin to those who have entered the religious order, he commits her to his brother of Ely, in order that the lost sheep may be restored to the fold where she was professed. And his Lordship of Ely—Heaven help him for a blundering bachelor!—directs that she shall be committed to the convent prison-house until she repents of her wickedness, and when she is loosed from it, shall make public confession in Chapter, and implore the pardon of the sisters for her enormities.

"Our Prioress was kinder to Margery than the Bishop meant—who could not be kind to her? Her prison life was no longer than would satisfy the Bishop's enquiries, and as for the confession in the Chapter-house—it never happened. There were some, though they liked not confession for themselves, who thought an opportunity was missed, and blamed the Prioress; for cloister talk is dull if we know not one another's failings. Still, the sisters were kind to Margery, and very kind when they wanted to get the secret from her. But she said never a word about it, unless it were to the Prioress. Beautiful she was as ever, but grief and humiliation were on her, heavy as death, and because she confided in none, she lost the friendship of the sisters. To me, who was but a child, she would talk, but scarcely to another, and her talk with me was never about herself.

"One other there was with whom sometimes she had speech, and that was old Thomas Key, maltster and trusty servant in general matters of the Priory. Him she had known in happier days when he was a tenant of the Caillys at Trumpington. Her family was too proud and too pious to remember the disgraced nun, and they never visited her; but from Thomas she learnt something of home and the outside world.

"Then came the dreadful year when the pestilence raged in Cambridge town. The nuns had been used to get leave from the Prioress to go out into the town, but there was no gadding now. The gate was closely barred, and none were admitted from outside except Thomas Key. We carried the Host in procession about the Nuns' Croft and—laud be to the saints!—it protected our precincts from the contagion. And while the sinful world without died like the beasts that perish, we sat secure, but frightened, in our cloister, and blessed our glorious saint for extending the protection of her prayers over the pious few who did her service in St Radegund's.

The Chancel Squint.

"You have heard how the parish clergy died that year. One, two, sometimes three died in one parish, and the Bishop found it hard to provide successors. Boys that had barely taken the tonsure a week before were sent in haste to anoint the sick and bury the dead in places where the plague had left an unshepherded flock. Sir John Dekyn, priest of St Peter's church on the hill, was one that died, and his successor did not live a fortnight after him. Then we heard from Thomas Key that a mere youth had taken the place, one Sir Nicholas of the Shelford De Frevile family, who had but lately been ordered priest at Ely. And we were told that he worked with a feverous zeal among the poor, the sick, and the dying of his parish.

"Now when this news was brought to sister Margery by Thomas Key, it was to her as a summons from death to life. Her eye brightened and her cheek glowed when she heard of the heroic goodness of this young priest. While the sisters shuddered and shrank at each morning's fatal news, she was consumed with a passionate desire to know what was passing in the plague-stricken town, and she plied my mother and Thomas Key with incessant questionings. 'Who was sick of the townsfolk? Were any of the clergy visited? How went it with the poor in St Peter's, where the pestilence was hottest?' For some weeks she heard that the light burned still at night in St Peter's parsonage, and that the priest was unscathed, incessant in his ministrations and blessed by his parishioners. And it seemed as though the sickness was abating.

"Then, late one afternoon in early August, there came a call for Margery. Thomas Key brought it, and whether it was his own tidings, or a message from some other, I cannot say; Margery never told me. But this I know, that she took me apart in the cloister and spoke to me, and she was terribly moved and her voice was choked. 'Little Alice,' she said, 'as you love me, get me the gate-key after Lauds to-night. It is life or death to me to go out into the town. Only do it, and say nothing—no, not to your mother.' Young as I was, I knew how the nuns were used to humour my mother into letting them pass the gate; but that was in day-time. At night, in our besieged state, with the death-bells tolling all around, it seemed a terrible thing to venture. But I asked no questions. Say it was the recklessness of a girl—say it was the love that I bore to Margery. I stole the key and gave it to her after sundown.

"What happened afterwards I will tell you as it was told to me by Thomas Key, who waited for her outside the gate. They passed along the dark, deserted streets. The plague-fires burnt low in the middle of the roadway, but there were none to tend them, and no living thing they saw but the starving dogs, herded at barred doors. They crossed the bridge and mounted to St Peter's church. The priest's manse—you know it—is a low house next the church. A white rose, still in flower, clambered on its walls, and, half hidden by its sprays, a taper gleamed through the open window; but there was no sound of life within. They pushed open the door and entered.

"Stretched on his pallet, forsaken and untended, lay the young priest of St Peter's, the pangs of death upon him. Margery threw herself on her knees by his bed-side, and Thomas watched and waited. For a time there was silence, for Margery had no voice to pray. Only at times the dying man grumbled and wandered in his talk; but little he said that Thomas understood.

"Then after a long time, he stirred himself uneasily and uttered one word, 'Margery.' And she—alas the day!—put out her arm and laid it on his shoulder. In an instant the dying man half raised himself on his bed and turned his eyes on her, and there was recognition in them. And one arm he threw about her neck, and felt blindly for the fair locks that had been shorn long since, and he said heavily and painfully, 'Margery, *belle amie*, let us go to the pool above the mill, where the great pike lie, and sun and shadow lie on the deep water.' So Thomas knew that they were boy and girl again by the old mill at Trumpington.

"That was all, and the end came soon. They two laid him decently beneath his white sheet, and Margery plucked two white roses from the spray that straggled across his window, and laid them on the dead man's breast. So they left him, with the candle still burning out into the dark.

* * * * * *

"There was a horrible dread in St Radegund's when, four days later, sister Margery sickened of the pestilence; and it was worse when we learnt soon after that Thomas Key was visited—then that he was dead. That was the beginning of our sorrows. You have heard, Lady Prioress, how three sisters died before August was out, how most of the others deserted the house, and some never returned to it. Our prayers were unheard, and to us who remained it seemed as if the saints slept, or God were dead.

"So it happened that when the plague abated, and the first meeting was held in St Radegund's Chapter-house, about St Luke's day in the autumn, there were only three to attend it—the Prioress, the Sacrist (Emma Denton), and Margery Cailly. For—wonderful it seems—Margery, who least needed to live, was the one spared of those who were taken with the pestilence. Presently some old sisters returned, and new ones took the place of the departed. But the sword of the pestilence cut off the memory of the old days, and the sins and sufferings, the virtues and the victories of the former sisterhood were a forgotten dream when the cloister filled again. So when Emma Denton passed into her lethargy, and Margery Cailly earnestly petitioned to fill her place in the Sacristy, there was not a sister to question her character and devoutness.

"Not yesterday, but forty years ago, Margery Cailly passed out of life; for you know that, save to me, she has spoken few words since. And though I have waited on her for most of those years she never breathed to me the name of Nicholas De Frevile, never hinted at the story of her unhappy girlhood. But once in the springtime, just after she entered her Sacrist prison-house, she entreated me to plant a white rose-bush on the grave of the young priest of St Peter's. I did so, and have renewed it since, and one day, by your grace, I shall plant a spray of the same roses where she lies apart from him. I have confessed my wrong in stealing the key and bringing death into the cloister. If you can forgive me, so; if not, all I ask is that you let your sinful servant depart in peace."

* * * * * *

There is a curious aperture in the outer northern wall of the chancel of the nuns' church which is now Jesus College Chapel. If it is examined its purpose is evident. It was the lychnoscope, through which the Sacrist watched by night the light before the High Altar. It is the sole abiding memorial of Margery Cailly, Sacrist of St Radegund.

Coachwhip Publications
CoachwhipBooks.com

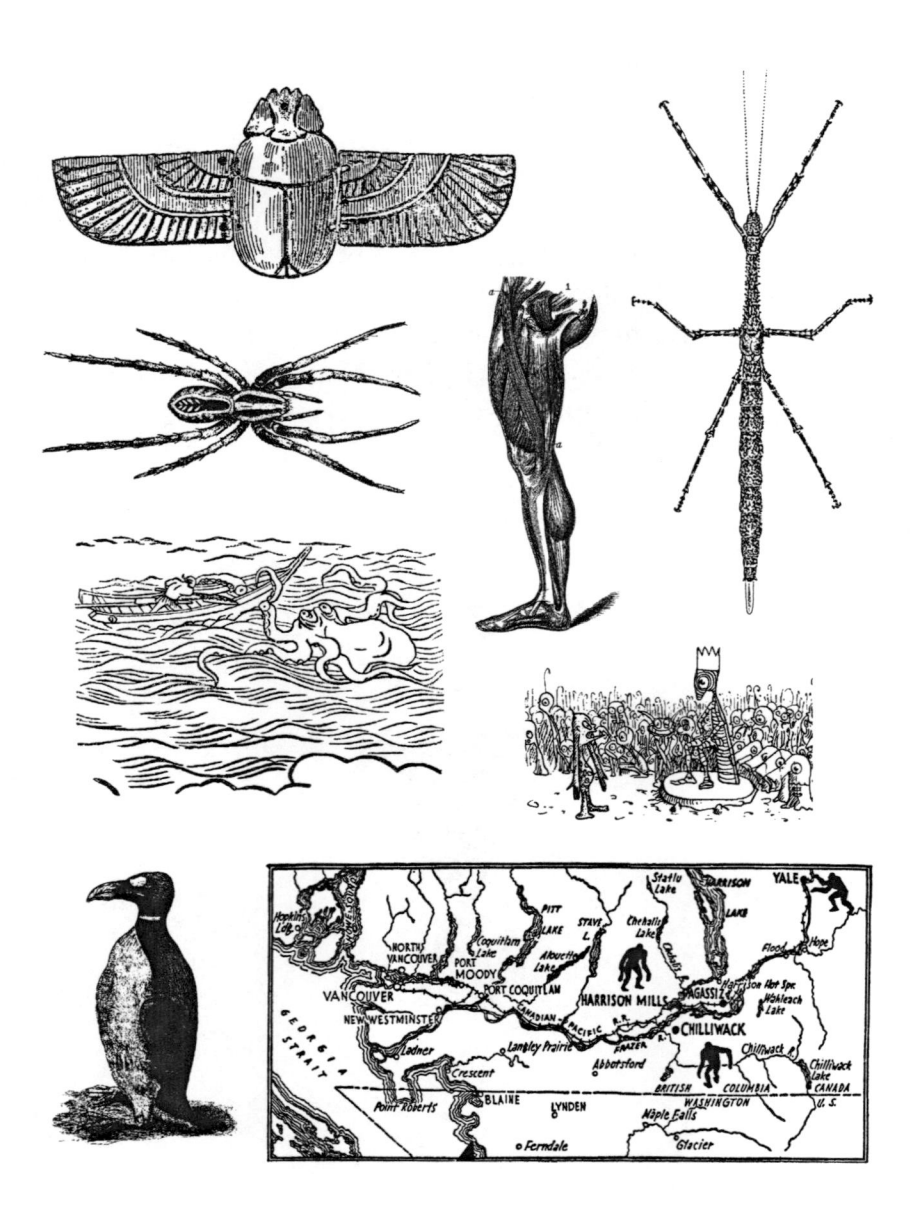

COACHWHIP PUBLICATIONS
COACHWHIPBOOKS.COM

THE SUPERNATURAL STORIES OF MONSIGNOR ROBERT H. BENSON

THE LIGHT INVISIBLE
A MIRROR OF SHALOTT

THE SUPERNATURAL STORIES OF
Monsignor Robert H. Benson

ISBN 978-1-61646-004-4